STEADY EDDIE

Also by T. Glen Coughlin

The Hero of New York

STEADY EDDIE

A Novel

T. GLEN COUGHLIN

Published by
Soho Press, Inc.
853 Broadway
New York, NY 10003

Library of Congress Cataloging-in-Publication Data

Coughlin, T. Glen.
Steady Eddie : a novel / T. Glen Coughlin.
  p. cm.
ISBN 1-56947-221-1 (alk. paper)
  1. Truthfulness and falsehood—Fiction.   2. Long Island
(N.Y.)—Fiction.   3. Male friendship—Fiction.   4. Working
class—Fiction.   5. Young men—Fiction.   6. Rape—
Fiction.   I. Title.

PS3553.O775 S73 2001
813'.54—dc21   00-059594

Manufactured in the United States of America

10   9   8   7   6   5   4   3   2   1

For Laura Coughlin Quinn

Special thanks to my friend, Tim Tomlinson,
and my agent, Tanya McKinnon.

Chapter One

Saturdays, I get paid. Next to the Pantry Pride's penny-candy machines, and the twenty-five cent pony ride, I count $220 in twenty-dollar bills. In my back pocket the money makes my wallet feel fat, nice and fat. Customers, pulling kids by the arm, steering squeaking shopping carts, push in, push out.

Between my fingers, fish scales stick to me like a second skin. Somehow they survived a thorough washing in the restroom sink. I flick them to the pavement. The smell of the fish department, the shop, the chicken walk-in box is under my fingernails, behind my ears, in my hair. A soak in a tub gets rid of the odor. My hands are swollen, a mess of small infected cuts. I form a fist and the pain makes me remember my boss's voice. Kurt calls me "kid." "Hey, kid, you got a truck on the dock with your name on it. Kid, I said no sugar. I don't take sugar in my coffee, go back and get me another. You got that, kid?" Reggie, one of the butchers, says I have to prove myself before I get any respect, before I cut red meat. But, bad as it is, that's how good it is. I like showing them I can lift and handle off-loads. I go crazy cutting and bagging chickens, probably setting records.

Street kids cut the parking lot and slam a shopping cart into the side of a dumpster. "Hey," I yell, just for the hell of it. "You think that's funny?" They see me and run toward the alley between the Grove Apartments. Probably one of them knows me or heard the name Eddie Trottman. In Freeport High School I had a reputation. It wasn't entirely earned. Some of it came from my father. Some from the guys I hung out with at the school. Last year I barely squeaked through and graduated Phi Beta Crappa. The school guidance counselor told me to get a job in the trades, meaning carpentry, electricity, plumbing. It was what they told all the guys they thought were going nowhere. He was right about one thing, I'm in a trade. I'm only nineteen and I'm going from apprentice to butcher. As soon as my one-year probation ends, I'll be a member of Amalgamated Meat Cutters Union, Local 342.

At the end of the supermarket, I sit on a concrete barrier. Egg-foo-something is in the air from the China Inn. The sun is low just over the Gulf Station at the corner. I loosen my boots and watch the traffic roll on Merrick Road. Every other car goes south on Grove Street down to the restaurants on the Nautical Mile.

Freeport is on the south shore of Long Island. Some people still call it a clam digger's town. The railroad slices the town down the middle. The north is filled with blacks who hang out on Main Street near the liquor stores, and the south is filled with clam diggers and fishermen who line the bars on the canals. There's some rich Jews who bought waterfront property near Cow Meadow Park when real estate was cheap. Behind the old movie theater across from Wetson Hamburgers, hookers stroll up to cars asking, "You need a date?" Just down from the library there's one house full of Hare Krishna that I've egged every Halloween since I can remember.

I live where the town is cut in half, in the middle of everything, where I belong. I'm half Puerto Rican, and half German. My father says I'm one of a kind, then adds, "Which kind I have no idea."

The sun disappears. Car headlights flash on me as they turn from the street. Loopy is late again. Nothing new. I'm losing a good buzz. I'm an hour into drinking beer. I slipped a few bottles under my butcher apron each time I went from the meat department out into the supermarket to straighten the meat case. The supermarket doesn't carry cold beer. I poured the beer into plastic chicken liver containers, then added clean chipped ice from the machine in the fish department. I tossed the empties into a hole in the wall. Someday someone will remodel the supermarket and there'll be an avalanche.

Saturdays, from eight in the morning to five in the evening, I'm at the bandsaw halving chickens. The saw is noisy, there's no point for a radio, or conversation. From five to closing time, I'm alone behind the meat case mirrored windows doing all the shit jobs: bleaching the boards, scrubbing the blocks, breaking the machines down, rolling the fat cans into the walk-in box. Last thing I do is throw down the sawdust. When I finish the place smells like a hamster cage.

Loopy rumbles in. The Hollywood mufflers on his GTO sound like hollow thunder. The rear bumper bears his life's philosophy, GAS, GRASS OR ASS, NOBODY RIDES FREE. He's wearing his standard muscle shirt, smoking a Marlboro.

"Asshole," he says.

"Douche." I hop in.

"What's up?"

"Nothing."

"You stink," he says, giving me a grin and a warm Miller bottle. Loopy is tall, lanky, and bow legged. His real name is Larry

Louperino, thus the nickname. On the dashboard a half-eaten hero on wax paper slides to my side as he turns out of the parking lot.

"Finish that, it's meatball," he says. "Still hot."

"Where'd you get it?"

"Screw you, 'Where'd you get it?' You want it, or not?" Tomato sauce is leaking out on the paper. "But, if you got to know, I bought it at Zuro's," he says.

I grab the whole mess and take a bite. Zuro's Deli, near the Freeport Raceway, has the best heros in town, better than 7-Eleven's.

We cruise with the windows open. Loopy's hair whips around his head. From the side all you see are hair and nose. Loopy's half Italian and his nose is about half the size of Italy. But nobody ever insults him to his face. He's got this stance, an attitude, like he's just about to flick his cigarette in your face. Since about the fifth grade, Loopy's done construction for some Mafia-owned company. The calluses on his hands are thicker than the ones on my feet.

At the beer distributor, I help Loopy fold the top down on the GTO. Sometimes we just hang at the distributor waiting for someone to come and pick up a keg of beer. Then, we follow the car to the party. On the hood we crack fresh beers. Across the street, the canal that leads to the Baldwin Bay is black and calm. It's late April. The really nice weather is still weeks off. The yachts, wrapped in canvas covers, wait like moths in giant cocoons. In June they'll be open, sailing to Fire Island for the weekend or Short Beach for a day trip.

Shotgun in the GTO, the engine presses me into the seat. I feel indestructible; a moving object at sixty-five miles an hour with a four-hundred-cubic-inch under the hood and a pose-traction rear. I slam in my eight-track. The Boss and a sad sax wail about the

Jersey Shore that I passed through once on a class trip to the Liberty Bell. Loopy puts up with the music. He's into Black Sabbath, Bachman Turner Overdrive, Meat Loaf, and shit like that. I bought the Boss's tape after I heard "Born to Run."

On Saturday nights, we hope that something will happen, maybe the two girls we hang with, Dirty Drawers or Armpits, will be at Violetta's. Maybe the boys from Merrick, with their Firebirds that their daddies bought for them, will cruise Atlantic Avenue and find the balls to line up next to Loopy's Goat and punch the gas pedal at a red light.

I open another Miller. The breeze whipping in the car sucks the cap away as we soar down Atlantic Avenue, past the hobby shop, Sam's Shoe Repair, the Galley Bar, the A&P.

We roll next to a Nova: lifted rear, custom air scoop, Cragar rims. Loopy revs the engine, makes eye contact with the other driver. The driver glances at us and burns rubber on his fat-boy slicks. Smoke rises from the dry concrete and smells like Saturday night at the Freeport Speedway. Seconds at the red light tick by slowly. The green light flashes. The cars explode forward. For a moment we're even, then the Nova catches rubber in fourth gear and blasts ahead. With another red light at the next block, the Nova decelerates. Wearing a giant shit-eating grin, the guy behind the wheel looks back at us.

"Think it's funny?" asks Loopy. Doing twenty, he bangs the GTO into the Nova's bumper, then hangs a quick right to Bayview Avenue. Nobody wins when they race Loopy.

Checking the rear view, he makes a few turns. I know where he's going. It's been on Loopy's route since Ginny and I broke up. On a narrow block, he coasts past large houses with porches, trimmed border hedges, and station wagons in the driveways. Ginny's house is coming up fast on the left.

Loopy's already downshifting from third to second to first. We do five miles an hour past the house. I know she's dating Jay. That sick feeling, like I just went up a fast elevator, begins to creep into the pit of my stomach. I can't think of them without that feeling. Saturday night is dating night for Jay, who picked a red VW Rabbit for his graduation present from his parents, and who can play the oboe, or the elbow. Jay, who I could blow away with a look, not even a look, I'd like to yell, Hey, Jay, you asswipe, come on out and . . . But, I am sealed tight as the Tupperware Ginny's mom hawks at Friday night parties. Ginny's mother, holding her glass of year-old California white, couldn't look me in the eye when Ginny suggested that my mother be invited to a Tupperware party.

"She's out with Jay," yelps Loopy, gunning the engine.

My sick stomach seems to twist. I'm sick over how we broke up, sick as I imagine them sitting in some wine-and-cheese place, or worse at the Met game, her wearing his baseball cap and him knowing all the players' averages, sick inside, sick of this town and cutting meat, not even meat, chicken. We sail under the trees and the black sky through Saturday night. "Let's go look up Pits," I say.

The GTO roars.

At the pizza parlor in the corner of the strip mall, Pits hangs on the pay phone yakking. She eyes us. We rip across the lot, right toward her. The car brakes and tires squeal, but she doesn't flinch. The Goat bumps her and she pounds the hood with her fist. I'd like to smack Loopy for getting so close, but I let it go. "Aw, it barely touched you," yells Loopy.

From her oversize flannel shirt, she flips us the bird and comes to my window. "If it had hurt, it would have been later for your asses," she says, trying to sound tough. She's really cute, with a big unearned reputation for B. O. Loopy came up with the nickname the day she climbed in his car with the top up. I found out later that she had spent a few days on the street because she couldn't go home. The nickname stuck anyway.

I snake my arm around her neck. Pits lives in Merrick, the town east of mine. In the mornings, almost every house has a pool truck or a lawn service in front. But, Armpits lives on the south end of Merrick, behind a golf course down by the dump. A garbage mountain rises right at the back fence of her house. About a hundred yards up, exhaust pipes let the gas out of the mountain. Her father is my mailman in Freeport and her mother gets the great honor to vacuum Merrick's custom wall-to-wall and scrub imported tiled walk-in showers and sunken Jacuzzi tubs with adjustable jets.

Tonight Pits' brown owl eyes are caked with blue mascara like someone in the bricklayers' union applied the shit with a trowel. Under her open flannel shirt, her tight-ass jeans and tube top show off her flat belly and navel, her usual uniform. Dirty Drawers is hanging on another pay phone, probably talking to herself. She's a flake. She tells everyone that she's nineteen but she's really twenty-two. I found out from Pits that her brother fingered her all through grammar school, which in a way was worse than rape, at least then she could have screamed rape. He's doing time upstate for ripping off anything and everything. A year ago he tried to pay me twenty bucks to distract a clerk at Richmond Hardware Store so that he could stroll out the door with a belt sander or set of socket wrenches. I told him to go scratch and Loopy wound up dropping a bin of nuts and bolts for Henry. The plan worked perfectly, all of it, except Loopy's twenty bucks.

On the warm hood, the girls fit themselves between our legs. Pits moons me with her owl eyes. "What'cha gonna do tonight?" she asks, smiling.

"What you wanna do?"

"Cruise." She puts her hand between my legs.

"But we got dates," says Drawers.

"Who the fuck would waste time and money on you?" asks Loopy.

"Dates with you two assholes," she says.

For no good reason, we head to Long Beach. I slide over the white leather seat, across the hump, and throw my arm around Armpits. Drawers takes her perch on the console and Loopy bangs the Goat's gears right into her crotch.

Roaring down Atlantic Avenue, Pits and me tongue kiss. Her mouth tastes like an ashtray. Her kinky-curly brown hair whips me in the face. Ginny doesn't smoke, has straight hair, and barely drinks. Pits didn't know about Ginny. That was one good thing about having girls in different towns. Sometimes, when the night was just about over, and Pits and I were saying good-bye, she would ask me when I would call, when I would see her again. I'd tell her I'll call, and for the tenth time slip her number in my wallet. Like I hoped Ginny would last, Pits must hope I'd call.

My hand is squeezing Pits' left breast. My fingers circle the nipple. With one quick move, I lift her tube top up. She's got pointy nipples with half-dollar areolas the color of calf's liver. Her flannel shirt covers most of her, but I see a guy almost drive off the road as he passes.

"What the fuck have you been smoking?" she yells, yanking down her tube top.

I kiss her again and her tongue swirls in my mouth like a live eel. Pits is so easy. It almost isn't fun. She's like one of those blowup punch clowns. No matter how hard you hit'em, they come right back for another smack in the nose. She once told me that I was the only one in the world who understood her. I pretended I hadn't heard.

Off and on, Pits and Drawers have been hanging out with us for a couple of years. We don't call them, write them, buy them anything, but still they're waiting every night at the pizza joint, drinking beer at a buck a bottle. Pits doesn't talk much, she just makes the heavy eyes at me as if they were answers to any question. She nuzzles her head against my chest. I give her a hug and she peers up. "I'm glad you came by," she says.

"Me too," I say. She smiles and pulls me in for a kiss.

We come up for air and I open her a bottle of Miller.

Drawers is a million-times worse than Pits. She wears the same baggy jeans every day with these two holes above the cheeks of her ass. As she walks, her drawers flash. Loopy bangs her when he wants, usually in the parking lot after the pizza joint closes. They are always fighting. Last summer, Drawers stabbed Loopy in the ribs with a Bic pen over some bullshit. I don't know what. Even at the emergency room she didn't stop. She jumped him, scratched his face in front of the doctors, and yelled that she would have him busted someday.

Stopped at a red light on Long Beach Road, a guy rolls up in a mint-green Bird. "Your daddy teach you how to drive," yells Loopy.

"Your mother."

The light changes before Loopy can respond. After thirty feet of banging gears, Loopy is side by side with the Bird. Pits's face beams. With barely enough space for the two cars to ride side by side, we charge past the parked cars. The Bird stays with us, sometimes a few inches ahead, then a few behind. If some schmuck were to open his door, it would be whacked into orbit. I'm not even horny, but I unsnap Pits's jeans and slide my hand down to the top of her panties. Watching the Bird, she power slugs her Miller. The angle is killing my arm. I inch down her soft stomach until my fingertips reach the top of her curly pubic hair, all the time half hoping she stops me, or at least pretends to care.

"I love Firebirds," she screams in my ear.

I pull my hand out. Loopy is a car length ahead when the Bird falls behind, then hangs a right.

"Pussy," yells Loopy.

In high school there were the jocks, the academics, the band, the leftover hippies, and the hitters. I was a hitter. None of us were black, Jewish, rich, or even middle class. None of us lived on the water, went on family vacations, or away to college. We went to high school for auto shop, or metal shop. The hitter girls went for cosmetology. A few hitters got into the community college for welding or computers and, every once in a while, a hitter made it big. But, most of the time, hitters got locked up for prying open the skylights on drugstore roofs or busted for beating their girl-friends. Some were killed in DWI accidents, or worse, got spine injuries from falling off their Harleys. Some of my old hitter friends are still in town, like the guy over at the Shell station pumping gas.

My official "hitter" label came in the ninth grade, after I did four months at the Westbury Children's Shelter. I got arrested for counting quarters, dimes, and nickels for two guys who were hack-ing heads off parking meters and beating them open with sledge hammers. Loopy and I got ten dollars for every one hundred dollars we rolled. Loopy didn't show the day the cops raided the house. It was just me, the guy who hired me, and his partner, a guy with pimples all over his face and neck.

My grandfather took a cab every Saturday, all the way from Free-port, to visit me at the shelter. In the dayroom, after long silences, he'd talk about repairing dry rot on his boat, tuning the old straight-eight engine, hooking fluke and flounders, or the price of fuel. Then, he'd lean uneasily on the Formica table and ask me, "Why'd you do it? Did you need the money that bad? Why don't you have a paper route? How did you get involved with those guys?"

To answer my grandfather's questions, I wanted to tell him that my father had once toppled the refrigerator down over my mother. Her legs were sticking out of the side and I thought she was dead. I wanted to tell him that my father had a blond-haired girlfriend. I wanted to tell him that when my mother drank Fresca with vodka, she went crazy and once flicked matches on my father when he was passed-out drunk. The couch caught fire and for a month its black springs stuck out like giant corkscrews and stank up our house. But all I asked my grandfather was, why didn't my parents visit me. Were they *that* mad at me?

Trying to make sense of it, my grandfather would look away at the caged windows. One afternoon after a slow Ping-Pong game in the recreation room, he gripped my hands and squeezed them. "You're from a no-good mix," he said. "But, you don't have to be bad." He told me that I wasn't like my father and mother. "You understand that?"

Back at high school, hitters hung by me. A rumor broke that in the shelter I shattered a kid's jaw. I have big hands and thick wrists—a gym teacher told me I was built like Jerry Quarry—so I rolled up my shirtsleeves and, without doing much of anything, my hair and my reputation grew. Kids passing in the halls nodded at me as if asking permission. Once after class, my tenth-grade English teacher told me I had scored high marks on a placement test. He said I was bright, I had a future, and had to shake off the shelter and the hitters. For a while, I studied, did homework, then my grandfather died and I started spending school days in Nunley's Carousel, grubbing money over the sound of the merry-go-round organ music, living on greasy pizza and six-ounce Miller ponies that

I carried in my army jacket like glass grenades. By junior year, the teachers didn't care if I was late or left early. When they called attendance, the teachers said *Trottman* as if not expecting an answer. The principal put me in the afternoon program, nicknamed the "Air Force" because by afternoon all the hitters were so high they were flying. I smiled through automotive classes rebuilding the shop teacher's '36 Ford three-window coupe that he sold and made a nice profit on.

Looking back, I realize I spent too many afternoons with one girl or another, too many nights standing like a jackass at the beer distributor holding a bottle of Miller, or riding shotgun in Loopy's GTO, blasting Bachman Turner Overdrive, shooting the shit about I don't remember what. I only wish I had paid better attention to my grandfather's lectures about dry rot and the old straight-eight.

Decrepit old-age homes line the street, blocking the ocean view. Behind them the weathered boardwalk stretches for a few miles. A senior citizen, pulling her gray poodle, eyes us. The dog, nails scraping for footage, struggles to squat on the sidewalk. On a street sign a seagull watches us cruise by. In the center of town an old man, wearing gray chinos high around his waist, crosses the street. I almost call to him. "Jesus, that guy looked just like my grandfather," I say.

"He looks like everyone's grandfather," says Pits.

My grandfather wore gray chino pants, a button-down shirt, and boat shoes every day. When I was fifteen, he died of a massive heart attack in his apartment. From his side window I saw him lying on the floor near the bathroom. I banged on the neighbor's door and they called the police. There was nothing much else to do. The cops took a lot of photos and rolled him into a vinyl bag with a long zipper. I was crying and the ambulance attendant kept

telling me that he was at peace and shit like that. During the
wake at the funeral parlor my father acted like an asshole, drinking
beer right next to the coffin, bragging that he knew all of Pops's
secrets. On the second night I smacked the bottle out of his hand
and it sprayed on the flower arrangements and across the thin red
carpet.

My father kept saying, "Eddie, you're pushing it, pushing it."

"Pops wouldn't want you here," I yelled. "Why don't you get
your scrawny ass out of here?"

"He's upset," said my father, smiling to the guests, swirling
around in his blue crushed velvet jacket and ruffled shirt. A few
days later, my grandfather's will was read and I inherited his thirty-
two-foot Egg Harbor cabin cruiser, named the *Glory*, and his 1968
Plymouth Fury that needs a transmission. My father tried to sell
the boat, almost gave it away for three thousand dollars to the first
guy who wagged cash in his face. But the title is in a vault in my
grandfather's lawyer's office and the deal fell through. My father
woke me up in the middle of the night and yanked me around my
room, screaming, "I was the son, I was the son." The next day he
gave me a phony apology and begged me to sign the boat over to
him. I got near the back door on the other side of the kitchen table
and told him to fuck off.

Loopy parks a few blocks down from the rides and the food
stands.

"Where we going?" asks Drawers.

"Where do you think," answers Loopy.

The salty breeze from the ocean seems to cheer us all up. I run
toward the boardwalk after Pits, grab her, and swing her around.
Loopy says something to Drawers. She smacks him with her big
leather bag that she lugs around. Waves pound the short, deserted
beach. Brown foam races across the mottled, gray sand toward over-

flowing wire trash cans. Night has closed in. Music and voices from
the amusement park drift in on the wind. The aluminum railing
that runs the boardwalk is lined with seagulls, all facing the ocean,
some standing on one leg. Sauntering lazily, arm in arm, Pits's sexy
hip bumps me. Loopy and Drawers come alongside. "I'm going to
give her the banging of her life," says Loopy in my ear. At the first
entrance to the beach, Drawers and the Loop slip under the boardwalk.

Out of the wind next to a closed concession, Pits lays her head
in my lap and I stroke her face. I wouldn't tell anyone but I think
she is beautiful sometimes. I like her full lips, crazy-owl eyes, and
small sharp nose.

"What are you thinking?" I ask.

"See that star." She points at the dark sky. "I wish that was me."
She rolls over on her side. "I was practicing today and made a demo
tape for my brother."

Pits wants to be a singer. Her brother plays guitar for some Los
Angeles loser band called Plastic Diamonds. He's got hair he washes
about four times a month that is down to his ass, and arms as thick
as elbow macaroni. I've heard Pits' voice a few times in her basement singing along with Gloria Gaynor and Carly Simon. She does
"Someone Left the Cake Out in the Rain," or whatever it's called,
better than Donna Summer.

"You want to hear my new favorite song?" she asks. "*Midnight
at the oasis,*" sings Pits. "*Send your camel to bed. You don't have to
worry, or hurry . . .*" She goes on singing and actually sounds like
the record.

"That was great." I kiss her.

"What are you thinking about?" she asks.

The ocean twinkles with light from the amusement park under
a round moon that puts a streak of shiny white all the way to the

breakers. "I wish I was out in the ocean fishing," I say. "Far out, where the big fish are."

"I never caught a fish," she says. "When I was a kid, I went to this place where the fish swam in one direction in this giant cement pool. All the kids put a little kernel of corn on their hooks. The fish were flipping all over the place. Kids were screaming. I didn't catch one."

I lean back listening to the wind whistle and the soft sound of the surf. "I've caught two fish at a time," I say. "My grandfather used to say that when you catch two at a time, you got to let one go."

Thinking about this, she lets her tongue rest between her teeth. "How come you never took me out on your boat?"

"It needs a lot of work," I say, which is half true. All the mahogany on the *Glory* is begging for a coat of varnish. Tied up in the slip, my grandfather spent spring and summer days working on the boat. In the winter, he worked on her in the boatyard. He showed me how to refinish the deck, how to repair dry rot, how to overhaul the motor.

"You probably take other girls out," she says.

"I don't take out girls that wear clogs." I stroke Pits's hair away from her forehead. She looks straight at me until I have to look toward the ocean. Drifting on the *Glory* in Reynolds Channel, Ginny caught her first fluke. In the bunk over the anchor storage, we made love as waves rolled into the boat from passing wakes. Taking Pits out on the *Glory* would be an official date; I don't even call her on the phone.

"I don't know, Eddie, sometimes I think you just come around because you got nothing to do."

I lift her head off my leg and stand.

"I got feelings, you know," she says.

At the boardwalk rail, the seagulls flap their wings clumsily and land on the beach. I grip the rail and I'm surprised it's still warm from the day's sun. I half expect Pits to jump on my back. I turn, she's lying across the bench. Down the boardwalk, the lights are bright. If I was with Ginny, I'd be at the rides and games, not here next to a closed knish place, waiting for Loopy. Walking slowly, I peer down through the dark slats in the boardwalk looking for Loopy and Drawers. I'm sure I hear Drawers scream, then it's quiet. A chill passes through me. I don't envy Loop, under there in the lines of light, in sand adorned with millions of cigarette butts, damp dark sand that never dries completely, and Drawers with her old jeans and panties around one ankle. Sometimes getting laid is worse than not.

After a block, I duck into a candy store that's called Saltwater Taffy and More. Behind the counter, a woman with gray hair and a gray mustache watches Edith Bunker argue with Archie on a small black-and-white TV. I stand there for a couple of seconds before she looks away from the screen. "There's a little bit of me in all of youse," yells Archie.

"Nice night," I say.

"I wish it were over. You're the first person that's been in here in an hour."

On a chrome scale she weighs a half pound of chocolate-covered jelly rings, then slides them into a white bag.

I hurry back to Pits. She's at the boardwalk rail. "Where the hell did you get off to," she says. "I thought you flat left me."

"Here's some candy."

"Take me out on the boat," she says, grabbing the bag.

"After I get it fixed up a little."

"You promise?" She opens the bag and bites a ring.

"Yeah."

On the bench she rests her head on my shoulder.

"You wanna go under the boardwalk?" she asks.

"Nah," I shrug. "I don't like closed-in spaces." Once I took a girl under and screwed her on a blanket. This girl was big, a German, her father was a doctor and had his office on the side of their house. She got whatever she wanted, so I let her get the top all the time. On my back under the walk, staring through her clean straight hair at the rotted boards and shafts of light, was as close to buried as I ever felt. She humped me like she was making butter, pounding the shit out of me. I didn't come, actually lost my hard-on, so she slapped my face. I drove her home and told her to have a nice life. I didn't care that all the guys thought this girl was so hot. I heard from one of her girlfriends that she nicknamed me The Corpse.

Pits pulls herself up and clicks her fingers in front of my face. "Hey, handsome," she says and kisses me. I attempt to finish what I started in the car.

"Do it like I showed you," she says in my ear. A few weeks ago in her bedroom she held my hand and showed me how to move it, told me to use just two fingers and the palm of my hand. It was the biggest turn-on. She moaned and broke out in a sweat. I try to maneuver my fingers around, but her jeans are tight.

Tonight Pits comes, maybe she fakes it. Sitting right there, she unbuckles my belt. When a couple strolls by, I raise my eyebrows to them as if to say, What are you going to do with kids now-a-days. Inside, I want it all to stop. I want Pits wearing a clean dress, maybe high heels. We could be in a restaurant, or even one of those clubs over on Hempstead Turnpike where the Jewish American Princesses go on Friday nights.

The couple hurries by and I know more than ever that Pits is wishing she were a zillion miles from here, a star in the sky, unreachable. She starts in again tugging at my pants. I see the ocean reflected in her eyes. I see a dozen nights like this one. I see Pits studying me. I feel myself choke up, my eyes almost filling.

"What is it? Did you know them?" she asks.

"I could have."

I buckle my pants. She covers my hands with hers. On each of her fingers she wears a silver ring. Some of them have blue stones, some black. I try to imagine her buying them, picking them out, trying them on for size. I touch her heart-shaped silver earring. "You don't have to do whatever I want," I say.

"I know," she says pulling out her cigarettes.

"Then why do you?"

"You know what your problem is, Trottman?" she says getting up. "You don't know what you want." She stares at me, waiting for a reply.

I put my head down and look between the slats at the darkness below.

"You're no better than me," she says, then goes to the rail and smokes. Her flannel shirt flaps behind her. It's not that nothing is good enough, it's just that what I've gotten isn't good enough. I get up and go to her, put my arm around her shoulder.

"And what about for you?" I ask. "Is this good enough?"

"You're good enough," she answers with her face next to mine.

I'm sorry about hurting her, but don't say it. Somehow, I feel better, about her, about the night. We kiss for a long time. She has that type of mouth that can kiss for hours.

Loopy and Drawers return. All Drawers needs is a broomstick and a wart on her nose. Her hair is every way, full of sand. Yellow cigarette filters stick to the back of her shirt that's ripped along the front and, she is pissed, major-league pissed.

"Eighteen dollars, Mr. Bigshot," she keeps saying. "Eighteen dollars."

Loopy finally opens his wallet and lets a few bills go blowing down the boardwalk. Drawers runs, stomps them with her sneakers and sticks them in her jeans pocket.

"That was like her favorite shirt," says Pits.

"I use nicer shit to wash the car," says Loopy.

In the Goat, Loopy drives the deserted streets back to Freeport, blasting his Zeppelin eight-track so loud the floor vibrates. Near Atlantic Avenue we blow through a red light. I look behind expecting to see flashing police lights. Pits snuggles against me, tucking her head half under my jacket.

We fly into the pizza parking lot. Drawers gets out without a word and slams the door. A second later the only thing near her is the burning rubber smell of the GTO's tires as we peel away.

Past the quiet streets, past the trim lawns, and dark houses with three cars in the driveway, Loopy takes the cut-off road behind the golf course. The dump hits us as if someone had opened a garbage pail. A dog runs in front of the Goat and Loopy swerves. Pits and I are slammed into the side of the car. She bangs her head. "Hey, Jerkoff, slow down," I yell.

At her house, Loopy leans over and watches us kiss. I put my hand over his face and he pulls my arm between the bucket seats.

"Why don't you grow up," says Pits.

"Me, grow up, me?" jokes Loopy. "How would you like me to show you how big I am?" He pretends to unbuckle his belt.

Pits climbs out of the backseat. "I'll see you tomorrow, Eddie?" she asks, ignoring Loopy.

Before I can answer, we're off. I look back and she's standing in the road.

"What are you in love, or something?" asks Loopy. "You got the same look as Drawers after I banged her."

"And what's that look?"

"Like you just found out the rubber broke." He laughs, drives with one hand, and locks his arms around my neck. "Hey, come on," he hugs me. I grab him and tug at his arm. He releases me and drives around the curve of the golf course. Suddenly, the air smells clean.

"We got to figure out a plan," I say, thinking out loud. "Maybe next weekend we could go into the city and hang out."

"With them?"

"Why not?"

"Didn't anybody tell you? Those aren't the type of girls you bring home to Mamma. You don't spend money on them."

"I know," I say.

"Let's go check out the girls," he says.

"What? The tittie joints?"

"Yeah, maybe that bald girl with the wigs will be dancing."

"I'm not in the mood."

"You got your cotton friend?" he asks in an exaggeratedly high girl's voice. I have to smile. He's such a nonstop douche bag.

"You want to go out on the *Glory* for some blues?" I ask, getting out in front of my house.

"What, you need a ride?"

"Yeah, I do."

"Are they running?"

"We could check, they could be in the inlet."

"What time?"

"Be here by seven, the latest." I say seven because he's always late.

"Seven-thirty," he says. Tires squeal and he's off.

Chapter Two

At home my mother lies passed out stone drunk on her side against the cabinets below the kitchen sink. The refrigerator door is open and AM News is blaring the traffic report. On the table is a half-finished glass of beer and an empty bottle of cheap vodka. I lean over her, making sure there's not a puddle of blood under her head. "Hey, Mom," I say.

She shakes her head as if dreaming.

In the refrigerator, I find cheese and bread and pour a glass of milk. Wash is piled on two chairs. My mother lets it pile up even though she does wash for a living at a dry cleaners called Laundry. I pull a chair next to her and stroke her black hair. It's soft and clean. Her breathing comes and goes and reminds me of a baby's.

Her maiden name is Rosalinda Rosado. Now, she's Rose Trottman. I have her coloring and features, dark hair, olive skin, but I have my father's squinty eyes and crooked smile. My father's name is Stan, everyone calls him Stan the Man.

With a shake, my mother's eyes open. "What, what happened?" she asks.

"Nothing."

"Where's your father?"

"Not here."

Coming around, her face shakes a little, sort of a mini convulsion. Floor tile patterns are pressed into her cheek. My father has moved in and out about two hundred times after about as many fights. Sometimes, he just goes to the grocery store and doesn't come back. The last time he punched my mother in the stomach then walked out. She lost her breath and rolled into a ball on the couch in the living room. The blow had been in the middle of a screaming bout over my mother's crazy superstitions. My father was hitting gin and milk, stewing because my mother had pushed a pencil point through the face of the queen of hearts in all the decks in the house. She was on a her second quart of Malt Duck, yelling that a queen of hearts, face-up under her bed, could dry her up, "like your girlfriends." My father sprang from the table, the chair fell over backward. When she pointed her finger near his nose, he punched her in the stomach and went out the door. I ran after him and grabbed his coat, trying to spin him around. I wanted to rip him apart, give him his own medicine. But he gave me a jolting push in the chest that knocked me off my feet. He got in his car and took off. I pictured myself killing my father, maybe with a knife. My grandfather told me my dad hadn't always been rotten. As a kid, he wasn't the apple with the worm in it, but that day I didn't believe it.

I help my mother off the floor, then go out the back door for some air and stand in the small overgrown yard. A few years ago I hit a tire iron with the lawn mower, the shaft bent, and the yard has never been mowed since. A loud jet streaks across the low sky heading to JFK. I've never been in a plane, but I lived my entire life under the flight pattern. I know there will be more fights, more planes, more days just like this one.

When I come in, my mother has the wrong end of a cigarette

in her mouth and is reaching for her beer. "Ma," I say, "you trying
for round two?" Her lips tighten as if she is going to kiss someone,
then she closes her eyes. It's an expression she makes when she's
drunk. She can't help it.

"What did you do tonight?" she asks.

"Went to the beach with Loopy and some girls." I pull the butt
out of her mouth and reverse it.

"That's all?"

"Believe me, it was enough, more than enough."

She lights the cigarette and takes a long drag. Biting her lower
lip, she looks me over. "Don't you want to *do* something big?" she
asks earnestly, opening her eyes. "Don't you want to *be* somebody?"

"The mayor," I say. "I wouldn't mind being the mayor."

She takes my hands. "I want you to be something big," she says.

"All right, the president," I say.

"Come on, come on," she pleads, trying to shake off my nonsense
and the booze. "What do you want?"

"I want . . ." Nothing comes out. I want Armpits to become
Ginny. I miss my grandfather, miss fishing with him. I want the
Road Runner, a hemi-orange '69 that's for sale down on Sportsman
Avenue that I test drove at ninety miles an hour. I want my father
to come walking in the door with a bagful of groceries and make
omelets like he did one time when I was a kid. I want to go back
and not roll stolen change for two thieving assholes and get locked
up for it. Not be labeled a Trottman. I tell her I don't want anything, not really.

I flick the kitchen light off and follow my mother down the hall.
Turning into the bathroom, she takes off her shirt and I see her
breasts. All my life she's been doing this. My father says it's because
she's Puerto Rican. Puerto Rican and German, a bad mix, my
grandfather used to say. My father met her in the service. When

they married, my father told her she was supposed to forget she was Puerto Rican. She wasn't allowed to speak Spanish, except to her relatives on the phone. I once heard my father tell his buddies that my mother was dark Irish, from Dublin City.

My mother tugs off her jeans and sits on the toilet. Listening to her go, I have a sick stomach for a second and shut the door in my room. I'm probably booked first class to hell for thinking she has a nice body. I slam my head back against the wall and it jars my jaw.

Outside, the traffic on Sunrise Highway whooshes by. A truck, air brakes hissing, pulls into the twenty-four-hour wash next door. I think about calling Armpits, but it would wake her old man and old lady. Nothing's good enough for you, Trottman. It's the first time Armpits ever got mad at me.

In the kitchen, I dial her number and hang up when her father answers. A second later, I dial Ginny's number. It can't make matters much worse. Her old man already thinks I'm a lowlife, and she probably believes it. After four rings I hear Ginny's voice: "Hello."

"It's me, Eddie, I know it's late but I . . ."

"I was studying for a test." I hear her yawn.

"College tough, huh?"

"Very." I see her lying on her bed in her pink shorty pajamas, books open.

"Ginny, I was wondering if you still think we need a break from each other. It's been six months. Maybe a movie or something?"

"That would be nice, if it could work."

"What is that supposed to mean?"

"Eddie, we had a lot of fun, and I really liked you, but I told you . . ." There is silence for a moment.

"What did you expect me to do? I saw you kissing Jay."

"It can't work, and it's late. Okay?"

I force myself to hang up the receiver gently.

Back in my room it stinks of dirty clothes, sweat, me. The room is rotting. Posters, of Bruce Springsteen, the Stones, the Who, have been falling off the walls since the ninth grade. They say nothing anymore, about me, about what I like, about where I am. I rip down the Boss and crumple him into a big ball. I shove the poster in the trash. I try to convince myself that, if I had gone to college, Ginny would have stayed with me.

"What's the racket," calls my mother.

"I just killed the Boss."

"The who?"

"The Boss," I scream.

"It don't matter. Always another boss," she says.

Chapter Three

My head is thick from last night and, I imagine, Loopy is probably in a coma from his thirty-one Millers. Still low over the hazy east end of Long Island, the morning sun pokes through a cloud. I wait in front of my house for Loopy to rumble up. A car with a fishing pole sticking out the window passes toward Grove Street, then makes a right to Woodcleft canal. Blues are running just outside the Jones Beach inlet. Most people think they are too oily and fishy tasting. But with my grandfather's recipe—get all the blood out of the spine, soak the fish in milk overnight, then wrap it in tin foil with onions and garlic, cook nice and slow in a low oven—I swear it's like eating king mackerel.

I've tried to teach Loopy a few things about the ocean, things my grandfather taught me, like a rope is called a line, a knot is a nautical mile-per-hour, the closet is a locker. Five minutes later, he's calling the stern the back and the hull the front. All he remembers is the toilet is called the head. But Loopy's got this respect thing about the ocean. He releases all the fish we can't eat, sort of wiggles them alive in the green current before letting them go, and he gets pissed off if the gas overflows into the canal or someone throws a bottle or can overboard. One time, a few miles out from the inlet, a big sunfish swam next to the boat like a slow-moving submarine. Loopy raced around, following that lazy fish, screaming his head off like he'd just won the lottery. Swaying its giant fins, the head—a mottled blunt bullet—vanished in the swelling sea. "I hope nobody ever catches it," said Loopy.

On the ocean, Loopy dreams about cutting out to Florida like in the movie *Midnight Cowboy*, except we'd go on the *Glory*, not on a Greyhound. I'd charter the *Glory* and he'd be my first mate. Anchored in the bay, I unrolled my grandfather's yellow intercoastal waterway charts, and Loopy and I plotted a course to Key West. We worked out some numbers for the cost of fuel and food on the back of a Twinkie cardboard. Loopy carries that piece of cardboard folded in his wallet.

The cars go by, bells for church start bonging, a pack of Jap motorcycles, motors ringing, speeds by. A Wetson's Hamburger truck pulls into the wash next door. My head pounds from last night and I go in the house squeezing my temples.

In the front room, I spin the TV dial through church programs and shut it off at *The American Farmer*. Coughing comes from the kitchen. What do I want? Since when does that matter.

"You up already?" I yell. My mother doesn't answer.

In the kitchen, she's at the table, smoking, drinking Pepsi from a can, her eyes fixed out the window like a zombie. "How's your head?" She still doesn't answer, doesn't move. I grab the phone and dial Loopy's number.

"You got to run out of here every Sunday?" she asks.

"Just the ones when it's not snowing."

"I heard the weather. Rain. You want to get hit by lightning?"

The phone rings in my ear.

"The beach," she says, resting her head in her hand. "You sit on a towel and watch the boats."

"Who is this?" asks Loopy's mom, answering the phone. I imagine her at her kitchen table smoking, holding her head.

"Sorry for calling so early," I say.

"Eddie?" she asks. "Oh, Jesus Christ Almighty, I'm having a morning," she says. "Loopy got locked up."

"Locked up? For what?"

"Were you with him last night?"

I can't think of any crimes we committed last night, but remember a few days ago Loopy tore ass out of the Sunoco station without paying Grady, the attendant. "Last night we didn't do anything."

"Was he drunk? Was he driving?"

"I guess they got him again," I say.

"If he had a brain in his head," she says. I stay on the phone until the dial tone clicks on.

"What's the matter?" asks my mother. "Your boat sink?"

"Loopy," I say, "he's in jail."

"Are you in trouble?"

"You think just because he gets locked up, I got to get locked up?"

"That's what I think," she screams as the screen door slams behind me. Outside, I study the traffic, hoping Loopy's red Goat will screech to the curb. I picture him on the side of the road, shitfaced, trying to walk a straight line, touch his nose, explain away the dozen empty bottles rattling around the floor of the car.

"What'd you two do?" asks my mother through the screen door.

"Nothing. Loopy must have got pinched after he dropped me off."

"What's this pinched?" She says the word like it smells of vomit. "Your father says pinched."

On his fingers, counting off from his pinky, I can hear my father running through all the guys he knows that got pinched. Louie got

pinched in that thing with the liquor store, Scotty got pinched and
bum rapped, Willie got pinched crossing the state line, cigarettes,
he'd say, pulling his middle finger back, Sally got pinched for lifting
from the till, "Believe that, it's the goddamn truth." Then he'd go
into his rules, "I'm only standing here before you because of Trottman rule Number One: Keep your mouth shut, and Trottman rule
Number Two: If trouble's on the stove, don't stay for supper." Day
to day, the rules change order, but he always starts with Number
One, which could have been Trottman rule Number Three the day
before.

"Well you know, Trottman rule Number One," I say. "If the
shoe fits, steal the pair." I turn around to see my mother's face.

"Pinched," she says. "Now, *your* friends are getting pinched?"

The screen door squeaks open. Clutching her pack of True and
matches, she settles next to me. "Boats sink," she says. "When I
was a girl I went to five funerals. All fishermen. No coffins, no
bodies, and they never washed up. A soul that dies at sea never
rests." She pulls her nightgown between her legs and turns to me.
"It's the same sea," she says. "The same one."

"Ma, it's the ocean." Her feet are tan, beat-up, bent toes, yellow
nails. I picture her toes on the sand, in the clear blue water of the
posters at the travel agent on Main Street.

"It's the same ocean," she says.

Standing, I hoist the cooler to my shoulder. "Listen, if Loopy
calls, tell 'im I'm at the boat." On the cracked gray sidewalk, I head
east and cut the corner on the movie theater's parking lot that's
turned into a Baptist church. The lot is half full with polished
Caddies and Lincolns. On the marquee it says, "When the time
comes, will you be ready?" Nothing against God, but I liked it
better when it was a movie theater.

South, down Main Street, in the hardware-store window are pictures of tools pasted to postboard. Years ago the tools had been real, but that was when the people that lived north of the railroad, stayed north. Now they're buying and renting houses all the way down to Atlantic Avenue. Even the liquor store put in bulletproof glass. If you want a bottle of wine, you've got to put your money in a slot, then wait for the clerk to fetch it.

Past the corner, a white station wagon pulls next to me. Figuring I'm going to get robbed, I back against a building. My boss, Kurt, leans across his wife, waving out the passenger window. "Hey, kid, you need a lift?" In the backseat, Kurt's kids are dressed like miniature sailors. His wife is a real knockout. I've seen her shopping in the store a few times. She's slender, has real long legs, and walks like she's balancing a stack of books on her head.

"I'm just going down to the canal."

"Get in," he says.

He lowers the rear electric window of the wagon. I put my cooler in. I don't really want to ride with them, but I get in the backseat anyway. I feel as if I'm bursting their private family bubble.

I've never seen Kurt out of the shop and, for some reason, he looks like he's shrunk. His hair is slicked down, and he's wearing a shirt with little umbrellas on it. The kids, both giggling, slide over to the other side of the car.

Kurt introduces the wife and kids and puts the car in drive. "Eddie does the work of two butchers," he says, smiling at me in the rearview mirror.

Trudy turns around and leans over the front seat. "Kurt's told me all about you."

"Kids nowadays lack conviction," says Kurt. "I went through a half dozen kids before I hired Eddie. And I'll tell you, I figured you'd last a week. What's it been now?"

"A year," I say.

"Trudy, you ought to get a load of the place on Monday mornings. Clean isn't the word for it."

"I wouldn't mind cutting red meat," I say.

"You will, believe me, you will."

"Just be patient," I say.

"That's right," says Kurt. "Good things come—"

"To those who wait," I mutter as he drives past the new recreation center at the end of canal, past the senior citizen development where my grandfather lived. I spot my grandfather's old apartment. A woman sits in a wheelchair in the open doorway. My grandfather used to say the neighbors went as fast as the seasons.

"I'll get out here," I say.

"We're going down to Jones Beach to walk on the boardwalk," says Kurt, pulling over.

"Before the crowds get there," says Trudy. Her skin is so white and perfect I can see the veins in her neck.

"Thanks," I say, opening the door. "Maybe sometime I'll take you out on my boat."

"How about showing it to us," says Kurt. "We got time." He looks at Trudy and pulls the station wagon off the road into the Old Oyster Wharf, a boatyard with dockage. We pass the Millers' house that must be a hundred years old. My grandfather and Mr. Miller were childhood friends. Mr. Miller only takes a quarter of the docking fee from me, a hundred bucks a season. In the winter I shovel snow for them. In April I painted the dock green and tarred the tops of the bulkheads. Usually, on Sundays, before I take the boat out, I haul their trash to the curb, or give the grass a once-over with their push mower.

Behind the house is another building where Mrs. Miller runs an antique shop. In the twenties, the Oyster Wharf was a bar and grill, during Prohibition it was a speakeasy. It's a relief to see the

CLOSED sign on the antique shop. I won't be asked to take out the garbage or sweep the walk.

"Kurt, look, an antique shop," says Trudy.

He winds the station wagon down the bumpy shell road, along a line of overgrown hedges. Beyond the hedges is a seafood restaurant, its exhaust fans blow an odor of garlic and fried fish. The kids hold their noses as the odor fills the car.

Kurt parks next to a red toolshed. A few of the boats are already out. On the light breeze, their tie lines swing in the empty boat slips.

The kids charge out of the car. Trudy grabs their hands before they get close to the water. Across the narrow canal, retarded kids dressed in jeans and white T-shirts roam in the yard behind the Martin Luther King Center. Some walk along a cyclone fence swinging their heads side to side. My grandfather said that they were lucky because they didn't know any better, claimed they were their own guardian angels, but I don't believe it. To me the kids are just more of the rotten luck in the world. Kurt and Trudy stare across the calm canal at the kids. Kurt raises his eyebrows, and his wife exhales a long breath. "You'd think they'd plant a few shade trees or something," she says.

I walk the dock to the last slip before the restaurant's property. The *Glory* sits high in the canal. The shimmering reflection of her white lapstrake sides and red water line is neatly cut in half by a pencil fish darting under the boat. Like the curve of a Viking's horn, her bow rises from the water as if all thirty-two feet of her just came out of a wave. On the side of her flying bridge are the script words *Egg Harbor*. She was built in '55, "When mahogany wasn't scarce and wood still had sap in it," my grandfather liked to say.

The kids are tugging and squirming, trying to break their

mother's grip. "They haven't been around the water much," she says, pulling her little boy to her shoulder. The girl manages to slide to the ground and bumps her head. The crying begins and Kurt rushes to the rescue.

After they are back in the car, Trudy lowers the window. "Kurt thinks you're something special," she says in a hushed way. "I'm very glad to meet you."

Shells crunching under the tires, the station wagon winds up the road. The kids wave. I wave back, wondering what it would be like to marry a woman who got dressed up on Sundays. I picture Trudy in the high-school band, marching straight down the center of the football field, chin high, raising her white boots and a sparkling baton. There were girls like Trudy in my high school, and the closest I ever got to one was Ginny. Hitters had their girls, the only batons they raised were Marlboros.

On the boat, I remove the gray canvas cover off the bridge. The varnish on the wooden wheel peels like translucent flakes of sunburn. Inside the cabin, I find sandpaper, a paintbrush, and an ancient can of my grandfather's varnish. With my shirt off, I sand the wheel with 180 grit. (My grandfather always corrected me—it's not a steering wheel, it's a wheel.) The retards patrol the fence one side to the other.

When he was alive, the other side of the canal was a beach where the white and brown ducks nested. At high tide, snappers jumped like bouncing silver dollars. My grandfather usually set a line off the bow of the *Glory*. Mostly he caught mucus-covered eels as thick as my wrist. They stayed alive a long time, wiggled even after they were skinned and put in a greased frying pan. He ate anything he caught: sea-robins, sharks, skates. He ate butterfish whole, on toast with mayo, head, tail and all.

Using an oily rag, I clean the instrument panel on the dashboard that my grandfather made from 16-gauge stainless steel. He was a machinist and could do anything with a flat piece of metal, a ball-peen hammer, and a box of rivets. For thirty years at a machine shop he made air-conditioning ducts and storm windows, while rock an' roll blasted above the noise of the lathes. He was the oldest worker in the place.

I finish sanding the wheel and hold off on the coat of varnish as it will take several coats to make it feel like glass. I'm too beat for fishing. I look at the sky and decide on just taking a nap.

With my clothes hanging over a line in the cabin, I crawl into the large bunk onto musty cushions. Rain pounds the hatches and deck. There are no visible leaks. Above my head, I read a yellowed list my grandfather tacked over the bunk space:

Preventive Maintenance Program
Spark plug cables
Loose fuel lines
Cracks in fuel lines
Electrical wiring
Steering mechanism
Lubricate components
Water intake
Zincs
Oil
Drive belts
Horn
Lights

There is another note on the rear of the door going to the head. I know it by memory.

Safety
Heaving Line
Life ring
Life raft
Life preservers—10

After I inherited the boat, I saw the lists and I realized that my grandfather must have known he was going to die. It was just too much of a coincidence. I had to ask someone at a boatyard how to check a zinc, and I still haven't found the life raft. Maybe I'm supposed to buy one.

I tuck my hands under my head and feel the *Glory* rock gently. I need to pull her out of the water, scrape the barnacles off her bottom, and give her another coat of red-lead. I have to sand the decks, varnish, paint the cabin. I drift off, making mental lists.

I wake up sweaty and open the brass porthole. It looks like the storm blew across the Island into the Sound. I've slept most of the afternoon. I turn on the water and an electric pump whirs and drops trickle into my palms. I splash my eyes. When I was a kid I'd imagine that I was crossing the Pacific to the Far East and no one, not even the Coast Guard, believed I'd made it. My grandfather said that if he had to cross an ocean, it wouldn't be the Atlantic. "Don't care for icebergs," he'd say, winking at me.

I lock up and step off the boat.

Towards Loopy's house, I cut through the senior citizen development, passing my grandfather's old apartment. The wheelchair that I saw this morning is folded, leaning against the closed door. The window is open a crack and I smell roast beef, or maybe stew. I swallow hard, remembering knocking on the door, my grandfather opening it, saying, "What are you knocking for?"

Loopy lives on the corner of Atlantic and Bedell with his mom and his fat little brother, Meatball. The house had a big front and side yard but the town widened both streets so that the Louperinos' stoop is practically on the sidewalk and the south side of the house is the shoulder of the road. From their kitchen window, you can watch the traffic light change. When Loopy's mom gets in the right mood, she talks about fixing the place and opening a beauty shop. Knocking the house down and rebuilding would be easier. In the spring termites swarm in the yard, the gutters grow two-foot maple trees. In the winter, the toilets and pipes freeze solid. Loopy doesn't do much around the place. If he shovels snow off the walk, his mother wants to throw a party.

I cross under the Louperinos' stone carriage port where electric green moss grows up the granite. The steps are rubbery and black from the rain. Using the lion's head knocker, I bang on the door.

Loopy's mother pokes her head out the porch window. She's got hair short as a terrier's, blond on top, dark on the sides. "Rape," she says, shooting her face at me like a guard dog. "Rape, the charge is rape." She pulls opens the door, stares straight at me, hands on her round high hips. Behind her, the enclosed porch is packed with broken bicycles, barbecue grills, stacks of newspapers, and piles of forgotten toys.

"Rape?"

"That's right." Mrs. Loop, on her long ostrich legs, strides down the hall. "That's what the detectives told me."

Rape. I see the cigarette butts sticking to Drawers's back, her ripped shirt. Then I remember that he went to a strip club, and wonder what could have happened.

Up the hall I have to pass the pull-out couch where Loopy's

grandmother sits on a rumpled cot in front of her walker. Loopy calls her "Grandma Cabbage." I try not to look at Granny, the tray of pills, the plastic bedpan, and the yellow sheets, but I smell her even over the smell of Champ, the Louperinos' German Shepherd. Granny releases one of the white plastic grips on her walker and raises her hand.

"My story?" she asks. "My story on?"

"Oh, shut up," says Mrs. Loop, spinning the channels on a small black-and-white TV propped on some phone books. "It's Sunday, your programs aren't on."

Granny puts her hand down, stares at a Met game.

In the kitchen, Champ pants under the glass kitchen table. He snaps at a flea that seems to be running up his back.

"This takes the cake," says Mrs. Loop, folding her arms.

"Who did he rape?" I ask trying to make it sound like a ridiculous question.

"Sandra Gass. You know her?"

"I don't think so." Then, I remember that Dirty Drawers's last name is Gass, and that Drawers' real name is Sandra. "Yeah, I do know her," I say.

"She's a tart? Am I right?" asks Mrs. Loop, pointing her long finger at me.

"We call her Drawers." Loopy's remark, "I'm going to give her the banging of her life," and the scream under the boardwalk rush at me.

"I knew it."

I sit at the table with Drawers's scream lingering like a camera's flash. Champ lays his head across my sneaker. On the stove a pot comes to boil and rattles. The pot's top rises and boiling water sizzles on the electric burner.

"Oh, look at this," says Mrs. Loop, grabbing the pot with dish towels on her hands. "Let me tell you, my Loopy would never rape a girl." Mrs. Loop opens a box of spaghetti and dumps it into the water. The steam rises around her face. "You were with him last night, what the hell went on?"

"Nothing. We went to the beach."

"Eddie, you're a rotten liar." She puts the top on the pot and turns to me.

"Nothing happened."

She looks at me as if she can see my thoughts. "Nothing?"

"Did you get him a lawyer?"

"No, I didn't get him a lawyer." She leans against the kitchen counter and lights a cigarette. "This is a real nice birthday present."

"It's your birthday?"

"Yeah, and don't ask. Don't even use your imagination." She bends into the bread drawer in the refrigerator. Her orange stretch pants slice the cheeks of her ass into two deflated basketballs. She comes out with a can of Black Label. Puss, their cat, walks the edge of the counter, daintily avoiding the hot stove. Mrs. Loop swats him to the floor.

"He raped Drawers," I say quietly.

"What?"

"I wish it *was* drunk driving."

"I just hope to Christ he didn't rape that girl," she says staring above my head. "Stay for dinner. I got enough." She lifts an aluminum colander of steaming cauliflower from the sink.

"No, I really got to go," I say, getting up.

The phone rings. Mrs. Loop snatches it off the wall. "Yeah," she says. "I accept the charges." She puts her hand over the phone and mouths, "It's Loopy," as if someone is listening.

I knew it was him because prisoners can only call collect from the jail.

"They're not tapped, you stupid ass," she yells into the phone, then she presses it against one of her flat tits. "Are the phones from the jail tapped?"

I shrug.

She gets back on the phone and, after a moment, says, "I don't have that kind of money. You must be confusing me with Jackie Onassis." She listens and puffs her cigarette, stabs it out in the clam shell on the counter. "Eddie is sitting right in front of me," she pushes the phone at me.

"Don't say anything, just listen, because the phones are tapped," says Loopy in a half whisper.

"How do you know?"

"Some dude that knows told me, okay?"

"Okay, okay, calm down."

"You calm down, don't tell me to calm down, I just spent a night in the tank with fifteen stinking drunks, and about twenty assholes in tie-dye that got busted at the Dead concert."

"The Dead were in town?"

"They were at the coliseum. You know I hate the Dead."

"Drawers really pressed charges?" I ask.

"I'm here, right?"

"Somebody must have put her up to it."

"Forget Drawers. Listen, the cops, they're going to ask you some questions. Just remember one thing, you were there, you saw everything."

"Were where?"

"There," he almost screams, "you know, under the boardwalk."

"I wasn't . . ."

"No, don't say that. Eddie, for me, do me this one small favor. Just say you were there, that you saw everything, that you saw that I didn't do a fucking thing."

He's waiting and I'm trying to figure out exactly what I'm getting into. "What did you do to her?" I ask.

"She's a whore."

I listen to his breathing and the hollow noises and voices in the background. What I don't understand is why he did it when she can barely give it away. "You want me to talk to her?"

"I swear on my mother's life," he breathes, "she's lying."

"I'll talk to her."

The phone sounds like it bounces off the wall. I hear him yelling at someone. "Look, I got to go, there's a line of Deadheads behind me waiting to talk to their mommies." He hangs up.

"What?" says Mrs. Loop. "What, come on?"

"He didn't do it. I'll talk to Sandra." I hand her the phone.

"You know he didn't do it?"

"I might have been there."

"What do you mean, you were either there or you weren't."

I back down the hall from the kitchen and almost trip over Grandma Cabbage's cot. She grabs at my jacket.

"Then that's it," says Mrs. Loop. "That's it. If you saw it you got to tell the police."

"I know," I say, unhooking Grandma Cabbage's fingers.

"Stay for some spaghetti," yells Mrs. Loop.

"I got to go."

"I have birthday cake."

I get to the door, the porch, and down the steps. Out on the sidewalk I walk against traffic on Atlantic Avenue. Loopy raped Drawers. Jesus.

Chapter Four

In the driveway trees burst with red buds. Black puddles from the afternoon storm reflect the orange and pink of the setting sun. The air is clean, full of the new night. Leaves, the color of limes, shine on the bushes against the garage. Weeds, beaten down from last winter's snow, have pushed through the fall leaves. In a few weeks the yard will be green. Spring has sprung. Fuck.

At the end of the driveway, on deflated tires, the Plymouth waits patiently for a new transmission. The once shiny paint is chalky. The longer the car sits, the more expensive it will be to get it on the road. In the steamy car window I notice the vinyl on the dashboard has ruptured, cracked like a miniature earthquake.

The front door is locked. Usually the house is open. Except for loose change and a few dollars hidden in my bedpost, there's nothing to steal. I yell in the window and, after a few minutes, go around to the back door. It's locked. I pop the window screen out and climb into the back pantry.

The house is quiet. "Hey, Ma," I call. Pots and pans are stacked neatly in the rubber drain board next to the kitchen sink. In the refrigerator there's a pot of black beans and rice. Under cellophane, a stack of pork chops cool on a plate that my mother usually uses only on holidays. I pull out a chop and take a bite. They are the center cuts that Reggie cut and trimmed special for me.

In the front room, the throw cover on the couch is tucked into the cushions. Newspapers are stacked under the window, even the TV *Guide* is on the TV set, not thrown on the floor. On the coffee table two highball glasses rest in puddles from condensation.

"You're back in one piece," says my mother, coming down the dim hallway, putting on her robe.

"You didn't hear me knocking?"

"Who couldn't hear your racket." My mother's flushed. Her bangs stick to her forehead. She tightens the terrycloth belt of her robe and takes my arm. "I got a friend here," she says. "Nobody you know."

"I don't want to know," I say.

"I'm thirty-nine years old," she whispers, grabbing my sleeve. "Thirty-nine. You think that's old, well, it's not."

How long has she known him? Two hours, three hours. I slam my hand on the cabinet door. The dishes rattle, something falls. "Jesus, Ma."

"Rose," calls a man's voice. "Everything all right?"

We both freeze, then she answers in a higher than usual voice, "Okay in here."

"Those were my center cuts," I say. "You were supposed to make them for me, remember?"

"This ain't about chops," she says. "You got your life. I don't take that from you."

I head out. The back door slams behind me. In front of the house I notice a baby-blue pickup truck. In the bed about a dozen empty Schaeffer cans have rolled to one corner.

Thirty-nine, getting laid from some loser at six thirty in the evening on a Sunday. Banged like some whore. Cooking all those black beans and my center cuts, cleaning the house. I look back, feel like screaming, but know I'm acting like a fool.

Past Wetson's hamburgers where the air is full of onions and grease, on the other side of the town's municipal parking lot, I enter the train station. The town bum is sprawled on a wooden bench. People call him the cowboy because he's always pulling an imaginary gun, pointing, shooting, then blowing across his finger. He's been the town bum since I was a kid. His eyes open and he sits up.

"Stan the Man," he says, calling me by my father's nickname.

"Eddie," I say.

"No, you're Stan." He points his finger at me and lowers his thumb like a trigger.

At the ticket window, I slide the girl a buck twenty for a one-way to Merrick, which is about a mile of straight track due east.

On the elevated platform the steel tracks lead west to Manhattan, east to Islip. Beyond the bowling alley and the fire department, straight down Main Street sits the Tropicana bar, where my mother probably met that guy.

On weekend nights, the Tropicana's D.J. plays disco records under a spinning mirrored ball. Old farts, thirty and up, crowd a dance floor that's about the size of two coffins side by side. But my mother doesn't go there when the place is packed and the music blasting. She's there during the day, when the front door is open, airing cigarette smoke and stale beer. Perched on a stool with a guy's arm around her shoulder, or alone watching the entrance, she spends her laundry salary at the happy hour special: SCREWDRIVERS HALF PRICE, TAP-BEER 2 FOR 1.

The train rushes in, hisses to a stop. The automatic doors slide open. In an empty car I sit next to a window. The train jolts forward

and Freeport fades in the darkness. The conductor doesn't punch
my ticket, so I fold it and put it in my wallet.

Pits lives in a one-story white house with black trim; the worst-
looking house on the block. The paint peels in hard flakes that
crack off the asbestos shingles and lie in the garden like odd-shaped
guitar picks. Overgrown evergreens, planted twenty-five years ago,
pull the rain gutters off the soffits and cover the windows. In the
side yard a swing set is bent like a giant, collapsed daddy long-legs.
In the shadows beyond, the dump looms, a sleeping giant with foul
breath. A breeze rustles the reeds and marsh grass that cover the
mountain, bringing the sour odor of garbage.

The street light on the corner illuminates a wooden boat rotting
in the driveway and casts my shadow on Pits's soggy crabgrass-and-
dandelion lawn. On the side of the house, I fight through the
bushes, past a Long Island Lighting electric meter that buzzes like
a dying bee, and peer into her window. At her makeup mirror that's
lined with light bulbs, the type in movie star dressing rooms, she
plucks at her eyebrow with a tweezer. She inspects her work, then
frowns. She crosses her bare legs, scratches her ankle, leaving white
marks on her tan skin. Her robe opens. The white cups of her bra
ride high on her chest.

Bottles of nail polish and large makeup cases that hold at least
twenty-five types of eye shadow glisten in the bright light. She
examines her front teeth. Somehow, even crooked, they . . . look
pretty good.

I tap on the window and she clutches her robe.

I put my fingers in the sides of my mouth and make a face at
her.

"You asshole," she says, pushing the window open. "You scared me to—Feel this!" She puts my flat palm on her chest and I feel her racing heart.

I slip in the window. With my hands on the floor and my legs out the window, I shimmy forward across the orange shag carpet. She grabs her pillow and hits me over the head with it, whacks me in the back, in the rear.

"Don't ever do that again," she says.

"Stop it, we've got to talk," I say, falling into her room. She tackles me on her bed and pins my hands down.

She tells me she doesn't like snoops, then kisses me. We roll over and she lets me pin her hands down. She's breathing hard and her robe is open, the skin above her bra flushed and red. "You know my father's not home yet and my mother's over at Gene's. You could have come in the front door."

"This is more fun."

"That's because you're a pervert."

"You should close the blinds. A real pervert could stand out there."

"A real pervert did!"

I grab her around the waist and slip my hands over her ass. She has an ass that fills out her worn Levi's with no room to spare. We kiss and my hands go inside her robe, to the arch of her spine, then into her bikini panties.

"My father could be walking in here any second." She pulls away. "So don't think you're going to climb in my window and—"

Kissing, we tumble around on the unmade bed. I slip off my sneakers. I think about Loopy, my promise that I'd find out the story. "I came over to talk," I say coming up for air, "about Loopy."

"Did you bring any . . . ?" she asks ignoring me.

"I didn't." Even though I've probably been with her twenty or thirty times, I've never had her so clean looking, fresh from the shower. Her white panties against her tan belly are glowing.

"You never do. Did you ever once? You make me. . . ."

Kissing her, I unsnap my jeans. She pulls them to my ankles, then off.

We don't really make love. I touch her the way she showed me. She grabs my hand and slows me down, guides me. Listening to the steady thump of her heart, I get into a rhythm, and, just before my hand cramps, she moans, shudders all over for a moment. Breathing slowly, her mouth opens, her top lip sticks to her teeth.

Across from me, her open closet is jammed with clothes, the floor covered with shoes. Yet, every day she wears the same couple of get-ups. I pull her head up and kiss her mouth. She rests her head on my chest and swings her warm leg across me. For a moment I think about mentioning Loopy and Drawers, but find myself too comfortable.

In the dark room I wake, make out the shape of the makeup mirror, and remember where I am. I reach for Pits, but she's gone. On the floor I find my clothes and I dress in the dark. It's the second time today that I've dozed off. I slip out of the room into the dark hall and walk toward the light. "Pits," I whisper, "Elena."

In the living room, projected on a fuzzy large-screen TV, Don Kirshner's *Rock Concert* features a repeat Elton John dressed as some asshole in a white wig and pirate hat. I swirl my finger in the murky five-gallon fish tank on the coffee table. At the surface of the water, two goldfish blow bubbles. Set in the blue gravel is a plastic NO FISHING sign. The veneer on the table is wavy and, where it separates, something's growing under the thin wood.

The toilet flushes and I freeze.

"You're lucky my parents aren't home yet," Pits says, coming down the hall. She hands me a glass of Coca-Cola and sits cross-legged next to me on the couch.

On a pile of magazines next to a Statue of Liberty ashtray, jammed with crushed Winstons with red lipstick stains on the filters, I pick up a container of fish food and sprinkle a few flakes into the tank. The fish dart at the flakes. Elena won 'em on the boardwalk in Long Beach. She had to pound a big hammer on a metal lily pad and bounce a bean-bag frog through a window.

The dark walnut-paneled walls tell a story with framed family photos: Pits as a wide-eyed baby, Pits's brother with braces, Mother with a beehive hairdo; Father and Mother in a stockade, their heads and hands sticking out as if floating in air. Mom in a bikini, looking two pounds heavier than a Halloween skeleton.

Along the windowsill are pots of withered brown cacti. I shift around and put my arm on Pits's shoulders. Elton does "Bennie and the Jets," a song that makes me want to jump out the window, but the house is a one story. I shut the TV off and tell her that I came over to talk about Loopy.

"I personally don't give two shits about that jerk." She gets up and flips through the albums stacked under the television table. She slips a record out of the cover, puts it on the turntable, then snuggles next to me. "I told Sandy she should charge him with rape."

"What?"

Donna Summer starts to sing, "Try Me, I Know We Can Make It," from her *Love Trilogy*, album.

"You were there last night. You think that was right, throwing money at her like she was some whore?"

"Sandy did charge him with rape. He's in jail."

Pits shoots me a look. "Then what's he doing driving around, going past here just an hour ago?"

"Tonight?"

"Yeah."

I lean back and stare at the ceiling. "Then he's out," I say. "His mother must of gotten his bail together."

"What are you talking about? Sandy wouldn't put Loopy in jail. She loves his ass."

I explain that Loopy called me from jail.

"I can't believe she didn't tell me," says Pits, smiling at me, her eyes shining. "Shit," she pushes my shoulder. "Last night she came by, madder than hell, madder than on the boardwalk."

I try to imagine Loopy cruising around and consider calling his house. His mother must have put the house up for collateral.

Pits goes on yakking about how upset Sandy was last night. I wonder if it's the first time Loopy ever raped her.

"Are you listening to me," Pits punches my shoulder. "Sometimes I think you've left the planet."

"Give me one good reason to stay."

She goes into this big story about Sandy coming over to her house last night and showing her bruises between her legs, purple and red bruises on the insides of her thighs. Pits says that Sandy said she wouldn't go out with Loopy again, even to a real nice restaurant. "So I said," says Pits, "that bastard ought to be put in jail. I just said it off the top of my head."

I try to picture Drawers's legs. "Between her legs?" I ask.

"Sandy said Loopy didn't have protection and, I know for a fact, that she's had three abortions, two last year. You know how stupid she must of felt going to the clinic three times. They have this bitchy nurse there who examines you before the doctor. She talks to you about birth control as if you were a moron, then makes you put a rubber on a fake penis."

Thinking about Drawers being led to the examining room gives me a sick feeling. I imagine the nurse's knowing eyes—just more white trash.

Donna Summer moans on and on. I turn off the record. In the next room a clock ticks. Outside, a car door shuts.

"You never find out if it's a boy or a girl, do you?" I ask.

"They do a D and C," says Pits. "The doctors don't even know." She's quiet a moment. "But, at least the babies never have to deal with all the shit we have to deal with."

I remember a movie I saw in high school Science class. It had close-ups of baby fingers and toes inside the womb, floating around like the astronauts in the Apollo missions. The film followed this kid through infancy, first grade, high school, college graduation, marriage, then fatherhood. The teacher made everyone write their impression of the film, hoping we'd understand that life was a cycle. I wrote that there were a lot of sick people in the world and it would be a better place if there were no men, women, or children, just animals and nature.

"I guarantee you, they must have told Sandy not to tell anyone about the charges," says Pits. "Otherwise she would have been over here blabbing every detail."

Loopy must have raped her. And Jesus, Loopy's story about me watching makes me feel like I'm trying to swallow a pill the size of a golf ball. I mean, it's not like he threw a dead cat in the town's swimming pool, or blew up a high school toilet with a cherry bomb.

My stomach growls. "You got anything to eat?"

"I forgot," she says in a real prissy way. "That's the other thing you think about."

I tell her I'm starving and she heads off to the kitchen in her bare feet and robe. "Do you want more soda?" she calls.

"Yeah, anything."

"How about cat piss?" she cracks herself up and giggles. She

comes in with a box of Kentucky Fried Chicken and a can of Coke.
I lift the lid, all that's left is a soggy tan drumstick.

"Loopy had this coming," she says. "I knew something bad would
happen to him someday. You get what you give. You ever hear that
expression?"

I tell her it's "You reap what you sow." But I don't believe it.
Nothing's fair and nobody gives a rat's ass, that's what I believe.

"Just today," says Pits. "This lady came in. Every week for a year
she's stiffed me my tip. She thinks the shampoo girl doesn't deserve
a tip. She thinks it's so easy bending over all day, testing the water,
putting your hands in other people's hair. Well, I'm washing this
lady's hair and she opens her eyes and says, like it's nothing, 'I
might have lice.'" Pits grimaces. "Just like it's nothing, that's how
she said it. You ever have lice?"

"No," I lie, remembering kindergarten when the school nurse
washed my hair in her office sink, then pinned a folded note on
my shirt that said, "Attention of Mrs. Trottman." I wore the note
home on the bus, hanging from me like a sign.

"I had 'em in second grade," says Pits. "They got in my armpits.
Believe that?" At the word *armpits* I spit out my chicken. She glares
at me and I pretend I'm choking. "If Loopy ever calls me that to
my face again," she says, "it's later for his ass."

"I just didn't think they went under there."

"I was a little kid," she says. "And they go all over."

Trying to sound sincere, I tell her that nobody calls her that
anymore and that I was really choking.

"I hate that nickname. Hate it." She leans her head on my shoulder and I look into her scalp, it's clean and white. One speck of
anything and I'd jump ten feet. "Eddie," she goes on, "this lady
had these little brown things, these little buggers jumping off her
head. I told the manager and she wrapped a towel on this lady's

head and put her out on the sidewalk. Just like that, still dripping. The whole shop was totally grossed out." We both start laughing.

The door rattles. Pits's old man trips in. His shirt is out of his blue postal pants. Pits says a meek hello and her father just stares at me. I sit up on the couch. "You know Eddie," she says. "You've seen Eddie." She takes my hand.

Our eyes meet and I look away. He scratches his crewcut, studying me. I've seen him in my neighborhood delivering mail, going house to house, following his pointy nose and no chin, just like a rat. "Do you know what time it is?" he asks.

She doesn't answer.

"Get out," he says to me.

"Dad!" squeals Pits.

"Elena, I told you. You don't bring his kind into the house."

"This is my house too. I'm nineteen years old," she says. "I pick who I want to go . . ."

Narrowing his eyes, her father steps closer, pointing his finger and his swollen pot belly at me. "I know where you live." He hesitates, then his eyes light. "Trottman, 257 Sunrise Highway, blue house next to the truck wash." A smile creeps across his face.

I swallow a bite of chicken. Pits squeezes my hand. I think of my father prancing around in his knit pants and silk shirts, pointing and accusing. With the coffee table between us, he steps forward, reeking of sweat and a bar room.

"Daddy, don't do this," she pleads. "He'll go. Okay? He'll go."

"He's shit," he mumbles, backing away. "He's shit. Get him out." He goes into the kitchen.

Pits and I are frozen, it's like we just witnessed a UFO. In the kitchen something falls, then it's quiet.

"He doesn't mean it," she whispers. "He's drunk."

"I'm going," I say, getting up.

Pits takes my hand. "He's drunk. He'll be passed out in a few minutes." I tell her I've got to get home, but she doesn't release my hand.

Just outside the door I kiss her cheek. "Let me ask you something," I say, "something personal." She waits. "You ever have an abortion?"

"No, why'd you ask that?"

"I just wanted to know." I pull her next to me. Abortion, I'd imagine it's something a woman carries with her like pins in a voodoo doll. Pits can only take so many pins.

"Bye," she says.

"Hey, Mr. Condemi," I call in the door. "Thanks for the chicken."

Pits pushes me, "Are you crazy?" She shuts the door.

For about five minutes I listen outside, for yelling, for a struggle. The night air is crisp. The sky dotted with stars, the Milky Way, the Big Dipper, the Little Dipper.

I bolt across the mown lawns and small gardens, leap some hedges. In the street, my sneakers pound the black asphalt. I hear her father, the mailman, calling me *Shit, shit, shit.* I turn the corner and run alongside the golf course. The air clears and I push it, pumping my arms, raising my knees. I make a turn around a tremendous swamp maple and pass large homes, their lit windows hidden in shrubs.

Chapter Five

Out of breath, I stop at a twenty-four-hour Carvel and stand under the plastic swirling cone. A woman and a child wait in their Volvo. A man returns from the Carvel counter with a tray of cones. The woman opens the car door for him. She is young, perhaps twenty-five. She looks over at me. I move down the sidewalk feeling like a wolf that just emerged from the woods.

When I was a kid, my father told me his German blood was stronger than my mother's Spanish blood. He said Puerto Ricans were dirty thieves who wore pointy shoes and drove Chevy Impalas with dinka-balls around the windows. My mother told me Puerto Ricans stuck together, never hit women, and loved children. I wanted her to tell me that the president, or the first man on the moon, was Puerto Rican, or at least fifty percent.

About a mile down, in front of a gas station, I call Loopy from a pay phone attached to a telephone pole.

"Yo-dee, Bro-dee," he says happily.

"You got out?

"Where the fu-gowie are you? I went over to your house and your mother was with some asswipe."

"Come and get me," I say and tell him I'm at the Chevron station on the Highway in Merrick.

"Stay there," he says. "Ten minutes."

At one o'clock in the morning, the gas station is closed. I think about sitting near the pumps but decide to just stand by the side of the road. I don't want anybody thinking I might break in the place. About a half-hour later I hear the Goat come rumbling. I hop into the white leather bucket.

Loopy, stoned or drunk, grins at me. "You look like you need some of this." From his top pocket he produces a crooked, bumpy joint the size of a Tipparillo cigar. "Man, it was the family to the rescue," he says, pulling out. "Fifty thousand bond and they put it up like they were buying a pack of butts."

"Who, the guineas?" I ask.

"You shouldn't call them that. Joe, Tony, Joey, Frank," he counts them on his fingers. "They heard you call them that it would be your last words."

"What do you think, you're one of them?"

"Let's just say the door is open," he says.

"Which one told you that?" I ask. "Because that's not you talking."

"Joey said it. He's gonna do right by me."

I let it go. Loopy's never been part of nothing except maybe a police line-up. If the guineas want him, more power to him.

On the elevated tracks that run along Sunrise Highway, the Long Island Rail Road speeds toward the city, rattling the empty cars. We pass the guy who sells trash cans and brooms from a trailer on the side of the road. A light shines from his window on his dog.

"Pits told me Drawers had bruises between her legs," I say. "How hard do you have to do it to bruise a chick's thighs?"

"How should I know," says Loopy.

"That's rape," I say.

"It wasn't rape." Loopy hangs an illegal U-turn and heads to Freeport. "She digs it. You think I got to rape that skank?"

"I heard her scream. She *always* screams?"

"You're supposed to be my stinking best friend," he says slamming the gas pedal. "You sound like the goddamn cops: 'And what happened next, and what happened next?' " he says in singsong. "You're supposed to help me outta this."

"Oh, yeah, I forgot I was there."

We blow past the little plywood cutout of a boat captain dressed in a rumpled blue uniform with drunken Xs as eyes, a liquor bottle tucked under his arm, his white captain's hat tilted back on his head. WELCOME TO FREEPORT, reads the sign. HOME OF FISHING, FINE DINING AND THE NAUTICAL MILE. At Bayview, Loopy makes a sharp right. Ginny's house is coming up in a few blocks. "Think she's out with Jay?"

"You know what, I'm not in the mood."

Ginny's house passes in a streak. I expect that sick feeling and it comes a moment later. I never told Loopy about my last night with Ginny. I think about it and realize I never will.

Loopy turns right at Atlantic and cuts off a girl in a Camaro. "Nobody believes me. The cops, they didn't even want to listen to my side of it. All they wanted was a confession. I told 'em she was the biggest loony that ever walked, but you know that cop Larson, the one from the high school, the one that snagged you that time in the park drinking beer? He didn't want to hear it. The guy is like one of those hunting dogs that has the scent. So I had to tell 'em you were there."

"You had to bring me into it."

"I needed a witness."

"A witness? Don't you think the cops took pictures of Dirty Drawers's bruises? How are you going to explain that?"

"You ever hear of two against one. Man, if it's our word against hers, they'll believe us."

"I didn't even talk to her and I believe her," I say.

"You know as soon as I got out of the jail, I went looking for you. Then you call me, one in the morning, and what do I say? What?"

I don't answer.

"Ten minutes, that's what I said. You're my main shit stain, my main man, and you start in just like the cops. What am I supposed to think?"

"I just don't like rape," I say.

Loopy pulls around a truck and goes into head-on traffic. For a few seconds, I see headlights and hear a horn blaring. He pulls back in the lane, and we sail all the way across the road, until the front tire slams into the curb. With a wild cut to the left, then the right, we are back on course. A thumping noise pounds the car. It sounds like there's a baseball inside a tire.

"You just screwed your alignment," I say.

"No shit, Sherlock." He turns on the radio, pushes the buttons, and has to settle for news or the Bee Gees.

"Take me home," I say, above the Bee Gees' fagged-out voices.

"You better go home and change your pad," he says, hanging a U-turn across a double yellow line. "You know why Joey bailed me out?" asks Loopy, grinning with stoned eyes. "You can't tell anybody, not Pits, not your mother."

"Don't even tell me," I say. "I don't care."

"I've been delivering these packages to Staten Island, these brown boxes. Tony tells me, if I lose one, or if anything happens, it's my ass." He laughs, then grins at me, waiting for me to say something.

"What was in 'em?"

"Fuck if I know." Loopy stops at a red light. "This past delivery, Tony paid me a pound of weed, usually he throws me a hundred bucks." Loopy takes out another giant joint from his pocket and sniffs it like an expensive cigar. "I had to swear to them that I wouldn't sell to just anyone. Tony thinks I'm not wound tight enough to do deliveries. If they ever knew I told you they'd cut our balls off and make heroes."

"How many boxes you deliver?"

"Just two. One on Saturday before I picked you up at work. They got real nervous when I called them from the jail."

Arms folded, I look straight ahead. He doesn't even know what he's delivering. "You ever get your IQ tested?" I ask. "Maybe you're delivering ears and fingers."

"The difference between you and a chickenshit sandwich . . ."

"Is the bread," I say. "Yuk, yuk."

Loopy turns down my block and slows at my house. The pickup truck is still outside. The house lights are on. I can picture my mother with her *West Side Story* record blasting, dancing around the house, while her new boyfriend watches in his underwear. But in the morning, my mother won't be humming "Maria" and cooking him an omelet. He'll be long gone.

"I changed my mind," I say. "Let's go out."

"Fucking-A," says Loopy, pounding the gas.

"Give me that joint." I press in the lighter.

"It's killer weed," says Loopy. "When I passed the church I thought I saw Jesus Christ standing out on the lawn."

"That's a statue."

"Maybe to you," he says.

I pull the smoke in and it burns all the way down. The shops, gas stations, the auto body places on Merrick Road blur outside the window.

* * *

Behind the Top Hat, a topless joint in Suffolk, three cars are parked in the lot. We pull in and the front end of the Goat bounces over a parking lot curb.

"Shit," we both say, then laugh.

Loopy lights up an enormous joint, sucks. Holding his breath, he passes. I pinch the joint, a seed pops and lands on the carpet. "The mob is coming to get us," I say. We crack up.

The next joint hits me like a right from Joe Frazier. I never was a pothead. I only smoke weed when someone offers it. In ninth grade for a few months I made fifty dollars a week selling loose joints until my mother found my stash in the house. She'd never admit it, but I know she smoked it. Loopy rarely smokes weed but thinks he's an expert.

"You should of made Tony pay you in cash," I say. My words sound distant, like there's an echo.

"I can sell the weed."

"You could get busted, then you'd be double screwed. You'd have rape charges and drug charges."

"We could both get busted right now. I got the pound right here." He picks up a shopping bag from the back seat and pulls out a brick of weed wrapped in clear plastic. We break out laughing. "You'd go down with me." Loopy laughs. "And no one would believe you."

I try to stop laughing but can't. I almost choke. Snot comes out of my nose. "It's not funny," I finally manage to say.

"I know, I know." Loopy throws his arm around me. "I didn't rape her," he says. "I mean it."

"You probably did and you don't even know it. You're a dope." We both break out laughing. "A dope-smoking dope."

"You got to tell the cops you were there, that I didn't rape her."

"If I say that, then I'm involved. Let me ask you something, what's worse, rape or murder?"

"Murder," he says.

"See, I think they're about the same. Rape, Loop, it's a woman's body. They got things going on inside. They're not like guys. A guy can wash his dick."

"Didn't you ever hear of douche?" says Loopy.

"I'm trying to be serious. Elena said you didn't have a rubber. Man, you got to know when to lay off."

"Since when is she Elena?" he asks.

"Since now," I say.

"Well, I didn't rape Drawers," he says. "And you were there, just remember that." He opens the door.

I wait a few minutes, thinking about those bruises between Dirty Drawers's legs. I try to picture them, but can't. I get out and spot Loopy near the door of the topless joint. When I get over to him I say, "You still didn't explain the bruises between her legs."

"She probably punched herself. Eddie, you know she's a sick-o."

"I know, she is, but still . . ."

"But, nothing. Man, come on." He hugs me and I feel his weight, his size. He must have kneed her, pounded her legs open with his knees. It's the only way to explain it.

In near darkness, we push stools back and stand at the bar. A girl sets us up with beer. A tall dancer with big tits is on stage snapping her g-string to Al Green. The dancer mouths the words of the song, "Let's Stay Together." In scuffed white high heels, she shuffle steps forward, then grabs the fireman's rail in the center of the bar. Somehow, she swings her leg above her head, hooking the back of her ankle on the rail. Like an animal caught in a snare, she snaps upside down, her legs apart, her brown hair hanging vertically inches above the stage. Blood rushing to her face, she smiles at us.

Loopy claps and throws a crumpled dollar bill. The girl unhooks her ankle and swings back to the stage.

"Oh man, you see that leg shot!" says Loopy.

The girl ducks behind a flower-print shower curtain that must lead to a dressing room. I stare into my beer and remember Elena's old man's remarks. I take a sip, gargle, and wash the weed taste out of my mouth. There's no sense in telling Loopy what Elena's father said. Being a Puerto Rican isn't like having a toothache or being broke. It's not going to change, no matter what anyone does.

A girl appears and begins collecting dollar bills in a hat from the few people at the bar. I toss a buck. She heads off, the cheeks of her ass waving good-bye. Loopy removes his jacket, showing off a V-shaped Harley engine tattoo that shudders when he flexes his biceps. Below the tattoo are the words, "Ride to Live, Live to Ride."

Loopy never owned a motorcycle. Whenever we go someplace and there's a lot of bikes, he rolls up the sleeve of his T-shirt and slips in with the bikers. He can talk all the lingo, panheads, flatheads, hardtails.

A dancer leans over the sink and beer glasses, squeezing her titanic tits together like dollar-eating blobs. Loopy stuffs a dollar in the cleavage. She caresses his hand as if they're sharing a tender moment, then pulls away with the dollar.

"You want to blow a doobie with us?" he asks, winking at her. "Let me know."

The night wears on. Girls take turns dancing to four songs, then switch. There's one blonde that wants to smoke a joint with us. She's cross-eyed, but real cute.

At closing time, Loopy and I wait next to the Goat for her. Everyone leaves, the lights go out, the cars pull out.

"She must of snuck past," says Loopy.

*   *   *

In the morning we are the only car in the lot. The bag of weed is on the backseat. The car stinks of weed.

I poke Loopy. He grunts. I push his head.

"Yeah," he says, coming awake.

"Let's get out of here."

He looks around. The traffic on Sunrise Highway is heavy. The sun is already over the topless joint. "I guess she blew us off," he says.

Loopy starts the engine and nails it into traffic. The front tire thumps like a bad headache. Hitting the curb seems like weeks ago.

"Man, I feel like I just went to war," says Loopy, massaging his temples.

In the back seat the weed is spilling out of the bag. My throat feels like I was swallowing swords. "What are you going to do with that weed?" I ask.

"That's money in the bank," says Loopy.

I look back at the sticky stems, leaves, and broken buds. The car reeks. I grab the bag and put it on my lap. It's almost hard to believe that for this bag of shit we could go to jail for a long time, for any length of time. I imagine Joey giving Loop the weed instead of money, and Loopy acting like he just received the key to Long Island.

As we cross into Nassau County, I throw the bag of weed out the window into the scrub next to the road.

"What'd you do," yells Loopy, hitting the brakes.

"It's done," I say. "Now you don't have to worry about selling it."

"Shit, I could have given it away at least." He swings the steering wheel, trying to turn around.

"You turn around, I'm getting out." Doing thirty-five miles an hour in traffic, I open the door, the gray road rushes by, and I realize I'm not going anywhere.

"Shut the freaking door."

At White Castle we stop for hamburgers. I eat eight belly bomb-

ers, Loopy eats twelve. The burgers are square, not very big, like
skin grafts on buns with pickles and grated onions. We wash them
down with orange sodas. "Eat 'em by the sack, blow 'em out the
crack," says Loopy.

I burp out the words "Murder burgers," already feeling things
moving in my stomach.

"What's today?" asks Loopy.

"Monday."

He pulls in front of the supermarket, but before I get out, he grabs
my coat. "If the cops come, what are you going to say?"

"I don't know."

"Eddie, come on. I could do time, real time—ten years."

I push the door open. "You should have thought of all that
before."

"So your gonna screw my whole story."

I get out of the car. Loopy gets out. With the torn convertible
roof between us, I take a deep breath. "I'll get Elena to talk to
Sandy. Why don't you go buy her some flowers, have them deliv-
ered to the house."

"Call me," says Loopy. The limping Goat pulls away.

It's "Super-Coupon Monday," so the parking lot is already hop-
ping. Old women holding carts wait at the automatic doors ready
to charge. I wind around them.

I punch my time card, just making it by a minute. I arrive a
half-hour before the butchers. Part of my apprenticeship is to be a
"setup man" for them. The air conditioner clears my head. Behind
the plastic curtain that leads to the meat department, Bell, the
meat wrapper, quickly snuffs out a prohibited smoke. "Jesus," she
says. "You just made me waste a good cigarette." Kurt enforces all
the rules and he's usually early.

"If you smoke, I will have to take measures," I say imitating Kurt. Bell laughs and shoos me away. I duck into the break room for my smock and apron. At the sink I wash my face, flatten my hair with water. I stare in the mirror, at the bags under my bloodshot eyes. "Puerto Rican shit," I whisper.

Behind the meat department, I open the chicken wet-box and the loading dock door. A refrigerated tractor trailer waits with waxed brown boxes of iced chickens. Today, I will split the chickens into parts, or bag them whole. It's a day's work.

Between the wall and the tractor trailer, I puke off the loading dock. The night pours out of me in reverse. No more weed. Ever.

"Hey, kid," yells Kurt, coming around the corner of the loading dock wearing his paper Pantry Pride hat like a cocky soldier. It's the kind of hat soda jerks wore in the fifties at hamburger joints. One size fits all. It's a store regulation that everyone in the shop wears the paper hat. No one likes them. "Kid, you know what today is?"

I shrug and wipe my mouth.

Kurt fastens a small pin on my butcher apron. The pin is silver and has three numbers, 347. "You're in the union, officially," he says. "You were supposed to get this a few months back, but you know how it is around here." We shake hands. Kurt heads off. I stand out there behind the chicken truck wondering if I should feel like I've won a million bucks. The tractor trailer driver comes around. "I got another stop," he says. "Let's get the birds off."

I open the back of the truck. With the hydraulic lift, I swing a pallet of chicken onto the dock, into the wet-box. Every couple of minutes, I see the pin on my apron. It's a piece-of-shit pin, but it makes it official.

Chapter Six

T wenty minutes later the truck pulls out and the sixty boxes of chickens are in the wet-box. I lean against the wall, wishing last night could be traded for eight hours of sleep. The wet-box smells of mackerel that didn't sell last week. Over the weekend, the ice melted into small piles and the slim blue-and-silver heads of the fish have poked through the ice like they're coming alive. It's sad, but Skate's department is always in the red and there's talk that he might be fired. I pass the loading dock door, then push into the swinging door of the meat department.

The shop is still clean from my going over on Saturday evening. An aroma of cedar hangs in the air. I get a new paper Pantry Pride hat out of a fresh stack and adjust it on my head.

I slide the blades on the band saws, adjust the tension, run my hand down the teeth, checking that they point down. Kurt said a guy lost his thumb because a blade was installed upside down. I scrape the plastic chopping blocks one last time. In the middle they are worn from the constant slicing and cutting. In the walk-in I put the chopmeat machine together. There are five main pieces: a screw, the screw box, a cap, a hopper blade, and the strainer. The pieces are clumsy and heavy. The butchers think putting the machine together is a pain in the ass, but I like it. I even like cleaning it with the pressure washer. The chopmeat machine is old and well made. I try to imagine how many thousands of hamburgers squeezed out of it.

I shove the bin under the chipper. The blades of the chipper are razor sharp. We use it to chop the frozen beef that goes into the chopmeat hopper. The chipper works on gravity. Frozen meat in a fifty-pound block is placed over the blades, the motor pushes a slide that works the meat back and forth until it's all chipped into little pieces in the bin. The chipper is the only piece of machinery I don't like cleaning. The blades have nicked me a dozen times.

In the fish department I put the bleached boards on the floor. I fill the fish display case with ice so that Skate can put the fish in and be ready when the doors open.

Across the counter I see Reggie come in. Reggie's six-foot-four and walks like he's about to go in any direction. He has a big smile and a big chin. My mother thinks he's handsome. She doesn't really know him, but she's in the store three times a week for cigarettes and milk, using my ten percent employee discount. My mother always waves to everyone as if they're family.

"Eddie Spaghetti," Reggie yells going past.

"Edgy Reggie," I say.

All morning Kurt flies around, putting meat out in the case. The production line is going. The butchers cut a piece of meat, position it on a Styrofoam tray, and then put it on a conveyer belt that moves toward two women who wrap the meat, weigh it, and tag it with a price. Most of the meat out in the case was finished Saturday. Meat keeps if it's kept cold.

In the mornings the butchers cut slow, their hands stiff.

"Still got your pin on," says Kurt, hitting me in the arm.

I split chickens on the band saw. It's the same, chicken after chicken: pull out the bag with the neck, heart and gizzard, split the chicken in half, place the halves on a Styrofoam tray covering the innards.

Over the conveyer belt, the machines, the band saw, Reggie is yelling something about some girl. I can barely hear him. "I left her sitting there. She thinks I'm coming back," he yells.

At ten fifteen I wash up and get the coffee, tea, corn muffins, and rolls for the ten thirty break. I hurry out of the store, cross Grove Street, past the Gulf station. I wear my white coat and butcher's apron, tied tightly around my waist. Across the street, in the Governor's Pub, I spot my father at the end of the bar. He hustles barroom shuffleboard on the regulation-size board. My father can slide those metal disks on the waxed runway as if they were on a remote control.

When I was a kid he'd take me with him. He stood at the bar, ready with a light for any lady holding a cigarette, ready to break up a fight, remind someone their money is untended, or their wife is on the pay phone. Pinching his Camel with his yellow fingers, he ordered, "Whatever is running good and cold." In his shined shoes, creased shirt and pants, one button open at the collar, white socks, Brylcream in his hair ("A little dab'll do ya," he used to say, winking at me), he'd break into a little Sinatra so sincerely that when he got to, *Each time I find myself, flat on my face,* people at the bar would make fists and join in with him—*I pick myself up again and get back in the race, that's life*—

If I go over for the rent money, I can just hear him: Look at this, my son, the workingman.

"Hey, Dad," I say, poking my head in the open door of the bar.

He swings around. One side of his face is swollen, almost twice its size. He tries to smile, but can't, and winces. "Eddie," he says.

"What happened?" I step into the bar. The few people on stools lean over their glasses. The bartender is watching *The Price Is Right* on a wall-mounted TV.

"I got run down," he says.

"With a car?"

"That's how it's done." His eyes smile. The skin on the bruised side is the color of beef. Along his neck, scrapes run up into his slicked-back hair. "A mix-up. It's straightened out. But I got the faces," he says and taps his head. "Up here. And I don't forget. You know that, I don't forget. Jeez, you look like you might need a little of the hair-of-the-dog that bit ya. Have something. You want a beer? A whiskey?"

"No, I got to go." Blood has dried on his collar and across the front of his shirt.

"Been one of those kind of nights for the both of us," he says and tries to smile.

"You ought to go home and get those cuts cleaned up."

"How's your mother?" I sit on the edge of a stool. "I told her I don't want her ass in the Tropicana," he says. "You know she was in there Saturday night stoned out of her mind, dancing by herself. By *herself*. Now, that's wrong, any way you look at it, that's wrong."

"If not there, it'd be someplace else," I say. "And she was probably looking for you."

"Wow," he says, moving his head as if getting hit by a hard right.

"I need your part of the rent."

"Stop by the motel. I'll have it then and I'll give you lunch." I turn, and he grabs my smock. "Heard your friend got himself arrested."

"Where'd you hear that?"

"Shit, that's already old news. Hope you're not involved in that. Because that's trouble, that's big time."

I run across the street to the diner and get inside fast. I order three teas, one light and sweet, two milk only, four coffees, one black, three regulars. From the bruise on his face, my father must have hit the pavement hard and slid. He remembers their faces. I try to laugh, but can't.

Before lunch the fat company truckdriver sticks his head in the meat department. "Pickup," he yells into the noise of the shop.

I split one last yellow chicken and shut the band saw down. Kurt tosses a trimmed chuck steak on a tray and wipes his hands on his apron. "That time of the week again," he says, like an apology.

On Mondays the full fat cans are put on a truck and replaced by empty cans. I tilt a black fifty-gallon can on its side and roll it out of the shop. The can has finished edges on top and is marked BIODEGRADABLE ONLY—NOT FOR HUMAN CONSUMPTION. All the scraps from six days of cutting, and the bad beef, spoiled pork, and rotten chickens are in the cans. As I turn the can, the fumes of decay and rot rise out like invisible smoke.

At the loading dock Kurt signs the trucker's receiving slip. I roll the can out of the store to the cement loading dock. The pressure in my lower back makes my knees wobble. The driver grabs the edge of the can and helps me roll it into the bed of the truck. That's as much help as he'll offer. Rolling the cans to the truck is one of *my* jobs, it's actually written in the *Local Amalgamated Meat Cutters Union Handbook*. Kurt showed it to me. Butchers don't have to move fat cans. Lots of guys pulled muscles, threw their backs out, or crushed their toes. A butcher on worker's compensation costs the chain big money, said Kurt. Big money.

With the first can on the truck, I go back inside for another. Skate steps out of the fish department with the deli girl. "Fat cans," says Skate.

"Yup, fat cans," I say going by. I roll the second can out of the meat department down the corridor toward the dock.

On the way back to the meat department, the deli girl passes me a pile of roast beef rolled between a sheet of waxed paper. I don't like eating when my hands have been touching the chickens and the cans, but I stuff it in my mouth anyway. Luckily I've never gotten sick. Lots of the butchers get skin rashes. The skin on their hands cracks and bleeds. The cuts get infected and small warts grow and spread. There isn't a butcher in the department without warts on his hands.

As I roll the second can to the dock, my wrist sends waves of pain into my arm. I stop and try to shake it off. When I was hired, Kurt brought me into the walk-in box and asked me to lift a tub of ground round and put it on the conveyer belt. I was so hyped up I tossed it like it was a box of pillows. Actually, I know, I'm not as strong as Kurt, or Skate. Forget about Reggie, I've seen him take a whole side of beef off a meat hook and carry it to the block like it was a forty-pound veal. The butchers are built thick. I'm built thin like my father.

I flash on my father's swollen face. It dawns on me that there's probably a hundred people that would like to kill him. He's been beaten in bar brawls, even beaten by clam diggers on Freeport Creek. Someone trying to kill him, not a big surprise. I tip the can. My wrist sends the pain down my arm. I lose it. The can crashes to the floor. Skate gets a shovel. "Go watch the counter," he tells the deli girl.

The stench moves around us like a ghost.

"What's the matter, kid? Some girl break your heart?" asks Skate.

"I don't know. I got off balance."

We scoop scraps of fat and the mounds of gooey crap collected in trays under the band saws. I see Reggie poke his head out. Kurt comes over, looking like a Nazi without trying. He stands with his eyes narrowed, his lips tight, holding his clipboard.

"What time did you go to bed?" he asks.

"To bed?" I repeat.

"Yeah, to bed. You have to get rest to work that saw, to move these cans. You have to concentrate. That could've broke your leg."

"I know," I say thinking of my father, across the street, probably leaning over the shuffleboard table. Sliding a disk. The disk stopping on the edge, hanging in the twenty-point zone. I am tempted to say, Someone tried to kill my father.

"Put that down and come over here," says Kurt. With his hand on my shoulder, he guides me to the loading dock. Outside it's spring, the air is fresh. "Cut the crap," he says pointing his finger in my chest. "You don't ever come to work in this condition," he snorts out his nose and shakes his head. "One mistake on that saw and you'll be walking around with that mistake for the rest of your life. You understand me?"

I nod. I do understand him and I know he's right, but it just seems there's no changing anything, at least not for me. "Sure," I say.

"Well, concentrate," says Kurt. "Concentrate and you won't get hurt." He heads down the walkway toward produce.

Chapter Seven

Past the Roadway Motel, past Phil's Auto Body, past Immaculate Used Cars, where my father once worked selling "cream puffs," the town is semi-industrial and the air smells of glue fumes from factories that make thermometers, patio furniture, and paint. In the morning, and after the five o'clock factory whistle, the sidewalks are lined with men wearing blue or green work pants, carrying lunchboxes or bags of food. During the day, chrome-coated lunch wagons, or "roach coaches," pull in and out, and at night hookers from the train station drag their johns into their by-the-hour rooms.

At the Amsterdam Inn, on the cement patch patio under the green shingled awning that spreads over my father's door, there is a hibachi grill and a chair. In the window of one of the rooms he rents, a faded cardboard sign reads, TROTTMAN PHOTOGRAPHY— FOR ALL OCCASIONS. The sign was printed when things must have been going better, when his customers dressed up for their photos, a time I can barely remember. I've driven by with Loopy and seen my father bent over in the chair studying the rust-stained cement. Sometimes Loopy pulls in, and I yell something like, "What you up to?"

"Slow today," he says, never being too specific.

Across the street from the Amsterdam, I lean against a telephone pole wondering if I should find a pay phone and call him. Even though he invited me, he doesn't like people dropping in. Last November the police hit his rooms with search warrants. They took his camera and a file of his photos. Now, to keep vice off his back, he pays a detective a hundred bucks a month.

After the Navy, my father worked in a corner photo store on Main Street. In the rear of the shop, he photographed babies, families, couples getting married. Weddings were my old man's speciality. He still brags that he was booked months in advance. Before I was five, he was fired for contracting referral work on the side, cutting out the photo shop owner. My mother's top dresser drawer is lined with my baby photos. When I was a kid, the photos were scattered around the house: on top of the refrigerator, in the knife-and-fork drawer, at the bottom of the napkin holder in the kitchen. Some are stained from coffee or burned by cigarettes. There's nothing extraordinary about them. Most are photos of me, a black-eyed, black-haired baby propped on a pillow holding a rattle, or a stuffed animal. In a few, my mother, with her shiny dark hair and big costume diamond earrings, holds me on her lap. When I look at them I imagine my parents as just a "normal" couple, my father going off to work in the morning, my mother strolling by the photo shop pushing me in a carriage and asking, "You want to go see Daddy?"

Now the photo shop is a head shop. Rastafarians plaster the windows with fluorescent Peter Max posters and sell rolling papers, incense, bongs, pipes, tie-dye T-shirts, and plastic marijuana plants.

All morning it's been raining on and off. The wet streets shine under the midday sun. People hurry by. I turn up the collar of my dungaree jacket and spot my father's red '74 Seville parked on an angle in front of his door. The Caddy was sideswiped. White paint runs down the side like streaks of light. My father burns through cars. It won't be long before the Caddy is replaced. My parents are as different as shit and flowers. She puts pennies and nickels in a coffee can, and little pieces of cloth away for a knee patch on a pair of old jeans. My father overtips every waitress, throws his money on the bar, buys drinks for strangers. Sometimes, he wears his underwear once then tosses them. My mother says he never learned to save.

I duck into the Salty Cod Lounge. At the bar a thick boa constrictor winds around the neck and green tattooed arms of a bearded biker. The snake looks as if he's interested in something out the window. The worst thing I've ever smelled was a seven-foot-long snake my father won from a guy in a card game. He left the snake in his trunk, and remembered it a week later. It was August and hot when he popped the trunk. The snake, black and deflated like an old tire tube, was curled around the spare tire. He poked the snake with a stick to see if it was still alive. "Goddamn it," he yelled, "a five-hundred-dollar snake." The odor wrapped around my neck, strangled me. My father hooked the snake with a shovel and shoved it down the sewer.

Next to the biker's ear, the boa's red tongue flicks into the air. The snake's expressionless face remains toward the window. On the bar in a puddle of moisture, the biker pushes his coins around with the tip of his finger. There's no telling if either of them is home.

I nod at the bartender and point at the pay phone next to the men's room.

"No drug deals," he says to me.

I dial my old man's number. After one ring, he picks up and I tell him I'm across the street at the Salty Cod. There's a moment of silence. "Should I come over?"

He says, "You see Roland from the tire place over there?" I look down the bar. Near the front window the light shines off Roland's round bald head. He's leaning over a beer and wicker basket of fried cod. "Tell him to give me another half-hour, then come over," says my father.

On the way out, I tap Roland on the shoulder and repeat the message. He lifts the worn sleeve on his blue hooded sweatshirt, looks at his watch. His hands are slick from the fish and black from handling tires. "He's already running fucking late," he says.

I dodge the traffic and jog into the motel's horseshoe-shaped parking lot. Two guys lean into the engine of an old Impala. Tools are scattered on the ground. On top of the car, empty beer cans are lined up as if for target practice. "Eddie," one calls.

"Screwy Louie," I say.

"Where you been?" he says, coming over, wearing the same waist-length leather jacket he wore everyday to auto shop.

"Around town."

We shake hands, thumb over thumb. The teacher used to say Louie must have played football without a helmet.

"You going to see your old man?" He bites his thin bottom lip like he always did, then smiles. "Shit, I saw him last week. His new chick, shit, she's good." Louie steps back and looks at me. "Shit, same old Eddie. Keeping to yourself, taking care of business."

"I've got to get going," I say. "I'm on my lunch hour."

"I'm between side jobs," he laughs, pointing toward the Impala. "That guy over there, he married my sister, and if we get the ride started we're going to the city."

"Some honeymoon." I back away. "Keep your tools clean," I say, because our teacher always said it.

"Good old Eddie," says Louie, smiling. "Steady with the wise cracks."

I hop over a muddy puddle and my father's door opens. A girl named April, who I haven't seen since we were students together in high school, peeks out. "My father in there?"

"You want your picture taken?" she says, smirking. April was two grades ahead of me and probably never knew I existed. I remember her strolling though the school's halls attached to a hitter guy like a hip-joined Siamese twin.

I push the door open. April holds her pink terry robe shut. Every two seconds she flips her dye-job blond hair out of her face.

My father emerges from the bathroom in his underwear, shaving cream on half his face. "Man, you smell like a can of Purina." He shakes his head. "Whew, what are you selling over there?"

The swollen part of his face is black. Rusty scabs run up his cheek like tire tread. He pats April on the butt and she tells him in a phony little-girl voice to stop. Women think he's a cure for loneliness. He can go into a bar, meet a girl, have a good time, go to another bar, meet another girl, party until exhaustion forces him to collapse. Two years ago he hit forty, but it didn't slow him down.

April, studying me, sits on the bed, resting against the headboard.

"April, stop staring," he says, leaning real close to the bathroom mirror, eyes bulging, the muscles in his legs straining like a frog's. "Eddie, have a cup of coffee, have a bagel."

"It's lunch, but he thinks it's breakfast," says April.

On the dresser is a hot plate from my mother's kitchen, a coffee maker, sugar in packets, milk in a waxed cup, coffee cake in a bakery box, bagels in a brown paper bag, and a tub of butter with a plastic knife stuck in it. April turns up the volume on the television bolted to the low dresser. A rerun of *My Mother the Car* is on. April sings along with the theme song.

"Mom says you stole the hot plate," I say, helping myself.

"Is that what she says?" He drops his razor in the sink. "She want it back?"

"Keep it, I'm going to get her one that does toast and baked potatoes."

"A toaster oven, stupid," says April, cracking up laughing.

"Here." From the nightstand he grabs his wallet. "Here's twenty bucks." He holds out the bill. "Get her one that makes spaghetti and meatballs."

"You ever coming home?" I ask.

"Maybe this is it," he says, going back to his shaving. "Maybe after that last time, I've had it. Your mother, she pushes and keeps pushing."

"You mean the queen of hearts fight?"

"Tell your mother I'm sorry, 'bout that," he says.

"Tell her yourself."

He nods his head. The water pounds into the sink.

"I should have kicked your ass for that," I say.

My father rinses his razor, opens the top, removes the blade, changes sides. He combs his hair and his biceps knot up like hard crab apples. "You want to go outside right now?" he asks.

"Just keep your hands off her," I say. My father hasn't hit me since my grandfather died. I didn't know it then, but I think he imagined he could fill in for Pops. Just a few days after the funeral, he bought me a Schwinn ten-speed English racing bike. "This is for all the birthdays I missed," he said, pushing the bike out of the kitchen into the front room.

"You think that I'm going to give you the boat for a bike," I said.

"It's a gift," he said, holding the sleek black seat. "No strings attached." Gears clicking, I rolled the bike out of the house like it was a grenade with the pin pulled.

My father slips on his pants, pulls them up around his small waist. "I might live right here," he says. "You don't want me home, that's for sure."

"That's for sure," I say.

"Get the oven for Mother's Day," April giggles.

I look at her pale face and notice her pupils are as big as the tops of pencil erasers, like Dondi's eyes in the comic strip. "What is she on?"

"What are you on there, April, my dear?"

"Just a little speed," she says, holding up her fingers an inch apart.

"You know, you look like your father." April leans forward and gets her face a few inches from mine. "Hey, I remember you, from high school."

"Yeah, good old Freeport High. What was the name of that guy you were going out with?" I ask, thinking about her miniskirts, her ironed straight hair, her leather pocketbook hanging from her shoulder as she looked out from under a cloud of cigarette smoke in front of the school.

"Frank. He's dead, car accident." She looks down for a second. "Half my friends in the class of 'seventy-four are either dead or good as. One of my best girlfriends has six kids. She majored in home economics, believe that?" She laughs. "I majored in cosmetology. It's something you can use for your entire life." She hangs her fingernails in front of me. On each pink nail is a tiny heart with a rhinestone glued in the middle.

"April's the new girl," says my father.

"The new model," she says, putting on a layer of pink lipstick.

From the corner of the drape, I see Louie out in the parking lot, holding a jumper cable. He leans under the hood of the Impala. Sparks fly and he jumps back a foot. Raindrops begin streaking the dark sky. Louie and his pal jump in the Impala and slam the doors.

"She's been in *Cheri*," says my father.

"Come on, you've heard of *Cheri*?" says April. "You ever hear of the movie, *Saturday Night Feel-up*. It's a whole series."

"I think I heard of 'em," I say.

"Stan, what garage is he from?" asks April.

"He's heard all of it," says my father, coming out of the bathroom. With his face puffy, his long sideburns and his hair combed back real high, he reminds me of Elvis. He rubs Aqua Velva Blue along his neck.

Under the night table, next to a battered gray record player with built-in speakers, are his albums: Chuck Berry, Fats Domino, the Mamas and Papas, the Coasters, the Orioles, the Vibrations, and of course Elvis. At home, when he's in a good mood, he puts on Little Richard or Elvis Presley and swirls my mother around, crooning in a deep voice.

"That stuff smells like dead flowers," says April.

"I like the way it smells," I say.

"Well, I'm the woman, and I should know."

"She's the woman," agrees my father, winking at me.

"And I bet you know that for a fact," I say.

My father looks at April with half-closed eyes, a look he wears when he sends a drink over to a woman's table, or offers a lady a light. Smooth Stan the Man to the rescue.

"You know, I don't know if I like you," says April to me.

"In two seconds I'm throwing you both out in the rain." He opens the gray, frayed drapes and looks out the window. It's raining like a bastard. Water rushes off the walkway terrace, splashes on the hood of my father's Caddy, and pounds the roof of the Impala.

April opens her purse and shakes a bottle of nail polish.

I stand next to my father. We're about the same size, same build. He's a little thicker in the waist, and his skin is ruddy, red. Out in the lot, the rain dances in the puddles. Louie and his buddy make a run for it across the road. Louie leaves the door of the Impala open. Should've worn a helmet, I imagine the shop teacher saying. "Louie told me he knows you and April," I say.

"Owes me fifty dollars," says April.

"He'll pay," says my father. "One way or the other."

Behind his buddy, Louie runs to the Salty Cod. They duck in the door. "You gonna break his thumbs?" I ask.

"Break his legs," says April.

"Eddie, I got to talk to you," says my father. "April, go watch that garbage in the next room, it's giving me a headache."

She gets up and changes the channel.

"I speak English, don't I?" he says.

"Jesus, you know," she says, getting up. "You think you got a right to your privacy, but if I want a little I have to pay holy hell."

My father stares at her, not moving a muscle.

April collects the nail polish and purse.

"I'll be over in a few," he says.

"Don't do me any favors." She slips out the connecting door across from the bathroom and purposely leaves it open two feet. The television goes on in the next room, something bangs. We hear a commercial for *Beatlemania*.

"April's all right," says my father, getting his Camels off the table in front of the window. "She has to be told twice but not all the time." He packs his cigarettes into his palm over and over, like a baseball catcher.

"Your face looks terrible," I say. "Does it hurt?"

"Nah, it's just road rash." He sits on the bed, leans back with the cigarette between his lips. "I was lucky."

"Who did it?"

"You don't need to know," he says. "Besides, you think you'd be better off without me anyway, right?" I don't answer him, although I think it's probably true. "I mean," he says, "I never was your grandfather, right? He's up there fishing with Saint Peter, Joseph, and Jesus Christ."

"Don't drag Pops into it," I say. "All I asked was a simple question. That's all. You don't want to tell me, don't. I'll live."

"You really want to know?" He shakes his shoulders like he just got a chill. "It's about April and the movie circuit. She was under contract and I pulled her out. You know how those boys play."

My father is sort of an agent for about a dozen girls who act in porno flicks and do spreads in magazines. I've seen some of the magazines. Compared to his work, *Playboy* and *Penthouse* look like eighth-grade health class textbooks. Once, all his girls did a spread for *Housewife* magazine—twenty pages of them cooking and cleaning naked, then somehow getting turned on to the vacuum cleaner or being horny under a dining-room table.

"They'd kill you over her?"

"She's got a quality."

"A quality?"

"Yeah, she'll do anything." He raises his eyebrows. "It's a rare quality." He sucks his cigarette and blows a large cloud of smoke. "In my business a girl like April could make me a rich man."

"Or dead."

"Trottman rule Number One: When it's my time to go, I'll have everything packed, except regrets. In the meantime, I have their faces, and they got to worry about me."

"You going to run them over with the Caddy?" I say.

"Not me personally, not my Caddy." He reaches into a brown paper bag. "You want a beer?"

I tell him again that I've got to get back to work. He opens a bottle of Piels with the wide chug-a-lug top and takes a long swallow. My hangover pounds in my head. "My detective friend in vice," he says, "told me you're all mixed up in Loopy's problem."

"I'm not."

"He says they're looking at ya hard."

"I'm shaking in my boots," I say, wondering if I should tell him about Loop's story that puts me at the scene. Instead, I wind up telling him about the boardwalk and Sandy's scream.

"And you had nothing to do with it?" he asks.

"Dad, I was with"—I almost call her Pits—"my girlfriend. She can back up my story."

"Who's this Sandra?"

"Merrick's town nut, a first-class flake, but she might have a case."

"Name, what's her name?" he says.

"Sandra Gass."

"Sandra Gass," he repeats almost spitting out his cigarette. "She got a brother that's doing time upstate?" My father smiles. He knows anybody that ever got in trouble. Under the nightstand, he digs into a pile of magazines. "Let me find this," he says. "You ever wonder what Miss Gass looks like under those old baggy jeans she wears?" He pulls out a slim magazine named *Hot Pants*. With his cigarette between his lips, he flips to a page and shoves it toward me.

In the photos, Sandy's sitting on a bed, dressed in baby-doll pajamas, sucking the corner of a large lollypop. Next page, her top is off and she's rubbing the lollypop on her nipples. The room behind her looks so familiar. Above the bed there is a picture of a horse-drawn carriage. Then I realize the pictures were taken right in my father's room.

"She had potential," he says. "She's no April, but she had potential."

I turn the page and Sandy has her legs open, displaying herself like a week-old ham sandwich. The smile she wears is as phony as the lollypop and the pajamas. "I took those last summer," he says. "Her brother brought her around. They were looking for some fast money."

I stare at the photos, expecting someone else, but it's her, same stringy hair, same teeth, same eyes. Only I never realized she had such a nice little body.

"It probably wasn't her first time," he says. "Girls in this business get raped all the time. My question is, why'd she report it?" He finishes his beer and gets another one.

"That's what didn't make sense to me."

"It got his fucking attention."

"She had bruises between her legs," I say.

"Shit," he shakes his head. "A lot of whores have 'em. Occupational hazard. You know, like Joe Namath's knees."

"I never thought of her as a whore."

"Knowing her brother, she's been selling that body since she was ten. Besides, in my business they're all whores." He closes his eyes. "As long as this is Loopy's problem and not your problem, forget about it."

"Let me keep this," I say, rolling up the magazine.

"How much do you know about your friend Loopy? You know he's running weed for the I-talians, you know that?"

"Where'd you hear that?"

"That rummy head never kept his trap shut. Listen, I don't give a fuck about Loopy, but you better watch your back. Those guineas pave people face down under the Long Island Expressway and plant exit signs in their asses."

"Like I'm supposed to take advice from you."

"Still with the smart mouth—I thought maybe a little hard work would cure you, but I guess Kurt lets you run the show over there." He laughs, coughs.

"Yeah, I run the show."

He takes out his handkerchief and brings up something. "If I could get rid of this fucking flu," he says.

"You ought to see a doctor."

"Half the fucking world should see a doctor." He gets up. "You came over here for the rent. I didn't forget."

I've still got twenty minutes. I sit backward on a metal-framed chair, two feet from him. He gives me his crooked smile, "So, your mother found herself a boyfriend?"

I don't say anything. As much as I don't like her bringing guys home, I can't give her up.

"Don't act dumb. Terry from the Tropicana told me the whole story."

"Like I said this afternoon, she probably went in there looking for you. And you know something, Dad, even after cheating on her, and hitting her, she'd take you back. You're the one that left."

He looks into the wide mouth of the beer bottle. "I'm going to let you slide on what you just said 'cause I'm in a good mood." He gives me this squint with a half smirk, like there isn't a damn thing in the world he doesn't know and if there was it wouldn't surprise him. I can put on the same look. If his teeth were whiter it would be like looking in a warped mirror. There's a knock on the window.

Roland is out there with rain dripping off his head. "That's my appointment," says my old man. "I'll have the money in a few."

I pace the room then sit on the unmade bed. The sheets are thin and slick. The pillowcase yellowed from a thousand nights. On TV, a scientist states that saccharin causes bladder cancer in humans and proposes a ban. They go to the street and one woman says she'll never stop drinking Tab.

My father's told me his "private shoots" are going to make him a "wealthy man," which means he can afford rent, beer, and cigarettes. Clothes over the door keep it open a foot and, in the adjoining room, I glimpse April on the bed holding her robe tightly like she's in a stiff wind. Big fat Roland stands at the foot of the unmade bed.

Smoking a butt, my father sets the camera on a tripod. "Show time," he says, raising one of the lights.

"Make him wash his hands," says April.

"I already just washed 'em," says Roland, heading into the bathroom.

I walk to the front window. The rain has let up. I remember Roland digging into the codfish and feel sick. I'm not sure if it's Roland or last night's partying. I go back to the door and peek around my father's black dress pants. April grabs a bottle of pink wine from the night table, swigs it, then rolls on her stomach and hunches up on her knees.

My father has had lots of models, tall, fat, thin, young, old. April is a close runner-up for the best looking, but she's ruined. My father ruins women. My mother says he ruined her. Robbed her life. When I asked her what she was talking about, my mother said, "My life. You know, life."

I knew. Years ago he brought a girl named Lisa to the house for dinner. My mother slammed pots and pans, cursed under her breath, but by the end of the meal we had all warmed up to her. Lisa was from Mobile, Alabama. She had been working as a stripper and heard the money was better in New York. My father told us that he'd double Lisa's wages and make her famous. At the time, my father had a year-old Caddy and a half-ass office over a pizza place on Main Street. Lisa just smiled and smiled, thanking my mother for whatever we were eating that night.

After that, whenever I saw Lisa pieces of her were missing: her strawberry-blond hair, the sparkle in her eyes, one of her front teeth. I saw her on Main Street standing at a pay phone holding up a leopard skin miniskirt that was slipping down her hips. About a year later she showed up in the diner. I convinced her to have a cup of coffee with me, and ordered her a slice of cheesecake. With all the muscles in her arms gone, and her eyes like dark holes, she smiled and said she had a new agent and was going to do a film. I never saw her again. My father said she had gone to the West Coast, but I believed she had lost all she could lose and was dead and buried.

My father crushes his cigarette and looks into the lens. He loves shoots like this. The guy at the Photo-mart in the next town gets paid per roll, no questions asked. April clears a fifty, my father takes the rest.

"April, the robe," he says. "Lose it." She hikes her robe so her brown bush pokes through her white thighs. Behind the tripod, I'm sure my father's got that look—crooked grin, eyes squinted from smoke. I try to imagine Sandy, putting on pajamas, posing. I realize I never knew her at all.

My father's dark figure behind the tripod becomes a silhouette.

His glowing cigarette goes slowly to his mouth, then down. I imagine him turning into a snake, slithering up the tripod, grinning, smoking.

Roland returns from the bathroom. He has removed his pants. His undershirt from the waist down is as white as his legs.

I step out under the awning into the drizzle. Despite the rain, the air smells like glue. A stiff warm wind howls through the walkway. I bang on the window and a few seconds later my father peeks cautiously out from the corner of the curtain, then opens the door a crack.

"Dad, I got to go," I say. "I only get an hour."

He sticks his head out, "I got half up front." He winks at me and hands me a roll of bills. "Tell your mother I'll send her . . . Better yet." He opens his wallet and gives me another ten. "Get her that good vodka she likes."

I take the bills and head off. I pass the Impala. Louie has left the drop light under the hood. The beer cans have blown off the roof of the car and lie scattered on the wet gravel. I kick a can and it goes a few feet. I will never let my father near any of my girlfriends.

I imagine Sandy in April's spot under my father's lights and camera lens and remember her scream from under the boardwalk. It stops me dead on the sidewalk. Standing in front of the telephone company behind Pantry Pride I realize that on Saturday night I could have done something, at least said something to Loopy.

From my back pocket I pull out the magazine and open the inside cover. The credits under "Lollypop Lover" read *Stan the Man Trottman*. The photos are like those kids' picture puzzles where at first glance everything looks correct, but at close examination women are wearing flower pots on their heads, birds have furry tails, and dogs have flippers instead of legs. Sandy's body is saying screw me, but her face is a blank, her eyes at half mast. It's not the same face that waited for Loopy and me at the pizza place. My father probably gave her a lude and a few shots of Mount Castle whiskey that's so cheap he only offers it to company.

I try to tear the magazine in half and finally just toss it into the dumpster next to the loading dock.

Inside the noisy meat department, Kurt doesn't seem to notice that I'm late. On his shoulder he carries a hindquarter of beef out of the walk-in box and slams it on the cutting block. "Hey, kid," he calls, "get those chickens going."

Chapter Eight

I flip a box of chickens on the cutting block, leaving twenty ice-crusted birds, breast down. Bagging chickens is the afternoon chore on Mondays—slip two whole fryers in a plastic bag, then tie the bag off with a metal wire twist. Outside the mirrored meat case window on the supermarket floor, Kurt straightens the rows of liver, lamb, pork, and beef. "The meat case is a showplace," is his standard line. "Present it correctly, sell it quickly," is another one he sings out, acting as if he's joking around. But everyone in the shop knows he's serious.

Reggie trims chuck steaks, on special for sixty-eight cents a pound, and whistles "The Hustle" over and over. At the chorus, he waves his knife in the air and sings "Do the Hustle."

The deli girl slips out of the side door from the deli department, tugging her smock over her hips. She's wearing a low-cut sweater and has the top buttons of her smock open. Reggie stares right at her cleavage. She smiles at me and heads down the blocks. She whispers something in Reggie's ear. They laugh.

The special service bell rings. "Got it," yells Reggie, sticking his knife in the holder on the block. The bell rings about four times

an hour. Week after week, it's the same people; and old lady in a
straw hat who asks if we have any "leaner chopmeat in the back,"
or a guy looking for bones for his dog.

Reggie slides the window open. From where I'm standing I see
Detective Sack and Detective Larson, the two who pinched Loopy.
When I was about ten, they busted my father for receiving stolen
car parts. I answered the door and my father bolted through the
kitchen and out the back. Before he went over the backyard fence,
Larson snagged my father's ankle. The two detectives handcuffed
him in the high weeds. I remember Sack coming into the house,
giving me a dollar bill and telling me to buy some candy.

I dry my hands on my apron and head over. It's either the crap
with Loopy and Sandy or they got my father again. I'm hoping it's
my old man.

At the window, Larson and Reggie are talking. Larson licks his
big blond mustache. He's wearing jeans and a sweatshirt. Sack puts
his hands in his pockets and shuffles around in his baggy suit. I
haven't seen either of the detectives since I left high school.

Sack leans across the pork chops in the meat case and shows me
his shiny badge in a beat-up black leather holder. A knot forms in
my stomach. "Detective Sack, Detective Larson," he says. "You
remember us? Don't ya?"

"Sure. You still giving out dollar bills?" I ask like it's nothing.

"Good memory," says Sack. "A good memory's what we're looking for."

Larson leans forward. "You got to come down to the station
house."

Sack tightens his tie that's about as wide as his neck.

"Did my father do something?"

"No," says Larson. "This is about your fun on Saturday night."

"Aren't these supposed to be on sale?" asks a woman holding a loin of pork. Everyone looks at her.

"That was last week," I tell her.

"Kid does have a memory," says Larson. "Remember anything about Saturday night?"

She puts the meat down on top of the chicken parts even though the pork section is two feet away. I lean out the window and grab the loin. Misplaced meat drives Kurt crazy.

"You want to talk somewhere a little more private?" asks Reggie over my shoulder.

"Sure. Talk. Talk is good," says Sack, smacking his hands together.

"Come on around," says Reggie. "There's a break room through the swinging doors."

"Meet ya," says Larson.

Reggie slides the glass window shut. "What'd you do?"

"Nothing."

"Hey, kid, do I look stupid," he says. "Those two guys aren't here shopping."

Just my luck, Kurt has met up with the detectives in the back hall and leads them through the plastic swinging doors into the break room. I slip around the small table. The detectives stand uneasily next to the rows of smocks, aprons, stacks of Styrofoam trays, and black sewer pipes running floor to ceiling. On the table, a fly moves across the white icing on an open box of hot cross buns. A cigarette floats like a buoy in a cup of coffee.

"I'm the manager of the department," Kurt says, holding out his hand. Everyone shakes hands. I even shake Larson's and Sack's hands. "Sit down," says Kurt, rubbing my shoulder. "He's a good worker," he says. I meet his eye. He gives me a face as if to say, I told you.

I look at the crushed cigarette butts and coffee lids on the floor. I think about Larson's comment, fun on Saturday night. I go over Loopy's call from jail, his one small favor.

"I know Eddie's father," says Kurt.

"It's not about Stan," says Sack looking at me. "It has nothing to do with his father. It's about Eddie here."

"And his friend, Larry Louperino," says Larson, bouncing his head back and forth on each syllable. "Best friend."

"Eddie, you're under arrest." Sack lifts my arm and his thumb twists my elbow. I turn and face the wall. "Before we ask you any questions," he says, "we got to read you your rights." I hear the clicking of the cuffs and feel cold metal tighten around my wrists.

"Under arrest?" I ask, with my face pressing into a white smock.

"You have the right to remain silent," recites Sack like a robot. He goes on quickly, with the words echoing in the tight room. "You understand your rights?" he asks finally.

"You can't arrest me," I say. "I didn't do anything."

Larson pushes me into a chair. I try to get up, but he holds my shoulder down. "Let's not get excited," he says. My metal folding chair scrapes against the floor.

Kurt's face has gone white. The detectives look at him. "Maybe I should give you some privacy," he says.

"Kurt, it's all right. I didn't do anything," I say.

He crosses his arms over his bloodstained smock, considering this, then shakes his head, opening the break door. "I got to get back to the line," he says in a high-pitched, shaky voice. I open my mouth, but nothing comes out. Kurt pushes through the doors. My stomach pitches and rises to my throat.

"Look, Eddie, I feel like I know a little bit about you," says Sack, hanging his big hands between his knees. "I know where your mother works. I know your father, where you live." He looks at

Larson. "Let's do this the easy way. Cooperate with us. You know a little bit about the system. You know what we want."

"What?" I ask. "What did I do?"

"The charges are accessory to rape," says Sack softly.

"Rape?" I ask.

"You know Sandra Gass?" asks Larson.

"You do know her," says Sack. "She knows you."

I focus on Sack's broad face and squinty eyes. "Why'd you have to do this here?" I ask. "You guys could have picked me up at my house, anywhere."

"Sandra Gass," says Larson. "Name sound familiar?"

"We don't call her that," I say cutting him off. "And I didn't have anything to do with that."

"Then it's the hard way," snaps Larson.

"Let me finish out the day?"

"Eddie," says Sack softly, "we've got to take care of this today."

I tell them that they didn't have to cuff me and swear that I won't do anything stupid. Sack grabs my dungaree jacket off the hook between the butcher's plaid jackets and drapes it over the cuffs so that it hangs behind my back. "That'll hide the bracelets," he says.

Sack steers me down the center of the shop around the fat cans. The band saws are quiet. Chuck steaks lie on the dead conveyer belt. Reggie, Skate, the deli girl, and the two wrappers are gathered near the scales. I try to make my face say, this is all wrong, a mistake. My eyes are filling. Skate stands stone faced next to Reggie. Kurt furiously unloads a tray of split chickens into the meat case. I see him and the butchers, like travelers on a train station platform, getting smaller and smaller, as the engine pulls away.

I'm led out of the store, into the sun. Shoppers pass. No one gives me a second look. I'm just the jackass that bags chickens and runs down the block for coffee with two sugars, tea light. I blink and swallow hard.

A Ford four-door is parked in the fire zone in front of the store. Larson opens the door. I duck and fall into the backseat. I stay there with my face on the thick vinyl, feeling its warmth.

Sack and Larson get in. The doors slam. The engine starts. We move. After about a mile we stop. Larson turns around and hangs over the seat with both elbows. "Sit up," he says, grabbing my shoulder. "Come on. This ain't nothing new for you."

I sit up.

"That was the hard part. Now you're going to tell us what happened to Miss Gass."

I bite my lower lip, wishing I could be someone else, someone without a juvenile record, anybody but Eddie Trottman.

"Speak up," says Larson.

We are in the middle of the boat launch parking lot at the edge of town. A few cars and boat trailers are parked near the canal. Across the street, the beer distributor, where Loopy and I started out on Saturday night, is open.

"Now, how would you like to go home tonight and forget about this whole thing?" asks Larson.

"I doubt that," I say.

"All you got to do is answer some very simple questions. Questions that you know the answers to." Sack eyes me in the rearview mirror. "Okay, now, let's start with your friend, Mr. Louperino, a.k.a. Loopy. That's what everyone calls him?"

"That and Douchebag."

Detective Larson smiles and elbows Sack. "Tell me about Saturday night."

"What about it?"

"What did you do, who were you with?"

"I went to Long Beach, to the boardwalk with Loopy, and two girls. One of them is sort of my girlfriend, her name is Elena, the other one is Loopy's girl."

"Sandra Gass," volunteers Larson.

I tell them about the night. I want to tell the truth about Loopy taking Sandy under the boardwalk, but it all gets left out. It's easier to drop the details. I figure they've heard Loopy's story about how I watched him do Sandy and she just moaned and groaned in the sand and cigarette butts. My account takes about ten minutes because Larson keeps stopping me with dumb questions like, "And what time was this?" or, "And whose idea was that?" When I finish, Larson smiles at Sack, who starts the engine of the car.

"You owe me five bucks," says Larson to Sack. Neither of them turns around. Sack steers the car into the late afternoon traffic on Atlantic Avenue.

"You think you could loosen these handcuffs some?" I ask.

"No," says Sack loudly.

We cruise down Atlantic past Loopy's house, then to Merrick Road. Larson sucks his teeth like something's caught. At a red light, Sack turns around, "Remember my name, it's Sack. I tried to be nice."

"No, you didn't," I say looking him right in the eye.

"Yes, I did," he says. "We treated you like a human being and you treated us like garbage."

"You arrest me at my job, arrest me for nothing. You think that's nice?"

With one hand Larson grabs my shirt and pulls me toward the front seat. "You heard the charge, accessory to rape. Five years because you can't tell the truth." He releases me and I fall back into the backseat. For a moment I am too stunned to speak. My heart's beating out of control.

Sack guns the gas, cuts two lanes of traffic, then hits the brakes, throwing me forward in the seat. He veers into the parking lot of the Villa Rosa Restaurant, jams the car in park, and turns around to face me. "Let me tell you the facts, son. I know all about Sandra Gass. I know she probably puts out seven days a week and twice on Sunday, but I believe she was raped. That's why I got the warrant. So if I were you, I'd think twice about that story you told us."

"Okay," I say, flashing on the cigarette butt sticking to the back of Sandy's ripped shirt. "I left some of it out."

"Thank you," says Sack, tightening his lips into a smile.

I take a deep breath. Loopy would say he was there for me, he'd do it for me. "Loopy took Sandy under the board walk," I say slowly, like the words are made of glass. "When they came out Sandy's hair was a mess, full of crap from the beach." I tell them about the torn buttonholes on her shirt and her yelling, "Eighteen dollars, Mr. Big Shot." I go on about Loopy's dollar bills blowing on the bare boardwalk, Sandy chasing them down. Then, I explain how she got out of the Goat at Violetta's, not saying anything, her face red.

"You saw them go under the boardwalk?" asks Sack.

"I saw them."

"What did you do?"

"I stuck with Elena." I release a breath I didn't know I was holding.

"Where?"

"On a bench next to a knish place. A couple walked by, they would remember us."

"But you didn't see anything? Right?" asks Larson.

"See what?"

"Louperino and Sandra."

"No."

"You still owe me five bucks," says Larson in Sack's ear loud enough for me to hear it.

"He doesn't owe you five bucks," I say, feeling blood rush to my face.

They both turn around.

"You weren't anywhere near Louperino and Sandra, right?" asks Larson.

"I wasn't."

Larson smiles at Sack.

"I swear to God on my mother," I say.

"You shouldn't swear on your mother," says Sack flatly. He throws the car in gear and we take off.

The brick precinct house in Baldwin, the town west of Freeport, is across from the movies. I've stood on line at the theater a hundred times and never given the precinct a second thought. Sack pulls the car into a lot marked POLICE ONLY and shuts off the engine. Larson gets out.

"You've got to do better," says Sack, opening the door.

Larson grabs my collar and yanks me out of the backseat. Holding the chain on my handcuffs, he leads me toward a battered green door. Going down a ramp, I follow Sack's enormous shoes. The hall smells of cleaning fumes.

Larson unlocks a holding pen that's about twenty feet across, ten feet deep. Inside, a guy sits on a gray bench, head between his legs. His wrist is shackled to a large metal ring on the wall that bends his arm behind his back. Larson takes my wrist and hooks me up to a metal ring bolted into the wall. The day swells up in my eyes. I try to swallow, but can't. Larson locks the cage then lingers on the other side of the mesh.

The other prisoner holds a bloody rag on his forehead and stinks of booze and sweat. Bloodstains have dried in large circles on his white shirt. Rows of black thread show in his white scalp like the stitching on a cheap baseball.

The guy lifts his head. "Please, for God's sake," he pleads. "I got three kids, a mortgage. I'm not a criminal, my brother-in-law is on the PD in Jersey, in South Amboy." He puts his head down and begins to moan as if he'll puke.

"Sobered up yet?" asks Larson.

"I only had a few," he answers.

"I don't think so." Larson heads to the office where Sack disappeared.

"I don't remember anything," the guy says. His cheek below his eye is swollen to the size of a small red apple. "I don't even know who hit me. What'd you do?"

"I was born," I say.

"I don't want any trouble," he says. "That's the last thing I want." His eyes are red, watery.

The cement block walls echo the people above, someone walking, a door slamming. For the first time in years the sounds from the children's shelter come back to me: keys jiggling, someone screaming, TV in the next room. There was ceaseless noise and waiting at the shelter. Waiting that would make me grit my teeth. I waited to go from the classroom to the gym, to the bathroom, waited to go down the hall to the next door, waited for dinner, waited for the television hour, waited to fall asleep, waited to get out. And, all the time the clickety-clack-slam of the doors being unlocked, locked. I break into a sweat.

"Accessory to rape," I whisper, just to hear the words. I try to get something from the word *rape*. It feels worse than the words *murder, kidnapping, robbery, stabbing, shooting.* It must feel that way to the detectives.

My gut tells me Loopy raped her. She was the only girl that would give Loopy the time of day. Together, they made sense. She's the girl wearing the most lipstick and eye shadow. She's the girl with the butterfly tattoo on her chest, who winds up in his car sucking face with him. She was Loopy's company when there was nothing to do. A warm body when the night was so over the crickets sang with the birds. And, now here I am, involved, chained.

I never thought about rape. Never thought Loopy would rape, could rape. I thought he was better than that. He never cared that I was half Puerto Rican. Never cared that my house was painted half yellow and half blue. Never cared that in the seventh grade I wore a shiny fake plastic-leather coat and the jocks called me "Pleather-Man." We were blood brothers in dungaree jackets and Converse sneakers. He would do anything for me. Anything. He gave me money, gave me rides.

"They don't believe me," says the other prisoner.

I look up from the cement floor.

"They want to crucify me for a few drinks," he says.

"You stink of it," I say. "Why don't you tell the fucking truth." I realize that's why cops don't believe anyone. I pull at my wrist attached to the wall.

"And I suppose you're telling the truth," he says, widening his eyes. Suddenly, he is sick on the floor. Puke pours out of him like someone emptying a bucket. Pieces splash on my jeans and sneakers. The stench makes me gag.

Sack comes out into the hallway and has to cover his nose and mouth. "Only a few," he says, and unlocks the door, bends slowly, and opens one of my handcuffs. "Okay, Eddie, let's get away from this mess. We got a date upstairs." He swings my arm behind me and snaps the cuff on my wrist.

Out the second-floor window, I see Merrick Road and the Baldwin movie theater. *Rocky* is on the marquee. I saw the movie alone one rainy Sunday. Sack takes the cuffs off me. Larson sips a black steaming coffee in a Styrofoam cup.

"Sit down," says Sack.

"Let me say something first," I say.

"Go ahead," says Sack.

"I didn't rape anyone, I didn't help anyone rape anyone, I didn't see anyone rape—"

"Hold on, hold on," says Larson. "We know you didn't rape anyone. Let's get that clear." As he speaks, his large crooked teeth seem to leap out of his mouth. He flips open a pad and Sack hands him a pen from his shirt pocket. "How well do you know Sandra Gass?"

I explain that I met her and Elena about two years ago at Violetta's when Loopy and I stopped for pizza. "We sort of picked them up," I say, "and been seeing them on and off."

"Elena's your girlfriend?" asked Sack.

"I guess you could say that." I think of Elena's face on the boardwalk, the couple strolling by, watching us.

"And Sandra is Louperino's girl?" asks Sack.

"Yeah, she is," I say.

"Is there any reason why Sandra would say that Louperino raped her when it wasn't true?" asks Sack, leaning on the back of Larson's chair.

"Sandy's a flake. She gets into crazy moods. I saw them go under the boardwalk. Loopy didn't drag her under. She knew what was up."

"That makes her a flake?" asks Sack. I think of the magazine spread.

"I know for a fact she did a spread in a porno magazine," I say, laying the fact out like a trump card.

"Yeah, your old man took the pictures," says Larson, without missing a beat. "So what?"

"I believe she was raped on Saturday night," says Sack. "And you were there."

"I wasn't there," I say, feeling exhausted. "They went under the boardwalk. I stayed with Elena."

"That's where our stories differ," says Larson. From his suit jacket pocket he removes a small tape recorder, places it on the table, and presses play: "My name is Larry Louperino, I live at. . . ." He fast forwards the tape for a few seconds, then presses play again. "She was the one who wanted to go under there in the first place," says Loopy. "When we go under, it's business as usual. We do it right on the sand."

Larson fast forwards the tape again, ". . . came down, he was there. Eddie saw the whole thing. If I was raping her, Eddie would have done something."

"So he watched?" asks Larson on the tape.

"Yeah, he was right there," says Loopy.

"That's Loopy's stupid plan," I say over the tape.

Sack asks on the tape, "Why would he just watch?"

"I don't know why Eddie does anything," says Loopy. "Maybe, Pits, I mean Elena, was holding out on him. Me and him, we're buddies from way back. Maybe he thought I was going to share."

"And did you?" asks Larson on the tape.

"No, Eddie just watched. He could tell you . . ."

Larson turns the tape off and takes a deep breath.

"That's all lies," I say.

"Do you know what the icing on the cake is?" asks Sack. "Sandra says you were there too." He raises his eyebrows, waiting for an explanation. "So, that would make them both liars."

"Yeah, it does, but, Elena, she's going to tell you the truth."

"You know something Eddie, I don't like cases like this one," says Sack. "Cases like this have me staring at the ceiling at three in the morning." He looks at me, "Really, even after twenty years. I get a case like this and my wife's getting nervous, my kids stay away from me. Now, I want to know the truth, what happened out there in Long Beach?"

"If Sandy said I was there, she's lying. I don't know why she would say it. Loopy that dope wants me to clear him." I put my head down, wishing they'd believe me. Five years in prison for rape. My mother thinking all the time I'm a rapist.

"I talked to Elena," says Sack, "this morning."

I look up, waiting.

"She said you got in a mood and walked off. You were missing-in-action for at least fifteen minutes. She said you could have gone under the boardwalk, gone anywhere."

"I didn't go under the boardwalk. All I did was walk down a little way, buy some candy, turn around, and come back."

"Let's go back to the boardwalk. What did Louperino say before he disappeared with Sandra?" asks Larson.

"Look," I say, with my throat thick. "When I was fourteen I did four months for being a Trottman. You think if some white kid from Merrick did the same thing I did he'd get four months? I can't go to jail again for some bullshit like this, for nothing."

"Don't worry, you won't go for nothing," says Larson, pushing his chair out. He licks his mustache, stretches, then opens a small dark window, revealing a brick wall a few yards away. "Come 'ere, I want you to lean back and look up this shaft, tell me what you see."

I poke my head out. All I see is a small square of the night sky.

"That's the way the case looks to us. We got one girl raped,

we've got two strong statements, one statement that is a bit un-
clear, then we got you."

Sack takes off his jacket. In his short-sleeve shirt his arms are hair-
less and tight as a fire hose. Larson brings the window down loudly.

"The world is bigger than that air shaft," I say.

"I'm tired," says Sack.

Larson takes out his handcuffs and twirls his finger, signaling me
to turn around. I don't move, so Larson turns me around and takes
my wrists.

In the empty holding pen, the floor glistens where the puke was
cleaned. Larson doesn't hook me to the wall. For about a half-hour,
I pace the cell, not wanting to touch anything. On the wall
scratched in the paint, among the hundreds of initials, something
catches my eye. I find, *Stan the Man* and know from the way the
S curves it was written by my father. I close my eyes. Sack and
Larson must be thinking, He's a Trottman, he is a Trottman.

I sit and remember my father talking about jail. "The joint, it's like
religion," he said. "Hour a day on the weights, hour in the library."
Then he tugged at the back of my hair. "Life, it's all balance."

The evening slips into night. Larson and Sack have probably
gone home to wives, to kids. They're probably raiding the refrigerator, watching Johnny Carson. Time seems to pass in large seg-
ments of nothingness. I think about going to prison, being
confined. In the dayroom at the children's shelter I remember writing poems, lousy ones about being alone, being in jail. I covered
my paper as if I was writing the next speech for President Nixon.

In the cell I twist and turn. I bite my fingernails, wishing I was
as tough as I acted. In four years of high-school homeroom, I don't
think I ever changed my expression. Steady· Eddie, with the wise
cracks. That was me, but tonight I'm scared. I feel small. The cops

don't care if I'm tough, they probably expect it. I feel chilled, but my underarms are soaked. My back aches.

A gray-haired cop in uniform comes in holding something steaming hot. I'm shaking and can't stop.

"Soup," he says, opening the cell.

"What time is it?"

"Eleven."

"Would you tell Detective Sack that I'm telling the truth," I say.

"I'm sure you are," he says.

"Do you know about the case?"

"Pieces of it. I was here when they arrested that other character, that Louperino kid."

"He put me here," I say. I take the soup and sip it. It's chicken noodle.

"I know your father." The cop leans against the wall and smiles. "A piece of work."

"You must think I'm from some kind of crime family."

"I don't think that, not at all."

"Not at all?"

He stands, tucks in his shirt tightly, and stares at me, waiting.

"When will I be getting out?" I ask.

"The evening docket judge called in sick, so it's the morning for you. I heard Sack's going to recommend a reasonable bond, but you're going to have to put something up, something more than a signature." He yawns.

I think about my mother, in the kitchen pouring her vodka into a glass of Fresca. There is nothing to put up, the house is rented. There's only the money I have saved for a car.

"Could I make a call now?"

"Wait to the morning. Everyone's sleeping." He turns the lock gently, and the door clicks. "Night now."

Chapter Nine

By eleven in the morning I've been in the courtroom two hours. All I want to do is go home and get into bed. I try to focus on accessory to rape, accessory to rape, but it still doesn't seem possible. The room is as cold as the wet-box at Panty Pride, and all I've eaten in the past eighteen hours is last night's cup of chicken soup. In the first row, Larson wears a powder-blue shirt, maroon tie, and tan pants. He folds his arms, keeping his chin in the air. He doesn't turn to look at me. That's a bad sign.

The judge, a tight-lipped grandma with an Ann Landers hairdo, bawls out some middle-aged father in a wrinkled suit for nonpayment of child support. "In a civil society the children are the victims. Society will pay your debt in the failure of these children," she says.

"All I can say is, my wife"—the deadbeat dad holds out a finger as if she's in the room—"she's living with another guy in my house and I can't even afford to pay *my* rent."

"Court records show that you are earning eleven hundred a week."

"I lost that job."

The judge takes a deep breath and eyes the state's attorney, who shuffles a stack of papers and meets the judge's eye. "We never received an updated record," he says.

"Send him to family services, get the records up to date," she says, tapping her pencil on the bench.

The court-appointed lawyer, who is also my lawyer, leans forward and whispers something in the guy's ear.

Next to me, a thin black girl, wearing a new denim jacket four sizes too big for her, is uncuffed by a court officer and led to the glossy wood table about ten feet from the judge's bench. She may be a girl from the halls of Freeport High who went by glassy eyed with an unlit cigarette in her lips, one of the hundred or so blacks in my ninth-grade class who disappeared over the four years. The judge glances at the clock, then back at the girl. "Is this her initial appearance?"

"Yes, Your Honor. Miss Reed was arrested for shoplifting at the Alexander's store at the Green Acres Mall."

"Mr. Schwartz, is she familiar with the complaint?" asks the judge.

"Yes, Your Honor. For purposes of expediency we waive the reading," says my lawyer, looking above his glasses from a folder of papers.

"How does your client plead?" asks the judge.

"Does any person running from somewhere got to be guilty of something?" the girl says, wagging her head from side to side.

"Excuse me," says the judge.

"Just 'cause I'm running from the store, that means I'm guilty?"

"Mr. Schwartz, how does she plead?"

My lawyer whispers something in the girl's ear. Narrowing her eyes, the girl seems to concentrate on bringing her lips over her teeth.

"I plead innocent," says the girl hesitantly.

"Not guilty," says Mr. Schwartz.

"Thank you," says the judge.

Smiling, my lawyer hikes up his pants and turns to the state's attorney. The judge asks the girl a series of questions that I've heard three times this morning. The girl is slow to answer. She can't remember her last address. "I think it was on River Street," she says finally.

"River Street where?" asks the judge.

After a half-hour, the girl is led away. I'm the last one up. "Court of Nassau County versus Edward Trottman," sounds the clerk. My name seems to echo in the courtroom. I stiffen on the hard bench. The court officer removes my handcuffs and leads me to the table.

A couple of heads turn to the large wooden door in the back of the room. My old man, wearing a Western get-up with cowboy boots and a stiff black hat, stands there as if he has just entered town square for a showdown. Our eyes meet. He nods at me, then comes to the mahogany swinging doors that divide the judge's area from the benches. The skin around the rusty scabs on his face is white as pork belly.

My father clears his throat loudly. Everyone turns. "Could I have a word with my boy," he says loudly. "Stanley Trottman, the father."

"Mr. Trottman, have a seat and wait for the end of the proceeding."

My father casts his eyes at the high white ceiling and large brass hanging lights, then at the judge. "With all due respect, two minutes with him?" My father's perfect pompadour hangs over his washed-out blue eyes like a question mark.

"Go ahead," says the judge, waving her hand. She leaves the bench.

"Could I have a little privacy," my old man says to my lawyer.

"Sure, of course." My lawyer walks over to one of the court officers and says something. They both laugh quietly.

"What did you tell the cops?" he asks, reeking of Aqua Velva and cigarettes.

"The truth, sort of."

He shakes his head. "You sign anything?"

"No."

"Good, don't. Trottman rule Number One—Don't ever sign nothing, never. You already broke Trottman rule Number Two: Keep your goddamn mouth shut."

"Take a walk, Dad," I say. "I don't need your help. I didn't do it."

"No one ever does it." He tugs at the back of my hair, something he's been doing since I was a kid. "Look, I got you covered on this one, okay? Just keep your mouth shut. You got money saved, right?"

"Money for a car, not money—"

"Andre doesn't come cheap, but he's the best. Just enter a 'not guilty,' get a bond set, then I'll call him."

"I swear to God I didn't—"

He raises his hand near my mouth and I swat it away. Our eyes meet. "I don't even want to know," he says, chopping the air with his hand. "Because it doesn't matter. I wouldn't care if you did a nun on the altar. Trottman rule Number One—Take care of blood and, goddamn it, if my own son ain't blood."

"All rise," announces the court officer.

"Mr. Trottman, have you had sufficient time with your son?" asks the judge.

"Thank you, ma'am, I have."

"Would you please take a seat in the spectator benches."

"I would prefer to stay at his side, if that would please the court."

"Only counsel can be at that table. Your son isn't a minor."

"Then, it's done," says my father, bowing. He goes through the swinging door and sits in the front bench about three feet behind me.

"Edward Trottman, I want you to understand that you have been charged with accessory to rape," says the judge, peering over her reading glasses. "You have been charged as one who worked together with another in the rape of a young woman. It is charged that you contributed as an assistant or instigator to the commission of the offense of rape. You aided, furthered, promoted the act of rape. Do you understand that?"

"I didn't do it," I whisper.

"Speak up," says the judge.

"I didn't do it."

"Mr. Trottman, this is not a proceeding to determine guilt or innocence. At this proceeding it is the court's job to inform you of the charges against you. Do you understand those charges?

I nod.

"Speak up," says the judge.

"Yes."

"Please read the sentencing guidelines," asks the judge.

The state's attorney stands. "A minimum of one year incarceration, with three years probation, and a fifty-thousand-dollar fine, up to a maximum of five years incarceration, three years probation, and a one-million-dollar fine, with a special court fine of fifty dollars."

"Let the record reflect that Mr. Trottman understands his charges and possible sentencing upon conviction. Mr. Schwartz, how does your client plead?"

"Not guilty, your Honor," says Mr. Schwartz, half rising.

"Now, the matter of bond," says the judge. "I have reviewed the pretrial report. Mr. Trottman holds employment as a butcher and maintains a household with his parents in Freeport. I find that he is no risk of flight, and, although the charges are serious, from his past record as a juvenile, I do not find him a danger to his community. He will be released on a ten-thousand-dollar surety bond." She stands.

"Ten thousand dollars?" I can hardly breathe.

"It's surety," says Mr. Schwartz, putting his hand on my shoulder. "Your father signs, and it's only paid if you don't show up at your next hearing."

The court officers approach, handcuffs already out.

"Does my father have to have ten grand?"

"In anything," he answers packing his briefcase. "Cars, jewelry, property."

"All rise," announces the clerk.

Before I get to my feet, the judge is through a hidden door. I'm cuffed and led from the room with the black girl and the deadbeat dad. I look back. My father gives me a thumbs-up sign.

Chapter Ten

Meadowbrook Parkway is practically empty. The trees are full of red and green buds, some have their summer leaves. My father steers with one finger. The stiff cowboy hat is in its box on the backseat. Elton and Kiki Dee sing last summer's song, "Don't Go Breaking My Heart." The Caddy is immaculate and smells like cherries from a naked-girl air freshener dangling from the rearview mirror. I turn the air freshener toward my father. "I hope Mom doesn't have to look at this."

"Just thank your lucky stars that I got this Caddy appraised for ten grand." He grins at me. "Had to slip the guy twenty bucks. New, this baby wasn't worth that kind of money."

It is time for me to say thanks, but I don't feel like it. I lean toward the door and fold my arms. North Merrick is coming up, Freeport next, then a straight run for Jones Beach. I lean back on the slippery leather seat and close my eyes. Even with everything on my mind, I could go right to sleep.

"So now you got yourself a real record." He tugs at the back of my hair and smiles.

"Cut the shit," I say, pulling his hand away.

"It's reality. Always deal in reality."

"Yeah, I know, that's Trottman rule Number One."

"You're learning," he says, winking at me.

"What's with the cowboy getup?"

"You don't like it? I took a road trip to Vegas, won big. April loves my ass in this. Man, Vegas. Cruise control on eighty, straight through, day and a half. Nobody ever made it faster than that. Every jackass in Governor's is bragging about making it to Miami in twenty-four hours. I tell 'em try Vegas in thirty-six hours." He presses the button on the radio, puts on 101, the oldies station. Cousin Brucie is yakking about the old Ferris wheel at Palisades Park, then he plays a corny oldie.

"Everybody's a goddamn cowboy in Vegas," says my father. "This sales guy tells me, if you can't eat breakfast out of your belt buckle, it ain't big enough."

"I think you look pretty stupid," I say.

"Well, if you think that then I must look good." He begins to sing along with the song: *"You'll never know how good a kiss can feel, when you're stuck at the top of a Ferris wheel, where I fell in love . . . down at Palisades Park."*

At the Freeport exit he cruises around the bend straight onto Merrick Road, past the Villa Rosa, without hitting the brake. "You think you know everything? Who sang that? Better yet, who wrote it?"

"I don't know, you're the expert at everything that doesn't matter."

He parks in front of Zuro's Deli. My father never shops in supermarkets. He'd rather pay top dollar in a deli. When my mother complained he told her, "I go in a deli and bing, bing, bing, come out with what I need."

"I'll give you a hint. The guy who wrote it has a TV show."

"Dad, just get me home," I say, looking at the bumpy road that leads into Industrial Park, then to the end of Freeport Creek and the water treatment plant.

"Shit, the guy who wrote it has two TV shows, *The Gong Show* and the *$1.98 Beauty Show*. Got it now?"

"Dad, I just got out of jail, for God's sake."

"Written by Chuck Barris, sung by Freddie 'Boom Boom' Cannon." I turn my head and look at the battered aluminum garbage pails at the curb. "You want anything?" he asks.

"No."

"I know just what you need," he says, jumping out.

"Shit," I scream when he slams the door.

Five minutes later, Zuro himself holds open the door to his deli. My father emerges carrying two brown paper bags of food. Balancing the bags in one arm, he slips Zuro a couple of bucks. Zuro's tan face and gold teeth light up.

My father puts the bags on the hood and opens his door. "Give me a hand," he says, but I don't move a muscle. This is his show. He pushed the packages between us and gets in. "Here," he says, handing me a submarine sandwich wrapped neatly in white paper. "Try that, ham with extra brown mustard." Next he pulls out a Hoffman's cream soda. "That used to be your favorite."

In my head I say thanks, because I'm hungry and because he signed for my bail and got me out. If I took off, became a fugitive, my father would be responsible for that ten grand.

At the end of the street, near the boat ramp, my father pulls between two cars with attached galvanized trailers. The water in the Industrial Canal docks shimmers like a rainbow from gasoline and oil. Across the canal, behind the reeds, is the Merrick golf course. South, behind the dump, is Elena's and Sandy's neighborhood.

My father turns the Caddy's ignition key, and with oldies crank-

ing on the radio, he unwraps his hero, a roast beef, mayo, salt and
pepper. "You remember the time I took you to Palisades Park?" he
asks. "I couldn't get you out of that salt-water pool."

"Cold beer and vinegar french fries. Man, oh man." He closes
his eyes. "They had all the names—Bobby Rydell, Frankie Avalon,
Fabian, Bill Haley and the Comets. I took your mother to the
outside theater to see the Lovin' Spoonful. What's that song she
was so crazy about?" He drums the steering wheel.

I think about Palisades Park and realize I only remember the
place by the TV commercial with all the kids jumping in the water,
and the jingle, "Palisades has the fun, Palisades has the rides, come
on over."

On the radio Cousin Brucie introduces the Shangri-Las and they
start singing, "Do-wop, do-wop."

"Seventy-one," says my father, "they shut the place down." He
unscrews his quart of Budweiser. "Built condominiums, thousands
of 'em."

"Dad, I don't give a shit about Palisades," I say.

"Why would you? You were just a little kid. That's the way it is
growing up, first you don't remember anything, then—"

"I remember plenty," I say.

My father grimaces, "Let's not start." He changes the station to
Cher singing that stupid Indian song, "Half Breed."

"You know, I've had some of my best meals in a car," he says,
biting into his hero.

"Why'd you even show today?" I ask. "When I was locked up
that last time, you never showed."

Chewing slowly, he places the sandwich on the white paper and
looks across the narrow canal. Below the reed grass on the other
side of the canal, a water rat shoots out of a hole in the bank,
startling a group of brown ducks. Wings extended, their webbed

feet skim the surface of the water. The rat, tail trailing, swims right toward us, then vanishes somewhere in the bulkhead.

"That time for rolling the quarters?" asks my father.

"There was no other time."

"I was strung out back then," he says. "Drugs and girls. All I ever did was run around town trying to get more of everything."

"That doesn't explain it."

"You had your grandfather, the greatest man on earth."

"And now I don't."

"Look, you can get the hell out of the car right now. With you it's always the same crap, different flies. I bail you out, try to do one goddamn thing right, and you're giving me a rash of shit? 'You weren't there for me,' " he mimics in a whining child's voice. "Let me tell you something, that holier-than-thou grandfather you loved so much, he wasn't there for *me*."

"That's bullshit," I say.

"Bullshit?" My father wraps up his roast beef hero so that one side is sticking out the white paper. "Bullshit?" he screams. "It's not bullshit, it's the goddamned truth!" His face is as red as his scab. He could hit me right now. That's usually the way it goes. I push him until he starts swinging, then I take off. "That was Pops's big secret," he says, "the big secret no one's allowed to know. Except I do know, that's the only problem with the big secret." He breathes heavy, and heaves his hero out the window to the blacktop parking lot. "You ruin everything."

"I'm thinking the same thing about you," I say.

A few times after my grandfather's death my father mentioned "Pops's big secret," then retreated, leaving it on the table like a dead stinking fish. When my mother was drunk and rambling, I asked her about the secret. She opened her eyes wide and said, "If

I told you, I'd go to hell." I worked on her for a half-hour until I convinced myself that there was no secret, that my parents had made up this tale to make them feel superior to my grandfather.

My old man grips the steering wheel with both hands. In his thin neck, one purple vein pumps. "Seasons in the Sun," that song about a kid dying comes on. I shut it off.

"What secret?"

He pushes his hair back with his hand, "Aw, nothing."

"You're always throwing this secret in my face," I say, hoping to finally have it out in the open. "Whatever it is, I wouldn't care."

"You think so?"

"I know so. Like you said, 'Same crap, different flies.' That ought to be Trottman rule Number One through One Million."

"This is something that would surprise you," he says.

"Like that train set?"

"You throw that goddamn train"—he yells, pointing his finger at me—"in my face one more time." He lowers his finger slowly.

One December, when I was a kid, my father carried on about Santa's big surprise. For weeks he worked the surprise, "Go to bed or Santa won't bring your surprise." But at the crack of dawn on Christmas, under a tree that was chopped down and stolen from a park, there was nothing except crap from a bird's nest that had fallen from the branches and a pile of new underwear and socks. "Shit," was all my father could manage to say. Shit, this, shit that, shit I'm sorry. Then, he told me the surprise was an electric train, one that did things, animals' heads went in and out, horns sounded. Shit doesn't always work out for Santa, is what he said.

"If you had this much faith in me." He holds his fingers apart an inch.

"Just get me home."

"Maybe you ought to know his secret," he says, talking though his teeth. "You're over eighteen. Maybe then you wouldn't give me your righteous bullshit."

"Forget it," I say, opening the door. "Forget it. You always have an excuse."

He grabs my arm. "Your grandfather wasn't there for me just like I wasn't there for you."

I try to pull out of his grip.

"Do you understand that?" he asks.

"I already knew that," I say.

"But you don't know why." He tightens his grip. "You want to know why?"

"Because you're a scumbag," I say, pulling away.

"He was in jail." He loosens his grip, then releases me. "That's right, in jail."

I watch his eyes, trying to detect a lie.

"Now you know why I'm so rotten. He's my excuse. I'm your excuse."

"You're full of it. Pops was never in jail." I sit back in the car.

"Let me tell you." He leans across me and shuts my door. "He went in when I was seven, did ten years for bank robbery. He was the tools man, the safe cracker. He actually got away with it for about a year, then one of the guys who did the job with him got pinched and ratted on him."

"Pops told me that one," I lie, opening the door.

"Those days bank robbery was a big deal, so he got fifteen years, got five off for good behavior. The Feds got him, so he was locked up in Texas. I couldn't even visit him. When he got out I was seventeen. I already quit school and signed for the service. I'm the one that had no father."

"He never went to jail." I break his fingers off the door and get out. "He just stayed the hell away from you." Everything inside me is emptying, running like someone just hit me with an ax. I look into the glowing water, trying to see my grandfather's face.

"Do you think Pops wanted to work in that factory?" my father asks, coming out of the car. "He was an ex-con—he couldn't get a better job. He raised you for me, because he never raised me. Now, do you understand it?" He puts his hand on my shoulder. "You're a smart kid."

"Keep your hands off me," I say. "You and me, we never had nothing."

He steps away and shoves his hands in the pockets of his tight blue jeans. His phony cowboy shirt and belt buckle shine in the water.

"You've got to ruin everything," I yell. "You ruined Ma, now Pops."

"You want to read the newspaper articles? I still got 'em."

I don't cry a lot, almost never. Last time I cried in front of my old man was at my grandfather's funeral. I was doing fine until the casket had to be moved from the funeral parlor to the church across the street. I feel that way again. It feels like I'm going to explode. So, I walk away fast, all the way to the end of the street, past the water treatment plant. At the end, the "treated" water pours out, foaming and swirling. I blow my nose onto the ground, and cough, then swallow.

My father has to be lying. The thought of my grandfather pacing a cell, sleeping cramped on a cell bunk, mixes with my memory of him in the cabin of the *Glory*, sliding into the V-bunk. I remember his old hands at the factory, the oldest worker, pulling the handle of the drill press a million times, the metal shavings curling around the drill bit like chrome snakes being born. A bank robber. The tools man.

My father pulls up in the Caddy. To go farther I would have to walk the sewer pipe like a plank on a pirate ship.

He beeps the horn, then beeps again. I turn and walk past the car. Tires squealing, he swings around and follows.

"Get in the car," he shouts, leaning over to the passenger window, gripping the wheel with a fist. All the way down the block, he keeps it up. "Eddie, come on, you had to find out. Come on, get in."

I cross the street in front of the car and he speeds off, almost hitting a parked car. I shoot the bird at the back of the Caddy.

Near Zuro's Deli, he comes roaring back down the block and slams on the brakes. "Come on, get in," he says. "There's more."

"More of what?" I say, still walking.

"More to it. Pops had his reasons." For a half a block he follows along with me. "Let me explain," he says.

I get in the car. On the seat is the tossed roast beef hero. All the red meat is piled on the long roll. "You want to know why? Settle down, then we'll talk."

"No, I don't have to 'settle down,' " I yell.

"It's in our blood, like the Kennedys, they all want to be president." He swerves around the corner near the retirement home. The door of my grandfather's apartment is wide open. I turn my head, looking for the woman in the wheelchair. My father guns the engine all the way to the corner. "It's not like we're evil, I'm not saying that."

"I knew this 'secret' would turn out to be a lie," I say, not wanting my father to get away with a story like this. "Pops told me you thought being bad was in your blood. We laughed about it."

"Don't be so hard-headed," he says, coasting into our driveway.

Before the car stops, I get out and walk into the house. My

mother is at the kitchen table. Her can of Schaefer sweats on the *Daily News* centerfold. The black-and-whites are of Son of Sam's latest victim. "You're home," she says, stamping out her cigarette.

"Did Pops ever do time in jail?" I ask.

She wets her lips and stares at me.

"Just answer me."

Her mouth opens but nothing comes out.

I go past her into my room and shut the door.

"You spoiled that kid rotten, rotten," I hear my father yelling. "Ungrateful little bastard. I told . . ." His voice lowers.

"Today?" my mother yells. "He had to find out today?"

I strip my clothes off and walk across the hall into the bathroom. I turn the shower on full force and step in.

"Eddie," my mother calls, knocking on the door. "Eddie."

"I'm in the shower," I holler.

"Eddie, I was just talking to your father," she hollers back. She pushes the door and the hasp lock I hammered into the molding falls to the floor. The door opens slowly.

"Don't come in here," I yell, closing the shower curtain. She enters and sits on the toilet seat cover, her legs pressed together. "Get out," I say peeking around the corner of the curtain.

"This isn't true? Is it?" she asks, rocking a bit, staring at the puddle of water on the floor. "It isn't true. All day I've been telling myself that it isn't true?"

"What isn't true?" I ask.

"That you raped a girl?"

I shut the water off, pull a towel off the rack, and wrap it around me.

"It's not the end of the world," says my father, standing in the doorway. "I'll call Andre. He's the best at these things."

"Rape," moans my mother.

"Accessory to rape," I say. "And I didn't even do that. Now get out." I try to lift her by her arms but she is dead weight.

"Even if he didn't do anything," my mother shouts at my father, "they'll think he did it. He's got your name."

My father rubs the steam off the mirror and examines the scab on his face.

"What happened to you?" she asks.

"Knocking around with the boys," he says peeling a piece of dried scab near the side of his eye.

"He's full of crap," I say. "Now, both of you, get out." I shove my mother. "Get out."

"That's the temper that got you in this mess," says my father. I want to grab him, push him out, but it would be a fight and I know he can beat me. He strolls to the door. I close it on them, wishing I could lock it.

I sit on the toilet. He's a rotten apple, I remember my grandfather saying about my father. The tools man calling his son a rotten apple. Perhaps my grandfather was framed, maybe he was forced to do it, maybe he owed someone money.

I pull my top dresser drawer open and dump my underwear into an Army-issue duffel bag. From the closet I collect my work shoes, jeans, and T-shirts. In a minute the duffel bag contains every stitch I own. I unscrew my bedpost and pull out a wad of money wrapped tight as a fist in red rubber bands. I stuff the money in my pocket.

In the kitchen my mother cuts half a stick of butter and scrapes it into a frying pan. The butter crackles, steam crosses her face, and she shuts her eyes. On the counter, next to a plate of onion slices, a bowl of black beans soak in gray water. My old man, in his usual chair next to the window, keeps an eye on his Caddy. When he's home he's either in that chair or asleep. He holds a Schaeffer with two hands as if he were praying to the can.

"Eddie," says my mother. "You grandfather was a good man, that's all you need to know." Teary eyed from the onions, she steps in front of me. "A good man."

I'm sure she knows something about why my grandfather would rob a bank, but I don't ask. Not today, not in front of my father. Instead, I hold her, smell the butter, cigarettes, and the chemicals from the cleaners in her hair. She feels smaller than my mother. I'd like to say, I'm leaving, that I've got to get out of here. But there'd be a scene. Yelling, explaining.

"I know you didn't rape," she says. "My Eddie never hurt a girl."

"I didn't, Ma."

"You wouldn't do that to me."

"I wouldn't."

"I never met a guilty man," says my father. "Believe that?"

My mother and I turn to him.

"I'm serious," he says. "There's always extenuating circum-stances." He gets up, stretches. From the bottom shelf in the re-frigerator, he grabs another Schaeffer. In his fancy jeans and embroidered shirt, he leans his ass against the kitchen cabinet. "You remember the time Mad Dog got pinched? His whole apart-ment, floor to ceiling, the tub, the closets, was jammed with hot stereos. When the cops came with a warrant, Mad Dog swore up and down he didn't know anything about the stereos." My father's eyes light. "And he actually believed that."

"Dad's girlfriend picked out that cowboy suit," I say. "You like it, Ma?"

"What did that cost?" she says. "Five nudie layouts?"

My father reaches and grabs her elbow. "And don't you love it," he whispers in her ear. With the back of his hand he brushes her hair away and kisses her neck just below her ear. I'd like her to smack his bruised face, but she leans back against the stove and lets him smother her like a boa constrictor.

It has always been this way. I've told her he's not going to change. She's met his girlfriends, seen him going by with his arm around girls in whatever car he schemed that month, but she goes back to him. I don't like to think it, but it could be the sex..

I pull the phone into the front room and dial Loopy's number.

"Maybe I need to set him up on a date with one of my girls," my father says loudly. "That would keep him out of trouble."

"Hey," says Loopy.

I press my forehead against the wall. "I spent the night in jail. You had to drag me into this. I'm charged with rape. Five years, asshole."

"All you had to tell 'em was I didn't rape her."

"Is that all?"

"You blew it, didn't you?"

"I told 'em I didn't see anything."

"Jesus, Eddie, you couldn't do this for me?"

"No, I couldn't. And why the hell did Sandy say I was there?"

"Look, don't worry, I'm working on her. I put a dozen roses on her doorstep. That's what you told me to do, right?"

"You bought flowers?" I try to picture him picking out a bouquet.

"Bought 'em? I took 'em off some Moonie at the train station."

"You're an asshole," I say. "Look, Loopy, I want you to go back to the cops and straighten this out."

"I would, if I could," he says. "Joey got me a lawyer. He's Joey's cousin or something, and he told me to keep my mouth shut."

In the kitchen my father lifts my mother and pins her against the counter. One of her yellow flip-flops falls to the floor.

"Loopy, come on," I say.

"Eddie, I got to go. I got to make one of those runs for Joey."

"You're putting Joey before me?"

"Look, I'll talk to my lawyer, he's a nice guy."

I hang the phone up. Screw him, screw Joey and his cousin.

My father's hands are kneading my mother's ass. She stretches her neck back and his mouth moves across her lips. Any minute now they'll be heading toward the bedroom. After, my father will be back in his chair next to the window, maybe thinking what a great lay my mother is, or comparing her moves to April's, who's got that quality. My mother will be on the stoop, carefully pouring a bottle of vodka into Fresca or orange soda. The trucks at the wash will pull in with hissing brakes, the traffic heading east from the city will build, then slack.

"Why don't you two give it a rest," I yell into the kitchen.

"What's the matter?" asks my father. "That big asshole friend of yours won't come to get you?"

I push past him and go out the back door. The late afternoon sun beats down on the weeds and the forever broken lawn mower. Down the driveway I take the license plates off my grandfather's Fury and go back into the house. The onions are steaming on low, rattling a mismatched top against the black frying pan.

Down the hall, my mother sits on the side of the bed tugging off her pants. My father comes out of the bathroom with his jeans open and his shirt off.

"Cowboy bedding down for the night?" I ask. He glances to the bedroom where my mother lifts her shirt over her head.

"You're getting a little too wise," says my father.

"I'm too wise and you're just too good," I say.

"Go find your retarded friend," he says. "Rape another slut."

"Pops couldn't have made you this rotten."

"Your grandfather never made me or gave me anything."

"This is your chance," I say flipping the keys of the Fury at him. "Call the junkyard. Get your fifty-dollar inheritance for Pops's Fury."

He swings and misses me. I retreat into my bedroom, slam the door, and hook the hasp lock.

"Come outta there," calls my father, "and I'll kick your scrawny ass up and down."

I wedge my foot against the bottom of the door and wait. After a few minutes, I sit on the edge of my mattress looking out at the truck wash. There is leaving, and then there is leaving for good. I have never left for good. A few times I ran off, slept at Loop's or at a friend's house, knowing I'd be back. This time I'm leaving for good.

My one trophy, won at a town picnic for the hundred-yard dash, I flip into the trash. Besides the red-white-and-blue STP oil and Thrush muffler decals over my "Impeach Nixon" bumper sticker on the back of my door, the walls are bare. Squares of the room's original yellow paint mark each place where a poster had been tacked up.

In my dresser, I check for money and find Ginny's high-school photo that she handed out during the last week of school. Her hopeful eyes and her optimistic smile reinforce that I had a snowball's chance in hell with her. The photo lands face down in the trash can. *With Love Always, Ginny* is written in on the back. Not quite.

My top drawer is full of junk: Johnny Lightning cars, matches from bars and diners, marbles, incense, baseball cards, a pack of Ginny's letters wrapped in rubber bands, an old Halloween photo of Loopy and me dressed like bums, a stick of Beechman gum, Hot

Wheel cars, a magnifying glass, a James Bond camera I sent away for and broke before the first roll of film was developed, two horseshoe shaped magnets. I dump the drawer in the trash.

My bedroom window screen pushes out easily and falls without a sound to the weeds and trash below. I hang my duffel bag on the cyclone fence that separates our property from the truck wash. I've climbed out the window dozens of times, sometimes just for the hell of it, but this time I won't be climbing back in before dawn. Without touching the ground, I hop over the fence into the dead bushes and what's left of the pine-bark mulch that smelled so fragrant for a few weeks one summer.

Walking backward, still watching my open window, in my half-painted house, with weeds three feet high in places, I step over soap suds running to a drain in the asphalt. The fact that I slept, dreamed of girls, dressed every morning and undressed every night, played with toy cars, read my first books, waited for Christmas mornings, listened to Fourth of July fireworks that boomed and cracked late into the night, in that small dark room inside that long window with the rotting frame, that it all means nothing, makes me weak for a moment. I swallow and I heave my duffel bag to my shoulder.

My mother will be fine without me. My old man will just have to take up my end of the rent. Don't worry about me, I imagine whispering in her ear. I love you, Eddie, I'd want her to say, but she'd start in: *You think you can run? You think that?*

Chapter Eleven

East on Grove Street with the strap of the duffel bag cutting into my shoulder, I pass behind the meat department and get a clear view of the loading dock. Reggie, in a bloodstained smock, leans on a fat can, smoking a butt. I'd like to yell, to run over and see his wide smile, but Kurt strolls out with his paper Pantry Pride hat slipping off the back of his head and his clipboard under his arm. I couldn't face Kurt today.

I continue east. Kurt probably won't want me back. For him, my arrest is like a self-fulfilling prophecy. No matter how hard I worked, no matter how clean the shop looked and smelled, he'd be thinking, I knew it, I knew a Puerto Rican kid from that family would be trouble. Kurt doesn't like trouble. According to Skate, when the store manager told Kurt about a stock shortage in the fish department, Kurt was ready to hire a new fish manager. Skate has twenty years with the company.

Before returning to work, it would be smart to talk to Reggie, find out Kurt's mood. Maybe, if all went as planned, I could go to Reggie's house tonight.

From Grove Street, I walk down Archer Street and make the turn on Sportsman Avenue. On the next corner in front of a small red shingled house with black shutters is a hardtop hemi-orange '69 Road Runner, chrome mags, black wall tires, louvered hood with a red-and-white FOR SALE sign in the window. I've looked at it a half dozen times this spring. Last month I took it for a test ride.

Along the front fender, there are old dents and scratches. The passenger side window is still cracked. A large piece of gray tape holds it together. The mechanic who owns the car spots me and lumbers down the driveway in a blue gas-station shirt, open all the way down. "So," he says. "You're back." I ask him if I could I see the engine again.

He pulls the hood release in the grille. "You know what it's got, the 440 Six Pac, three two-barrel Holly carbs, special aluminum intake manifold." The hood opens revealing a mass of orange paint, chrome, and decals. "The Coyote Duster," he says. I'd like to point out some flaw in the engine, but it's all gleaming clean. Touches of chrome dot every corner; the air filter, the valve covers. Everything else is orange. "Finishes the quarter-mile at ninety-eight," he says.

"The seat needs repairing," I say. "The window, I'd have to re-place that. Anyway you look at it, I'd have to put money into it." In my pocket my money feels fat as a baseball.

"Kid, this here is a giant, no frills, Chevy-, Pontiac-, Ford-eating machine. Raw power," he says. "If that's what you're looking for, then this is your car. Either you want it or you don't."

"Will you take eleven?"

He closes the hood gently, like he's tucking a dozen eggs in their carton. "Eighteen hundred," he says. "Take it or leave it."

"It ain't new," I say figuring I've got nothing to lose.

He stares down the block as if he's expecting someone.

"It has fifty thousand miles," I add.

"Highway miles," he says. "All highway."

"Look, all I've got is twelve hundred."

"It's not Christmas." The guy heads up the driveway, his blue gas station pants falling off his ass.

I throw my duffel bag on the curb and sit. I could run after him and offer him more, but I'll need money, for food, for gas, even to register the car. I lean back on the duffel bag. Starched summer clouds, white as the bleached towels and sheets my mother brings home from the laundry, drift in the blue sky, giving me the feeling that the earth is moving and the sky is standing still.

"This your first car?"

I spring up.

The mechanic holds out a can of Budweiser.

"My second, but my first car never ran." I pop my can and put the beer tab in my pocket.

"What were you planning to do, street run it?"

"Maybe." I sip the foam off the top of my can.

"Promise me one thing." He sucks his teeth. "Don't beat it, treat it like a lady," he holds out his hand. I shake it and the guy hugs me with his other arm.

In front of Elena's house, I beep the horn, *meep, meep*, which sounds just like the cartoon character Road Runner. The steering wheel vibrates in my hands. I feel the smoothness of the skull shift handle, press the clutch in, and go through the gears. *Meep, meep.* I open the window and rest my elbow on the door.

The front curtain moves in the window. A second later the front door flies open and Elena rushes down the walk.

"Get in," I say.

"Where'd you get the ride?"

"Just get in."

Before the door shuts I bang into second gear, leaving rubber. She slides across the wide black-vinyl bench seat.

"Where'd you get it?" she asks.

"Don't worry about it." Heading toward Merrick Road, I blow the stop sign near the end of the dump. "All you got to know is, it's mine."

"Eddie, don't run that line with me. You sound like my father."

"I bought it," I say, smiling. "Twelve hundred dollars cash, cold cash."

"Where'd you get that kind of money?"

"What do you think I'm doing dressed in the white smock behind the meat counter?"

"Playing doctor," she says and kisses my cheek. "Yesterday the cops came around," she says, "asking a whole bunch of questions about you and Loopy."

"Let me guess," I say, rolling up my window so that I can hear her. "Two detectives, Sack and Larson?"

"Yeah." She turns toward me. "Are you in trouble?"

"I spent the night in jail," I say, and she pulls away from me. "For raping Sandy." I ease up on the gas. "You told the detectives I left you on the boardwalk," I say. "Loopy tells them I was with him. Two minutes to buy you candy. Two minutes and I lost my alibi."

"I just told them what happened." She clutches my hand. "I swear to God. Eddie, I swear." She closes her eyes and takes a deep breath. "Why didn't you call me?"

"For what?"

"For what?" she yells. "Jesus."

"Don't start. Not today, okay. I don't even know if I still have my job. The cops arrested me at the store with everyone watching. Believe that?" She shakes her head. "The judge said I 'contributed as an assistant.' " I try to laugh but can't. "Accessory to rape, five years, a million-dollar fine."

"A million," repeats Elena.

"I know, it's ridiculous, where am I supposed to get a million dollars?"

"I'll tell them you didn't do it." She slides over on the seat. "I know you didn't do it."

"Tell that to Sandy," I say. "She said I was there."

"She said that?" Elena shakes her head. "I mean, you didn't go under the boardwalk, did you?"

"I went to get you candy. That's it."

I stop across the street from Sandy's house. The foot-high lawn is a sea of fuzzy dandelions. Thick plastic is stapled over the front windows and halfway up the roof there's a sting-ray bicycle. Rust bleeds down the shingles to the aluminum gutter.

"Why are you stopping here?" asks Elena.

"Go see if she's home," I say. "Tell her we got to talk."

"She won't want to talk to you or Loopy. I know that for a fact."

"Just do it." She eyes me then gets out of the car.

"Waste of time," she mutters then crosses the street and heads up the walk. The wind blows and dandelion seeds float across the street. The door opens. Elena says something, then the door shuts. She shakes her head at me and comes down the path.

"Not home," she says, getting back in. "Her mother said she hasn't been home since Saturday night."

Because I can't think of anywhere else to go, we're flying down the Wantagh Parkway headed to Jones Beach. Light poles, the green marsh and the bouncing buoys in the channels flash by. I round the Jones Beach water tower and continue past Parking Field Four, then Three. In light traffic I pull into the left lane and bounce over potholes on the Drainage Bridge. For a few miles we drive without talking or looking over at one another. The parking fields and beach concessions are all empty. A gull, pulling apart a dead crab, takes off from the concrete road. "Let's walk on the beach," she says.

At West End Two, the last beach before the Jones Beach inlet, I park past the concession. We get out and I sit on the hot hood. Elena fits between my thighs and gazes at me with her owl eyes. I kiss her and she puts her arms around my waist. A cool ocean breeze whips her hair across her face. Beyond the dunes there's a few people on blankets and a guy flying a box kite. The ocean is a good half mile down the beach.

"Why would Sandy say you were there?" she asks. "That's what I'd like to know."

I rest my head on her shoulder. After a few minutes of just holding each other, we kick off our shoes and toss them on the backseat. Under my feet the cement is still warm from the day's sun. I cuff my jeans up a few turns, then we walk along the smooth painted parking lot lines to the sand and follow the red hurricane fence.

We cross the soft white sand, where the shells have smooth edges and don't cut our feet, down to the hard muck area between the dunes that fills with water when there's a storm. Elena takes my hand and bumps me with her hip.

Like white paper airplanes, terns streak over our heads and begin to dive at us. We break into a jog, then an all-out run. Birds are coming within two feet of our heads. At the edge of the dunes, the terns withdraw to the tall grasses and we break out laughing. When I was a kid I'd come to the bay in the *Glory* with my grandfather and dock near the Short Beach Coast Guard Station. I'd cross from the bay over to the ocean, cutting through this nesting area. The terns attacked and I had swung a towel over my head.

I'd like to tell Elena about weekends docked at Short Beach, eating orange creamsicles, digging clams in black gooey mud, fishing for snappers off the bow. But it feels better to just listen to the cutting wind.

"Hey," says Elena. "Where'd you go?" She pulls my arm.

"What?" I say.

"You do that. You disappear sometimes."

I turn to her and place my hands on her shoulders. "You believe me, don't you."

"Of course."

"Not so fast," I say. "I really need to know."

"Look, Eddie," she says. "You've always treated me like I was missing a few body parts. I wait for you every Friday night. You think I don't have anything better to do?" Her eyes demand an answer and seem to read my mind. She pulls away. I catch up to her and take her hand. "So don't tell me I answered too fast," she says.

The ocean is rough. A hundred yards out waves break at a sandbar, then race in, churning white water. A mile off, the beach turns like a fluke hook and the manmade jetty of boulders juts into the ocean. At the edge of the water the beach is empty. No umbrellas, no people, no dogs, no flying Frisbees, no joggers. The cold ocean water races to our ankles, then streams out, sucking the sand away from our feet.

"Let's skinny-dip," says Elena.

"Skinny-dip? It's freezing." She runs up the beach to a white life guard stand and takes off her shirt. "You're crazy," I yell.

She unsnaps her bra, throws it down, pulls off her jeans and panties. She charges toward the water, her breasts bouncing, her skin glowing, and dives under breaking water. I hold my breath waiting for her to surface. She appears in the foam and calls me a chicken. In two seconds I'm naked, my dick and balls tight between my legs. I dive in, come up, and grab her. A wave rumbles by us, knocking us forward. The water, supercharged from the cold, turns my skin to solid goose bumps.

I tug her out of the waves to the beach. Dripping, shivering, we stand over our clothes, the wind whipping us. I use my hand to wipe the water off my body, then pull her into me. Even ice-cold, I get a hard-on. Elena reaches down and grabs me. "You want me to?" she asks.

I don't say anything. There's no one coming, but I realize I could get arrested for doing this in public. "Somebody might see us," I say.

Elena looks up the beach. "You worry too much." She kisses me.

Wet, cold, her hair pressed flat against her head, she kneels and takes me. I feel the warmth of her mouth, it's smoothness, and I think it's somehow wrong that she's doing this just to please me, doing this out in the open, but I don't stop her. I just hold each side of her wet kinky-curly hair, just enough to let her know I'm there. I bite my lip and concentrate. Come on, come on.

Looking out at the green ocean and the white rolling waves that just keep coming one after the other, I come. Just a few feet from the water, a mottled herring gull swoops a fish from the shoreline. The bird swallows the fish whole then takes off into the wind.

For a while we stand there, her breasts on my chest, the wind drying our bodies. Her forehead reaches my lips and I keep them pressed against her salty skin.

"You like that?" I ask.

"I'm supposed to ask that," she says.

"Come on, did you?"

"Sure," she says smiling.

"Really?" Liking it is something I can't begin to imagine.

"If I didn't, I'd tell you," she says.

"But you'd do it anyway," I say.

"Maybe," she says. "If you liked it."

"Sometimes I think you just do things to please me, like every minute you've got do something just to keep me around."

"What are you talking about?" she says.

"I want you to do it for yourself, not because you feel you have to."

"Myself?" she says. "Eddie, let me tell you, girls don't do that for themselves."

"Okay, forget it," I say.

"You don't know what you want, even when you get it." She brushes at her legs, from the knees down they are full of sand. Naked, she heads to the water. She's right, I don't know what I want. Just Saturday night, my mother asked me what I wanted. "Did I want to be someone important." I wanted the Road Runner, a steady girlfriend. I didn't want to be fired or in trouble, big trouble for being what, friends with Loopy, his "accessory?"

At the water she bends her slender waist and delicate shoulders, and splashes. The ocean streams up her strong legs. She's built like two different people joined at the waist. Yet, there's a daintiness in the way she moves, in the delicate shape of her breasts, and the dark triangle where her legs meet. She runs back to me. "What are you looking at?" she says.

"You."

"Well, stop," she says.

We pull on our clothes. I'm still light-headed from the cold water, so I don't say much as we head back to the car. She holds my hand tightly and purposely bumps me with her hip. "That doesn't bother you?" she asks.

"No, not at all," I say.

"Maybe I was doing it for myself," she says, bumping me with her hip again. "You ought to stop thinking you're so smart."

"If I said you had a nice body, would you hold it against me?"

"Corny." She gives me another bump.

Elena and I head to Reggie's house in Baldwin Harbor to find out what the talk was around the shop. I've been to his house twice to help build a deck around his above-ground pool. On the way, I pull into the Shell station on Atlantic Avenue. Grady, another guy from my auto shop class, comes out wearing a KISS T-shirt with the sleeves ripped off. "The Trottman," he says. "Where'd you get the ride?"

"I stole it."

"That figures." He picks up the pump.

"Yeah." I step out of the car. "Why does that figure?"

"I don't know, you said it." I stare at the numbers on the pump clicking over, wondering if he sees a Puerto Rican with a stolen car and a white girlfriend. I get back in the car.

"Who's he?" asks Elena.

"A hitter," I say.

The car sucks up ten gallons and the fuel needle only moves from empty to three quarters of a tank. Gas prices are up. I peel off four dollars and get twenty cents change. When Grady checks my oil his jaw drops open. "Man," he whistles examining the engine. "Where'd you get this thing, from the Indy 500?"

"I told you, I stole it."

"Yeah," laughs Grady. "Right."

With Elena glued on my right side, I drive into Baldwin Harbor, around the curved sidewalks, past the lawns groomed like golf courses. Reggie docks his cabin cruiser thirty feet out his back door.

A butcher makes good money, but not enough to afford Baldwin Harbor and a boat. Guys at the store say he married money. One of the meat wrappers said he was born into it. I pull past a lawn service truck and park behind Reggie's Monte Carlo. Between the houses, the sun glows over the glistening bay. In another hour it will be dark.

We ring the doorbell. No one answers. I take Elena's hand and follow a pebble path to the back of the house. A round Weber grill smokes with the cover closed.

"That smells good," she says.

I lift the cover of the barbecue. Lobster tails sizzle in aluminum foil boats. "Five ninety-nine a pound," I say.

Next to the grill is a brown box full of empty waxed papers. The box is marked FROZEN MAINE LOBSTER and stamped PANTRY PRIDE. The box is from the fish freezer at the store. Skate doesn't sell the lobster by the box, no one could afford it. The lobster tails are rewrapped in packages of three and sold by the pound.

I remember Skate's face when his books come up short each month.

At the canal, Reggie drops a hose and climbs off his boat. I wave. He marches straight toward us, crossing the thick lawn, past the decked pool and lounge chairs.

"What, you just walk back here like it's Eisenhower Park?" he says. Black hair runs up his chest and neck where it meets his five o'clock shadow.

"No one answered the bell," I say.

"No one's in the house." He folds his arms, waiting for a better explanation.

"What's going on at the store?"

"Eddie, we all got problems." He walks past me toward the patio and the smoking lobster tails.

"What a prick," says Elena, just loud enough so that Reggie hears her.

Reggie lifts the cover of the grill and turns down the heat. With fancy barbecue tongs he places the tails on a large white platter. The burnt red shells are still boiling in butter.

"That box holds a lot of lobster," I say. "Skate orders that much for a month." I look at the supermarket stamp on the box.

"This isn't from the store," says Reggie. "This is from a wholesale place. Same boxes, that's all." There's a moment's silence. The orange sunset hangs over the bay. "And, who's this pretty little piece?" asks Reggie.

"Elena," I say. "My girlfriend."

"What are you doing mixed up in that mess," he whispers in my ear. "If you got this piece of ass?"

"I heard that," she says. "And he's not mixed up in it."

"I'd say he was mixed up in it," says Reggie, smiling.

I realize everyone at the store—Kurt, Skate, the deli girl, the meat wrappers—must think I'm a rapist. "Reggie, the whole thing is total bullshit," I say.

"Yeah, well, like my mother used to say, 'It'll come out in the wash' " Reggie eyes Elena up and down. "Look, ah, I'd say stay for dinner, but my wife has friends coming." I think about Reggie relishing the stolen lobster, about Skate losing his job over it.

"Kurt say anything about me?" I ask.

"We all read the newspaper at the break table." He scrapes the grill with a wire brush and watches my face. "Story's in *Newsday*, I got it inside." He goes in the house with the lobster tails.

"You get all this when you're a butcher?" asks Elena looking at the boat and the bay.

"It's like *The Wizard of Oz*," I say. "You're not supposed to look behind the curtain."

He returns with the paper and walks us to the front of the house. "I don't have to worry about you talking to Kurt," he says in my ear. "You know, about the tails?"

I put the paper under my arm and pull my car keys from my pocket. Elena slides in the passenger side. When I get to the front of the car, I turn and walk back to Reggie. "I wouldn't want Skate to lose his job," I say.

Reggie lowers his dark eyebrows then smiles, "That's a big threat coming from a rapist."

"I know." I wink at him. "But you got everything to lose, and I got nothing."

"You got your life," he says leaning forward.

"Tell your wife and her friends that the rapist says hi."

At a red light on Atlantic Avenue I toss Elena the paper. The story is on the third page. " 'Two face charges in Long Beach boardwalk rape,' " she reads. " 'Two Freeport teenagers were charged with raping a young Merrick woman under the boardwalk in Long Beach. The victim received care at St. Peter's Hospital Rape Trauma Center. Larry Louperino, 19, of 2993 Bedell Street, was arrested early Sunday morning. Edward Trottman, 19, of 1144 Sunrise Highway . . ." When Elena reads my name I pull the car to the curb. " 'Was arrested,' " she reads, " 'at the Pantry Pride Supermarket in Freeport yesterday afternoon, where he is employed as a butcher's apprentice. The duo appeared separately before Superior Court Judge June Moses in Mineola. Louperino is charged with one count of aggravated rape. Trottman, who appeared,' " she points to a word.

" 'Subdued,' " I say.

" 'Sub-dued,' " she reads, " 'at his court hearing, is charged with one count of accessory to rape. The rape was reported at 1 a.m. on Sunday at the Merrick Police Station. Later that morning, police, acting on information provided by the victim, arrested Louperino at the Top Hat Go-Go Bar located on the Nassau/Suffolk County border. Bail set at the time of their arrests remains at: Louperino $25,000 and Trottman $10,000.' " She rubs my leg.

"Man," I say. "That's bad." I take the paper and reread it silently, picturing Kurt reading the article aloud over an eye-round roast, his tall wife standing at the stove in her print dress remarking, "And he seemed so nice."

Chapter Twelve

I follow Elena down her basement stairs. The air is cool, thick with the smell from the oil burner, thousands of loads of laundry washed and dried, the wet earth. She finds the lights. Colored bulbs cast beams of green and blue on the peel-and-stick floor. Like rings on a tree's trunk, chalky water lines around the bottom of the knotty pine walls mark yearly floods. Wicker chairs are stacked near the bar, and along the walls are boxes overflowing with porcelain-faced dolls, Elvis collector plates, and other crap. Elena kicks a box as she passes. "My mother's collections," she says. "She's got to have one of everything."

I haven't been in the basement since last spring, when Elena threw a party. I was dating Ginny then, just going to the party for lack of anything better to do, using Elena for a quickie, as Loopy likes to call it.

"When my parents come home, we're going to have to be quiet," says Elena. "My father doesn't even want you on the property."

I wonder if he hates me because I live in a run-down house. At the small bar in the corner of the room, I fish around for his ancient booze that was under the bar the night of the party. I find a bottle of Rock and Rye that's half turned to sugar. The oranges in the bottle are black and it pours like pancake syrup. All the "Rock" is out of the rye. I slide Elena a glass. "Tell your father that, soon as the landlord gets his price, my house is going to be knocked down. That's why no one puts any money into it."

"It's not that," she says. "I got my father to admit that the house isn't your fault." I sip the candy-sweet whiskey. Elena sits on one of the stools. "If I tell you," she says, "promise not to get mad."

"Jesus, come on, just tell me."

"You're Puerto Rican."

"Half," I say.

"He says you can't be half pregnant, and you can't be half Puerto Rican."

"It just shows you how stupid he is." I drain another inch of the bottle into my glass. Elena doesn't say anything. I've always wished I was a full something. The best would be Indian. I would have my own kind. I could live on a reservation where everyone was the same. I'd name my kids Red Arrow, or Flying Hawk or Flying Ass-backwards, and teach them all the Indian customs. "Sometimes I hate being me. You ever feel like that?"

"All the time," she says. "I used to watch *The Brady Bunch* and wish I was Marsha." I remember Greg Brady trying out for the football team, or the debate club, then winding up team captain. "Just suppose," says Elena, "just suppose this, okay?"

I drain the bottle.

"Just suppose we got married," she says quickly. "Our kids would be only one-quarter Puerto Rican, and our grandchildren would only be one-eighth."

"Marriage," I say. "This got serious fast."

"I'm just trying to say, our kids—"

"What if I was full Puerto Rican?" I ask.

"I'm just trying to make you feel better."

"Well, don't," I say.

"If you weren't Puerto Rican I probably wouldn't even like you," she says. "You're like the toughest guy I ever met. You can take anything. That's why I told you what my father said." Her brown eyes wait for me to say something. She puts her hands on mine.

"Just don't start talking about marriage," I say. "Okay?" Married, Jesus. The only way I'd get married would be to have everything set—a job, a house, a backyard.

Elena practically has to get on her hands and knees, but comes out from under the bar with a bottle of Wild Turkey. I pour an inch in my glass.

"You want to know what the funny part is?" I ask. "My German half, I think that's the rotten half."

"You don't have a rotten half," she says. I reach behind her head and gently pull her to me. We kiss. I grab her around the waist and we wrestle to the floor. She laughs and I begin kissing her. For a while we make out like two thirteen-year-old kids. We kiss and kiss, then kiss some more.

When we come up for air I pour another Wild Turkey. I feel like getting drunk. The plan Elena and I worked out, involves me starting the night in the basement, then sneaking up to her room, then sneaking out of the house in the morning. I wanted her to spend the night on the *Glory* with me, but her mother still gives her a hard time if she stays out all night.

Already, I'm dreading being down here under the house, hiding out in the dark in a place I don't belong. There's always the chance Elena's old man could stumble down and find me.

The record player's needle scratches and she hurries over to a rusted microphone stand that's attached by a curled wire to a two-foot-high Fender amplifier that belonged to her brother.

"Now listen," she says putting on a deep voice. The music starts and she bends her knees, bouncing right and left in her tight blue jeans. *"So I'd like to know where, you got the no-tion, said I'd like to know where . . . to rock the boat, don't rock the boat, baby . . ."* She clicks her fingers to the beat.

With her arms outstretched, she leans into the mike. *"Our love is like a ship on the ocean, we've been sailing with a car-go full of love and devotion."* Under the colored lights she spins, keeping perfect time with the record.

At the end of the song, she lifts the needle on the record player and asks me if I think she's good. I think she should try some Steely Dan or Fleetwood Mac, but tell her she's better than the record. With our arms around each other, we press our foreheads together. "You're the best," I say.

Elena's mother calls down the stairs, and her voice makes my heart leap. We look at each other. "I'll be right up," answers Elena. "Wait a little while, after the TV goes off, then come up," she whispers to me.

"You're sure your father won't come down here?" I ask.

"My father hasn't set foot in this basement in ten years. My mother comes down once a week to do the laundry." We kiss. "Are you gonna be all right?" she says.

"Yeah, I got the rest of the whiskey."

She smiles, then climbs the stairs two at a time.

"See you in a little while," I say when she's already gone.

In the basement I sit at the bar and sip another inch of whiskey. Above, on the first floor, a chair scrapes, then the floor creaks. I try to imagine Elena's parents walking from the TV to the kitchen or to the bathroom.

Someone, maybe twenty years ago, spent a lot of time and money fixing up this basement. The knotty pine walls aren't that paper-thin garbage paneling that the landlord put in the hallway at my house. I rap my knuckles gently on the wall. Solid. Relatives probably crowded down here under the house, counting down to midnight on New Year's Eve, while Guy Lombardo's Royal Canadians whined "Auld Lang Syne" on the black-and-white Emerson over in the corner. Elena would have been running around in pajamas, with the feet built in 'em, and her brother would have been called down to play "Moon River" or some Christmas song on the guitar.

But, the party's been over a long time. Everything down here is from the early sixties. The tax stamp on the Wild Turkey is 1965. On the bar, I wipe a dusty lava lamp with a paper towel, then plug it in. The lamp glows an eerie green, like the color of the Hulk's skin in the comic books. The lava is a ball of immobile goo in the bottom.

I'm so overtired. I cap the Wild Turkey and put my head on the bar. Spinning slowly, like a weightless astronaut, a ghostly glop floats in the lava lamp. I say Elena's name. It sounds French, and Italian; my two favorite kinds of cooking. French in her lips and eyes, Italian in the ass and bush.

When the TV goes off, the house falls quiet. I keep my head on the bar. Stan the Man scrawled in the paint of the jail cell floats in my mind. "She's got a quality," I hear him saying. "A quality."

In the glow of the lava lamp, I creep up the stairs. Being drunk in a strange house is tricky. The door hinges whine and I trip into the hallway. On my toes, I pass the parents' bedroom. The door is open and I peer into the darkness, hoping to see sleeping shapes, but only catch the bloom of the street light coming in the window.

Without knocking, I push her bedroom door open. In the moonlight she's sitting on the end of her bed wearing baby-doll pajamas.

"You really think I'm good?" she asks in a whisper.

"At what?" I say.

"Singing."

"I'm going to pass out." I sit next to her and close my eyes.
She holds my hands on her lap. "I'll never sing in a band."

"Why not? You're good enough," I say, because I know she needs
to hear, this. I don't know if she's good enough.

"Eddie, I'm not talking about record contracts," she says. "Just
a bar band."

I lean back and the bed feels better than any bed I've ever felt.

"My father says I'll be washing hair when I'm fifty." She rests
her head on my chest.

"Just let me pick your music," I say, yawning.

"Eddie, come on, wake up," she shakes my shoulder. "This is on
my mind."

I open my eyes and prop myself up on my elbows.

"The thing about my father," she says, "he thinks I'm a loser."

I picture her old man in his truck eying the houses like he's trying
to levitate the mail into the mailboxes. She turns and puts her face
in a pillow. It takes me a moment to realize she's crying. I listen
to her soft sobs, then lift her face gently. "What?" I ask. "Did he
do something to you?"

"Eddie," she says, "when I was little he always said I could be
anything I wanted. He bought savings bonds and put money away
for my college. After my brother went to Los Angeles, my father
changed." She sniffles and swallows. "He spent the bonds on a
camper, not even a new one. The place that sold it to him hid the
the rust with body putty and paint. His foot went right though the
floor on our first camping trip."

Like a bad dream, I imagine her father making breakfast and in the middle of scrambling eggs, his foot going through the floor. "Look," I say. "You can still be anything you want. He's a mailman. What does he know?"

"He used to like being a mailman," she says.

"Tomorrow he'll be lugging his canvas mail sack up Sunrise Highway," I say, "catching his breath at every telephone pole." When I think of him this way I can't hate him, even though he hates me. "It's like all fathers are cursed by God or something," I say.

Chapter Thirteen

My eyes open on Elena's Jefferson Starship poster. Leaning over her, I pull the blind away from the window. About a half mile away, a line of gray sanitation trucks labor up a winding road to the top of the garbage heap. Frenzied seagulls dart and dive into the trash.

I place my head back on the pillow I'm sharing. My mouth is so dry you could strike a match on my tongue. Hangover. I need about ten cups of coffee and two bottles of aspirin. I squeeze my temples remembering the Rock and Rye and Wild Turkey.

Elena turns, so that we lie side by side. The cheeks of her ass press against me. I wind one of her brown curls around my finger. "What time is it?" she asks, stretching her arms over her head. She climbs over me and out of bed. A faded tan line from a bikini top runs across her back. She pulls on a robe. "Be right back," she says.

The clock radio flips to 07:46. If it weren't for Loopy's stupidity, I'd be leaving my house, walking to Pantry Pride for another day of cutting chickens and fetching coffee. "Hey, kid, this ain't light and sweet, I said light and sweet. Didn't I say that?" For all I care the butchers can all drink piss-water. I roll over and examine the small cuts on my hands. A few remain red and infected. Maybe leaving that shop is a blessing. Maybe I don't need to be trimming chuck steaks for the weekly special, waiting for a fifteen-minute break so that I can remove my paper hat, lean over a cup of coffee, and pick warts on my knuckles.

Elena enters the bedroom with a towel around her body and one wrapped on her head. She shuts the door. With the makeup mirror flipped to the magnifying side, she brushes out her eyelashes with a tiny brush. Her eyes are like the rear fins on a '59 Caddy, a little too big, but the best feature anyway.

"I wrote my brother last week," she says. "I read in the *Rolling Stone* that a lot of bands are looking for female singers."

"You sure I shouldn't be sneaking out of the house?" I ask.

"Don't worry," she rubs cream on her cheek. "My father is doing an early shift and my mother's still in a coma." Smiling, she stands, opens the towel, and does a quick turn around peep-show. I grab her wrist and pull her into bed. We kiss, squirm around. She's fresh from the shower and the smell of soap floats on her skin.

"Wait, wait, wait," she says reaching into my underwear, grabbing me. She leans out of the bed and comes up with a rubber and tears the package open with her teeth.

Keeping our mouths locked, one on the other, we kiss. She works the rubber on me.

It's like I just got out of jail after twenty years. I move faster and faster trying to hold out, trying with all my concentration. I watch Elena's face, hoping she'll come with me. I think about the Road Runner, about the work I could do to cherry it out. I go over the engine, each piece of chrome, the feel of the stick shift. She squeezes her eyes shut, and begins to gasp, just then I'm history.

"Keep going," she moans.

I maintain the rhythm, knowing I'm fading. Finally, she opens her eyes and kisses me.

A minute later, her mother stands in the doorway, robe open, revealing her baggy pajamas, her hair in yellow curlers with pink foam in the middle, her eyes wide open, mouth open. I yank the covers up to my shoulders. Elena's mother's face, the color of a smoker's fingers, maintains the same expression. I'm unable to unlock my eyes from hers. She looks like Elena, except her eyes are sunken like she's collapsing from the inside.

"Your mother," I mouth.

"Mom!" cries Elena, leaping out of bed. "Get out of here."

Elena's mother takes a step back and Elena slams the door. With her ass on the back of the door, her face flushed, she catches her breath.

"I'll go out the window," I say.

"She knows you're here," she says. "You might as well go out the front door."

"For God's sake," says her mother through the door. "For God's sake, not in my house, under my roof."

In record speed, Elena slips on panties and a bra. I'm pulling on my pants and shirt.

"That isn't that Trottman boy?" yells her mother. "The one arrested for raping Sandra?"

"Tell her no," I mouth.

"He didn't do it, Ma," says Elena, opening the door a few inches.

"It's him?"

"Ma, he didn't do it. I know for a fact that—"

"Get him out of this house," she yells.

Elena slams the door. We listen to her mother screaming, raving: "Get him out, get him out."

"She's going to call my father," says Elena. "They have radios in the trucks," she says. "Believe me, she'll call him. If she runs out of cigarettes, she calls him."

"I'm gone," I say pulling on my work boots. "I'm going out the window."

"What do you expect me to do?" asks Elena, putting her hands on her hips.

"I'll take you to work."

"That's real nice of you," she says, spitting the words. "My father's going to throw me out, maybe kill me, and I get a ride to work?" She picks up her brush and begins pulling it through her wet hair.

"Elena, I called your father," screams her mother through the door. "I can't have a rapist," she says with her voice getting higher and higher, "a rapist, in this house in bed with—"

"Shut up," screams Elena, opening the door. "You had to call him. You couldn't, just for once, be my mother."

"I was always your mother," she says. "You didn't want me, you didn't."

"And I was always your daughter." In her bare feet, Elena steps into the hall, backing her mother up. "Your daughter," screams Elena.

"And you've never changed." Her mother's arm swings and I hear the smack on Elena's face. Elena falls against the wall and a shelf of knickknacks unhooks and drops to the carpeted hallway without a crash or a noise. "You're a slut," yells her mother. On her knees, her mother gathers the pieces of little boys and girls sitting on stools or holding hands. She holds one girl's olive-sized head, and tries to fit it back on a small pair of shoulders.

"This one was discontinued," she says.

"I'm sorry," says Elena, dropping to one knee.

"Get away, get away," says her mother. "The damage is done."

In her room, Elena pulls clothes from the closet and piles them in a suitcase.

"It was a dumb place for a shelf," I say.

"Every inch of the house is jammed with her collections. That's what she does—collects, collects, collects," says Elena, loud enough for her mother to hear. "Everything is a collectable, or a fucking limited edition." She sweeps the top of her dresser—makeup, sprays, splashes, perfumes—into a shopping bag. "She wants everything, except me." She pulls on her jeans, throws on a sweatshirt, and takes one last look around the room. "I'll have to come back," she says.

I carry the suitcase down the hall. The knickknacks have been picked up. Elena's mother smokes at the kitchen table, a cup of coffee and a small glass of something, what my father calls a "whiff," sits next to her ashtray. The knickknacks are spread across the table.

"You better not be running away again," says her mother. "It'll kill your father." She drags on her cigarette.

"You had to call him," says Elena. "I'm nineteen years old and you had to call him."

"I want him out of the house," says her mother, pointing her cigarette at me, "and those suitcases back in your room."

"You're like a freaking fifth-grade hall monitor," says Elena. "Reporting to the teacher. Dad's going to have—"

"A fit in his pants," she says, raising an eyebrow.

A thunderous crash from the street outside startles us. Elena goes to the front window. I imagine a blue-and-white mail truck swinging into the driveway, maybe dragging a galvanized trash can under the bumper.

"The garbage men," she says.

I let out my breath. "Are you really leaving?" I whisper.

"One time," says Elena, "my father threw my brother into the wall." She points to the partition between the living room and the kitchen where the sheetrock above the molding has been patched.

Elena moves the drapes to get a clear view of the street. The hands of the pot-belly stove clock above the refrigerator are at nine o'clock. I pick up her suitcase.

"Put that goddamn thing down," shouts her mother.

At the side door in the television room, I put the bag down. Elena's carnival goldfish is floating at the top of the bowl, its eyes white like pearls. I pull the door open, clearing a path for a quick get-away.

Elena's mother finishes her whiff and places the glass in the sink. She stubs out her cigarette butt, squashes it, smearing ashes across the tops of her nails.

"You never, never were there for me," says Elena, her voice rising. "You never came to one of my basketball games. Not one."

"You didn't want me," yells Elena's mother.

I'm sure she doesn't want it to end this way. I always hoped that my mother would change, that she'd wake one day, come to her senses, and realize that she was a mother first and girlfriend to every scumbag in town second. I move Elena's suitcase so it's half in, half out of the house. In the distance, the garbage trucks climb the steep mountain of trash. Seagulls glide on currents, darting at the mountaintop. My grandfather watched the seagulls on the ocean because they follow the top feeders.

"You're so stupid," says Elena. "You were supposed to love *me*. It wasn't my job." She begins to cry.

"You loved your father," she says, "and he adored your little ass."

"I feel sorry for you," says Elena. "I really do."

"I feel sorry for you, dressing like a whore, coming home at all hours, stinking of drink."

"You were a great teacher," screams Elena. "Eddie, come in here."

I don't move, so she takes my hand and pulls me into the living room, the nicest room in the house. The velvet red curtains are layered like a funeral parlor. The coffee table shines from thousands of coats of spray wax.

"You hear that sick bitch," she says, breathing and trembling like she's freezing.

I put my arm around her and see my face in a mirrored row of glass shelves that hold a collection of small shells, each with its own stand. The shells and shellacked seahorses are balanced as if created to sit on a shelf and not at the bottom of the ocean. "We should get out of here," I say. "Your father—"

"You saw her smack me," says Elena, pressing her face into my shoulder. The collection makes me wonder why anything or anyone is where they are. Maybe God just shakes everyone up in a giant paper bag and dumps them out.

"If you leave with that rapist," says her mother in the doorway, "you're never getting in that door again."

"No loss," I say.

"I want him," Mom says, eying me, "out of this house." She heaves a heavy breath. "And you—"

"Shut up," screams Elena.

"He's got," she says, "two minutes." And she turns her back.

"Let's go," I say, looking at the patched wallboard. I take her arm and we cross the kitchen toward the side door. Her mother's back in her chair, the whiff half full. "Tell Dad," says Elena, "I'll call him."

"You know,"—her mother shakes her head—"I don't do anyone's dirty business."

When we reach the door, I grab the bag.

Elena's mother comes out of the house after us. "You think you can just walk out of here with that spick, huh, Elena?" The corners of her mouth twist. "A rapist is the lowest you can go."

A car rounds the corner, past the large swamp maples that have lifted and cracked the sidewalks. I consider making a run for it. My car is only twenty feet away. If it's Elena's father, I could make it. I'm relieved when the car continues down the block.

"Come on." I pull Elena's arm and lug the bag a few steps toward the front of the house. Over the bushes the orange top of the Road Runner gleams under the sun. Elena grits her teeth and turns.

"The lowest," says her mother, clutching her robe around her. "The lowest."

Elena breaks away from me and with both hands shoves her mother in the chest. Her mother falls against the stiff hedges.

I yell for them to stop but they struggle, twirling on the small walkway between the house and the hedge. It ends when Elena's mother leans over in a fit of coughing. Behind her on the hedge are her curlers, stuck like Christmas ornaments. Her mother straightens and pulls her pajama top together.

With Elena sobbing, we hurry down the path to the car.

Chapter Fourteen

"It's like we left the world," says Elena, chewing a french fry. A Garvey skiff passes, loaded with burlap sacks of clams. The wake gently rocks the *Glory* and Elena grabs her wine.

"We're not going to tip over," I say. "At least not anytime soon." We touch paper cups of Reunite red. There is no *tink*, no sound at all.

Evening has killed the breeze. The flat canal dances with water bugs and dragonflies. Mosquitos buzz my head and, every minute or so, I nail one on my arm or neck. At the Old Oyster Wharf the docks are quiet during the weekdays. Next door, the Yankee Clipper Restaurant packs the dinner crowd at the tables with a view. In the patio picture windows, candles glow at the tables where couples and families are being served drinks and salads.

I rub my fingertips over the top of the sturdy wooden folding table that my grandfather made without using a nail or screw. Every corner and joint is joined by dowels. The legs lock open with small pins attached by nylon string. Elena shifts in her wooden folding chair, the kind that were at the back of the church when I was a kid.

I tell her about the table and she halfheartedly examines the dowels and feels the smooth varnished wood. "He could make any-thing," I say and describe a toolbox he made from a flat piece of scrap metal, explaining that he used a ball-peen hammer and tapped it into shape, then pounded rivets to join the sides.

She fills her cup with wine.

"You're upset about your mother," I say, picturing Elena hanging on her mother's robe. "Just forget about it," I say.

"Great advice. You ought to be on the radio," she says.

"Come on, this is supposed to be a celebration."

"Of what?"

"Of leaving," I say. "Getting out."

"I've left before," she says. "You'd think it would be easy." She finishes her wine. "I'm too old to run away." She bites her ham-burger and gets ketchup on her lips. "I'd like to go see my brother, get away from here."

"Maybe he'll come home," I say.

"He won't," she says. "He's got a temper like my father's. They'd kill each other."

"He doesn't hate Puerto Ricans, does he?"

"Eddie, shut up." She grabs my face, pulls me across the table, and kisses me. "My brother loves everybody—he's a hippie," she says. "My father used to say he looked like a Barbara, not a Bobby. When his friends called on the phone my father would yell, 'Bob-ra, telephone,' at the top of his lungs."

I smile, knowing it wasn't funny.

"My father just kept riding him and riding him. One night my father dragged the lawn mower in the house and put it on my brother's bed." Elena picks up her cup of wine then puts it down. "The next day Bobby moved out." She lets out a breath. "My family is so screwed up."

On the back of my hand I nail a mosquito. Tiny dots of blood splatter on my knuckles. I don't know why I thought this dinner would be a celebration. But I guess that's my dopey way of looking at things.

After dinner Elena curls in the scoop of the V-bunk where the hull meets at the front of the cabin. I screw the top on a jar of pickles and throw uneaten slices of onion, Elena's burger, and mushy french fries in the canal. I cover the coleslaw, or "cold" slaw as my grandfather called it.

In the cabin I light a Coleman lantern that's bright as a spotlight. Although I aired the bed cushions and pillows on the deck, they still have an odor of mildew. I close the portholes above the V-bunk and settle next to Elena, who's leaning on her elbow, wearing my hooded sweatshirt. I toss my grandfather's coarse Navy blanket over her.

"You coming under?" She lifts the blanket.

With an ancient deck of cards that have pictures of the Empire State Building under construction on the back, I deal a round of rummy. After a few rounds, I tell Elena that my grandfather did ten years for bank robbery and she says that her father did thirty days for drunk and disorderly because he had a prior and the judge wouldn't cut him a break. "It's not the same thing," I say and explain that my grandfather had to plan this crime, plan it with other guys, that he just didn't get drunk and go out and get arrested. She sits up and breathes heavily. "Excuse me," she says.

When I ask for a card, she ignores me, so I try to pull one out of her hand and she yanks them away and says, "Don't you dare." I lean back, wishing I could start over, and explain that I found my grandfather the day he died. Anybody in the world could have found him, but I looked in the window and saw him on the floor. I tell her how my father threw his beer at the wall of the funeral

parlor with my grandfather lying right there in an open coffin, tell
her about the responsibility of getting a gift like the *Glory*.

"If your grandfather was so smart, he wouldn't have done it and
he wouldn't have gotten busted," she says. "And you know something else, you've got an inferiority complex." She says, getting up.
She puts on a fake laugh, "You're so easy to figure out."

Pulling on my jeans, I realize I could remind her that just a few
hours ago she was twirling around on her front lawn with her
mother. We bump shoulders and she pushes her hip into me. "Just
cut the shit," I say. "Okay?"

"Want me to split?" she says. "Just show me how to get outta
here and I'm history."

"I don't know what I want, remember?" I leave the cabin and
climb to the flying bridge. The tide has risen and the stern is a
foot higher than the dock. In the night sky the stars are thick as
buckshot. I try to figure out our argument, how it started. I remind
myself that she's the shampoo girl, tight jeans, red bikinis, and a
lot more "street" than some of the girls that come around the
volunteer firehouse on Friday nights. But she's so damn right. If
my grandfather was so smart, he wouldn't have done it in the first
place.

I swing off the bridge, leap to the dock, and head to the street,
climbing up the shell driveway past the hot exhaust fans from the
restaurant on the other side of the hedges. Crickets, thousands of
them, end their racket as I pass, then crank it up again.

I cut across the lot of the Yankee Clipper and someone runs
toward me calling my name. I squint into the bright restaurant
lights and recognize Whitehead, Loopy's old buddy, wearing a valet
jacket, over a white undershirt. His hair, once down to his ass, is
just over his ears. Chills race up and down my arms and on the
back of my neck.

"Man," he says happily. "I can't believe it's you. Jesus, man. I read about your ass in the paper. Rape." He laughs. "Oh, man."

"What are you parking cars?" I ask, knowing the obvious.

"Yeah," he smiles. "Ya want a Caddy?" He dangles a set of keys and we both laugh. "What happened to you? he asks. "I mean, raping Sandy?"

"Drop it," I say. "Nobody raped nobody." He's skinnier than ever, and his toes are sprouting like mushrooms from his Converse sneakers. "So, this is what you do?"

"I know," he says. "It bites, but sometimes these rich fat mothers come out all juiced up, stuffed with lobster tail, and shove me a twenty." He looks down at the ground. "Ya still hanging with Loopy?"

"Not like the old days," I say. "I got my own place. My girlfriend's shacked up with me."

"Jesus," he says. "Leave it to Trottman." He shakes his head. "Hey, you remember that cheerleader chick you were hung up on?"

"Cheerleader?"

"The one with the black hair, that lived off Bayview."

"Ginny?"

"Yeah, Ginny. Am I right, or what, didn't she look like a cheer-leader?"

"Yeah, I guess she did."

"She's here tonight," he says. "Inside with the whole family and that little prick from the drama club. The one that was always running for 'stupid' council president."

"Jay?"

"Yeah, Jay," he says. "Remember him with the corduroys and the VW Rabbit?"

I nod, remembering hearing the story that he could have had any car he wanted and he picked a Rabbit. I follow Whitehead across the parking lot between a big Electra 225 and a Park Avenue.

The restaurant's lights shine through the picture windows. Images shimmer and dance on the ebony canal like flames from a fire. "Right there," says Whitehead. "See her?"

Ginny's back is to me, but there's no mistaking her thick black hair, cut straight across her shoulders. Jay's there, wearing a tan disco suit with six inch lapels and a flowered tie. Her father waves a wineglass, using it to make a point.

Reflected in the window glass are the *Glory*'s cabin lights at the Old Oyster Wharf. On deck, the glow of Elena's cigarette moves slowly to her face then back to her side. For a second I can't move. I'm stuck between Ginny and her family cracking Alaskan crab legs, and Elena smoking, waiting for me.

At a green metal door, held open by a crushed cardboard box, I duck into the kitchen. I pass an army of waitresses dressed in black uniforms, and push straight ahead through swinging doors into a carpeted hall.

Everything seemed possible when Ginny was around. She told me not to take a job, claiming I was smart enough for college. "My father says that college isn't a choice," she said. "It's an obligation."

A waitress arrives at their table and pours a magnum of champagne. Over a toast, Ginny's father says something, probably witty, he's a smart guy, reads the *Wall Street Journal*, plays Scrabble, has a lawn service. Ginny's mother raises her glass. The champagne is the exact color of her beauty parlor hair. I don't want to gawk at Ginny, but I'm not ready to go back to the boat. I decide to call my mother. We haven't talked since I left and she's got to be wondering what happened to me. I hang on the pay phone in the hall, listening to the ring, until some guy answers. I ask for my mother. The phone drops.

"Hey, hey," says my mother, which means she's been drinking. She never says that to me when she's sober. "So, that's it," she

says. "You just leave. No good-byes. How do I pay the rent money,
the electric, the food?" Ginny's table erupts into laughter and I
wish I was in on it. "Where are you?" asks my mother. "I went to
the boat, I didn't see you."

For a moment there is an awkward silence. I ask her how work
is going. "The ladies at the laundry, they all read the paper. What
do I say?" She breathes heavily into the phone.

"Who answered the phone?" I ask.

"Can't I have a little life?" she asks. "I got to turn into dust,
because of you." I tell her I've got to go, but she goes on. "You
found out about Pops, that why you left?"

"No," I say. "I just had enough."

"You want to know why?" she asks. "Why Pops robbed the bank?
Pops's father," she says, "was a crook. He needed Pops in the job.
Pops was good with tools." Silence. "Pops was no crook," she says.
"Believe me."

"You mean, my great grandfather was a bank robber?"

"Into everything," she says. "No good, like your father."

"Jesus," I say. "Three generations?"

"Get off of me," she says to someone, the phone bangs on something.

I replace the receiver and rub my fingers over the fancy wallpa-
per. Not for a minute did I ever consider that Pops even had a
father. He never talked about him.

"Eddie?"

I look up to Ginny's shining eyes.

"I can't believe it's you," she says.

"It's me." I'm against the wall, wishing I could make a break for
it, but she's a foot in front of me.

"Are you"—she points her finger toward the kitchen—"working
here?"

"Just filling in for someone." I can hardly speak. My mouth has gone dry. She's the same, her face and eyes shining against her black hair. I'd like to reach out and touch her, feel her heat. I ask her if it's a special occasion.

"I made a three-point-five cumulative," she says. "It's like an A, sort of."

"I know what it is," I say.

"I still can't believe it's you." Shaking her head, she goes over my ratty black T-shirt, jeans, and sneakers, and I look at her short dress and high heels. On her finger there's a diamond engagement ring that could take someone's eye out. She raises her hand. "Jay gave it to me," she says. "He's full of surprises." She looks back toward her table.

"Full of crap is more like it," I say.

"I saw your first mate," she says. "Looks like you're doing all right for yourself." She turns to go and I step in front of her. "Please," she lets out a breath. "I know you're in trouble, Eddie. I read the paper. I had to promise my parents I'd never talk to you again."

"Believe me," I say. "I didn't do—" A woman comes down the hall and Ginny steps around her.

"You never do anything, right?"

Ginny winds her way back to her family, the champagne, and Jay. For her, it all fits. She thinks people make their own luck and, now she thinks I'm a rapist. Whatever we had might as well have never existed.

Clouds cover the moon and the darkness thickens. In the light from the restaurant, Elena waits on the transom. Like a fighter on the way to the ring, she wears my gray sweatshirt with the hood up. "Hey," I say, tugging a line.

"Where'd ya go?" she asks.

"For a walk." I step aboard the transom and hop to the deck.

"For a walk?" She flicks her cigarette in the canal. "Maybe I should go for a walk." She twists out of my reach. "I'm not a trash can, Eddie." Rage gleams in her eyes. "You can't run away because I say something that pisses you off."

"I was only gone—"

"Long enough for the lantern to burn out," she says. "I was in there in the dark."

"There's a light," I say. "A switch."

"So what's it going to be?" she asks. "You either care about me or you don't."

I realize she's not that girl yakking on the phone, hanging around just for a night of cruising in Loopy's Goat, bumming beers and cigarettes. Maybe she never was. Elena waits for an answer. There are tears in the corners of her eyes. I need to say the right thing. I don't want to lose her.

"I care," I say. Slowly, like the *Glory* drifting on the still canal, she moves into my arms. Ginny's face floats in and out of my mind, but I don't want to think about her.

"I was scared," she says. "Scared you might not come back."

The smell of shampoo in her hair reminds me of this morning when she was in her room fresh from the shower, naked, playing peek-a-boo with her towel. She was beautiful then, pink from the hot water. I move her hair away from her face and fit my mouth around hers. I make a promise never to lose control with her. With her I feel some kind of beginning.

In the cabin the electric lights are out. "Battery's dead," I say. I re-light the lantern, and Elena's face in the warmth of the yellow light is flush and rosy. She slides into the booth and I lie across the V-bunk. "You tired?" she asks. "You want to go hang out at Violetta's?"

Chapter Fifteen

I rub a circle on Violetta's steamy window and peer out into the L-shaped shopping center. In the empty lot, the Road Runner is parked under the light in front of the Peking Palace, a Chinese joint that has two big red phony-baloney dragons guarding the front door.

"Hands off the glass," says Vinnie. From his sauce-stained smock he pulls an opener and nimbly works it over the tops of two long-neck Cokes. Italian horns on layers of gold chains jingle around his neck. "My wife shows me the paper," he says. "She says to me, 'Those boys, they're the boys from the store.'" He slides the Cokes across our table.

"Don't always believe what you read in the paper," I say.

"I can spot trouble. Always drinking, leaving beer cans in the lot. Who do you think has to clean them up?" He waits for an answer. Loopy's famous for tossing beer cans, and I'm not far behind. "I tell my wife I'm not surprised at all."

"Look," I say. "Your trash is blowing all over the parking lot."

"So," he says.

"You don't even have a garbage pail out there."

He shakes his head, then goes behind the counter.

Keeping her face at her plate, Elena pulls a slice out of our pie and dangles it, dripping oil. She's still upset over me leaving her on the boat.

"So what happened?" asks Vinnie. "You going to jail?"

"Eddie didn't do it," says Elena. "I was there." Vinnie gives her a crooked look of disbelief. "Then why'd you ask," she says.

"Okay, okay." Vinnie puts his hands up. "Maybe nothing happened." He picks up his Coke and drinks, staring straight out to the parking lot. He must have that lot etched in his brain.

"Thanks," I say, reaching for Elena's hand.

"Forget it."

Outside a car screeches, then parks in two spots in front of the Peking Palace. The engine rattles, backfires, and shuts off. Along the side of the car a streak of white paint goes from the front bumper to the back.

"What's the matter?" asks Elena. I tell her that my father just arrived. She peers out the window, "What's he doing here this late?"

"Late?" I say. "He probably just got up."

The Caddy's passenger door opens and April climbs from the car, tugging her miniskirt. She zips up her jacket, a white rabbit fur.

"That's his big-money girl," I say. "She's been in *Cheri*."

"*Cheri?*"

"The screw magazine."

"She's pretty," says Elena. "I know she doesn't do her own hair." April's hair is twirled on her head like a gold screw.

Hair and a pair of tits. It's about all she's got going.

The Caddy's driver's door opens and my father comes out of the car quick, like he just dropped his cigarette on his lap. Hatless, cowboy belt buckle sparkling under the store light, he ducks into the backseat. A few seconds later from the rear of the car climbs Sandy. Drawers herself!

She's wearing the same ripped, hip-huggers, black T-shirt, and a giant flannel shirt that she always wears.

"Your father knows Sandy?" asks Elena.

April, leading the way, covers the rough asphalt with long strides. My old man, swaggering in his ass-kicking pointy boots, follows Sandy. If anyone can get the truth out of her, it's my father. I'm relieved and anxious at the same time. His solutions have a tendency to foul things up even worse.

April crosses the sidewalk. At the window glass, she removes a gold lipstick from her shiny white pocketbook, touches up her bottom lip, then puckers. Sandy spots us and turns to walk away, but my father grabs her firmly by the arm.

"Is he hurting her?" Elena asks, pushing out her chair. The black scab under my father's eye has left a patch of shiny skin. In a few weeks there'll only be a small scar. I take a swallow of soda. "Eddie," says Elena. "He hurt her."

"That's what he does," I say. "He hurts people."

Elena shoots me a look, then glances back out the window. "You're not going to do anything?" My father knocks on the glass and Vinnie shakes his head. My old man yells to open the door and I tell Vinnie to let him in.

"I'm closed," says Vinnie.

"Come on," yells my father, rapping his keys on the glass. "Open up."

"Closed," repeats Vinnie. "Twelve o'clock, closed."

"I don't care what Sandy did," says Elena, "your father has no right to hurt her."

"She put me in jail," I say. "Got my name in the paper, for nothing. Maybe she should have thought of that." Elena lowers herself back into her chair. I don't want to tell her that against him I've always been powerless, that in my bed I've plotted his death, wished him locked up in jail forever, but never could do anything. "I'm gonna shove your smart mouth up your ass one of these days," he'd yell. All I ever had against him was my smart mouth, and a couch or table to run around.

A queasy feeling passes through my stomach. It's the uncomfortable sensation I always get before a fight. My father strides out to the parking lot, spins a shopping cart around toward the door, and hops the curb. Without missing a step, he rams the door with the chrome mesh of the cart. Amazingly, the glass doesn't break.

"What, you crazy?" yells Vinnie. "You crazy?" My father backs up and threatens to bang the glass again.

Vinnie turns the key in the lock and April pushes around my father and into Vinnie, who's trying to block the door. "Bathroom," she says, rubbing her thighs together, and slides past him toward the back of the store. "I'm closed," he calls after her. My father leads Sandy into the store. "I said closed," says Vinnie, blocking his path.

"Dad, please," I say, stepping between them. "I don't need any more trouble."

"I'll call the police," says Vinnie.

I get Vinnie to back off and give us ten minutes. He uses the phone behind the counter and begins speaking in rapid Italian. My father pulls two chairs up to our table. "This must be Elena," he says, holding out his hand. Elena, eyes like two full moons, doesn't move. "I don't bite," he says. She takes his hand and they shake over the pizza. "You sure are pretty."

"Dad, cut the crap," I say.

He waves me off. "When I see potential I owe it to that person to say something," he says, looking at Elena. "Part of my job is

spotting talent, maximizing potential. That little honey in the ladies' room already had two centerfolds. But Eddie here, he doesn't
like easy money. He thinks everyone's got to be ass deep in a chopmeat machine."

"Just leave Elena out of it," I say.

"Hey, all I did was call her pretty." The pizza parlor lights shine
on his watery eyes. Elena tells Sandy that she called and that we
went to her house.

Sandy shoves her hands into her hip huggers. "I couldn't call
you," she says, sniffling. "I was at a shelter. The counselors told
me not to contact anyone." She pushes her stringy black hair from
her face and closes her flannel shirt across her chest. "I signed
myself out," she says. "I couldn't take it anymore. Sitting around
listening to how this one got beat up and thrown out, or this one's
husband smacked her." She goes on to tell us that she was walking
around all day, until she turned into Governor's for a beer.

"I was looking for her for two days," says my old man. "Then I
look up and she's sitting right in front of me."

"Jeez, Sandy," I say. "You got me in a lot of trouble."

"She's got a lot of balls," adds my old man.

"Get me a beer," says Sandy.

"What's the pizza man's name, Tony, Vito, what?" asks my father, motioning toward the counter. "Vito," calls my old man in
his phony velvety voice. "Calm down and come over here."

Vinnie approaches the table.

"Give us another pie," says my old man, "and get everyone a
beer."

"I told you," says Vinnie. "Closed."

"Charge me double," says my father, smiling. "Double the prices
and I'll leave you a nice tip."

"You don't hear so good," says Vinnie evenly. "I'm closed."

From his front jeans pocket my father pulls a wad of crisp one-hundred-dollar bills in a money clip. He wets his finger and snaps off a bill. "That'll cover it, right?"

Vinnie turns the bill over then stuffs it in his pocket.

Like a freshly clipped and perfumed poodle, April returns from the ladies' room. "In case you're wondering why I'm so dressed up," she says sitting down, "we're going to Studio 54 tonight, right, Stan?"

"Disco," he says. "That's not my son's style, is it, Eddie?" He removes a plastic toothpick from the top pocket of his cowboy shirt and works it over his teeth like he's scratching off a lottery ticket. Everything, except his teeth, is immaculate. Greased back, his black hair shines like water. He's always been immaculate.

"Still wearing that cowboy suit," I say. "You ever take it off?"

"I like cowboys," says April. "I'm his cowgirl."

"Gettie-up," says my father, raising his eyebrows at April.

Sandy sits on her hands and leans forward. Perspiration beads her forehead. "Sandy, you okay?" asks Elena.

She sniffles and picks up her beer.

"She's fine," says my father. "Just got to get something off her chest, that's all."

"If I did what she did," says April, flashing her long red finger-nails in front of her face, "I wouldn't feel so good either."

Sandy pushes her hair away from her face and takes a long slug of beer. She puts the bottle back on the table.

"Eddie," says April, "you just ought to be thankful your father cares."

My father waits for me to say something, but thanking him is like admitting that I need him and I don't. He was never there for anybody except his second-rate girl friends. Studying me, he waits. When I was little his gaze would make me nauseous. I'd ask my mother to make him stop. After I turned twelve or so, I figured he was looking at me because I was half Puerto Rican. He didn't want to believe that I was his son, living proof of his stupidity, his lack of control.

"No, I'm not Eddie's grandfather," he says. "No glowing circles over my head." He takes a sip of his beer and watches me. My father's smile fades, his eyes sort of shimmer. At the jail in the visiting room, he once gave me a house about six inches tall constructed of glued match sticks. The doors worked, and the windows, made from cigarette pack cellophane, slid up and down. The expression he wears now, he wore that day.

"Eddie, I just want you to know," says my old man, looking at Sandy. "I never believed her. Maybe you figured I did, but I know you better than you think." He glances at Elena. "He's the kid that got mad at me when I whistled at a piece of tail going down the street. When I heard this little whore dragged my son through the mud." Sandy shoots him a look that could cook a chicken, but he continues, "Shit, that pissed me right off, really pissed me off."

"She's not a whore," says Elena. "Maybe someone at this table is, but she's not."

"What's that supposed to mean?" says April.

I tell everyone to simmer down. "Maybe Sandy has something to say."

"It wasn't my fault," she says. "At first I told the detectives you weren't there, I was sure you weren't there. I told 'em and told 'em. Then they showed me Loopy's statement about you being there and then I wasn't so sure." She takes a swallow of beer. "The cop with the mustache"—she squints her eyes remembering—"said you were there and kept saying it. He must'a said it a million times." She leans forward. "I didn't want to sign my statement."

I release a deep breath. An easy sensation in my neck and shoulders feels like I just rose to the surface of the water. Sandy takes a pack of Kools from her shirt pocket and taps one out.

"Loopy really rape you?" I ask.

"I told him to cut the shit," she says, and counts on her fingers. "We didn't have a blanket, the sand was wet, I had on a new shirt. And I wasn't in the fucking mood."

"Aw, nobody raped nobody," says my old man. "So let's stop the nonsense. You're banging the guy eight days a week."

"Eddie," says Sandy, "I didn't see you dragging Elena under there. What, I gotta put out every damn time?" She crosses her legs and lights her cigarette, blowing the smoke across the table.

"I don't see what that has to do with it," says Elena. "Eddie lost his job because of you."

"Could I get a Kool?" asks April.

"Don't tell me," says Sandy. "You left yours in the machine?"

"You hear that," my father laughs.

"Cheap little—" says April, getting up. At the cigarette machine she opens her purse and begins dropping in quarters. The back of her skirt is hung up on the rabbit jacket. The bottom of her ass cheek, where her panties are crushed under the tight, dark tops of panty hose, is showing. I remember her on her knees with Roland, my father smoking behind the movie camera. April tries hard to be sexy, it's almost sad. There's no girl left in her.

She returns to the table, gives Sandy the evil eye, and packs her cigarettes. "It would have just been common courtesy," she says.

"Com'ere honey." My old man smoothes her skirt. "Don't give any for free."

Unaffected, April sits and lights her cigarette, blowing smoke into the air. Sandy holds her elbows, looking at the table.

Vinnie asks everyone to move their bottles. He takes away the half-eaten pie and replaces it with a new, hot one.

"No sausage?" asks my old man.

"You never said sausage."

"Throw something on it, pepperoni, sausage—something." He raises his eyebrows. "It's laying out here naked as an autopsy."

"Next time you want something, say it." Vinnie lifts the round tray, removing the pie, and heads back to the counter.

"Italians," says my old man. "Pizza and digging ditches, that's all they've ever been good for."

"Columbus discovered America," says April.

"Look at this," he says, smiling. "I'm hooked up with a historian." My father rubs his hands together. "Tomorrow I'll take Sandra down to the police station and get this straightened out."

"Should I show them what your father did?" asks Sandy, tugging the neck of her T-shirt and revealing a black bra strap and a row of red bruises. Elena gets up and examines Sandy's neck. "He choked me," says Sandy. "Almost killed me."

"Nobody choked nobody," says my father. "How do I choke somebody by grabbing the back of their neck?"

"Nobody choked nobody," says Sandy. "Nobody raped nobody. Everybody here can go to hell."

"You bring her down to Larson with marks on her neck, you think he's going to believe her?" I ask.

"You worry too much," says my old man. "She can wear a turtleneck."

"I've had enough." Sandy heads to the door.

"You better go to the police in the morning," my father says.

She turns, looks at all of us, then to Elena.

"You better," says Elena.

Sandy rushes out the door, across the parking lot to the pay phone in front of the Chinese joint.

Elena gets up. "Maybe I should—"

"Don't," I say.

"More problems than goddamn algebra," says my old man.

"You promised. Studio 54," whines April.

Vinnie finally comes back with the pizza and my old man tells him that if there were an Italian Hall of Fame, the pie would be in it. My father invites Elena and me to Studio 54, tells us the bouncer used to work at Uncle Sam's and "owes me a favor." I tell him it's late, that I've had a bad day, that I'm not dressed up enough, but he pushes. "You don't have to be dressed up. Shit, none of the stars are dressed up." But, I'm not going and no matter how he tries he can't convince me. I've seen the place on the news, all these "disco ducks" leaning over crowd control ropes waving their hands trying to get noticed. I could just see it—April and my old man would waltz right in, Elena and me left in the mob.

None of us notice Vinnie's brother-in-law, Pete, and the two guys behind him come in the door. They just appear two feet in front of us. During the day Pete's behind the counter, dressed in whites, tossing pizza dough with his spare tire hanging over his pants, but tonight he's dressed for a wedding: blue suit, tie, shined shoes. In his hand he holds a wooden ax handle.

Pete's son, a kid with wavy black hair and dark eyes, sticks his hands in the pockets of his chinos. The other guy coolly looks me over and shuffles his big Frankenstein boots.

"You think you can try to break my window and disrespect Vinnie over there?" asks Pete. No one, not even my old man, moves. "This is my establishment. This is how I feed my family."

"They must be sick of pizza." My father smiles and pushes out his chair. "I paid a hundred bucks for this pie." My father shoots his eyes toward me then back to Pete.

"You think I need your money?" asks Pete with a strained smile.

"Stan, if there's trouble," says April. "We'll never get—"

"Shut up," says my father.

"I'm not the one asking for trouble," says Pete, raising the ax handle. "You come in here and—"

My father strikes, fast as a snake, and the ax handle is in his hands and Pete is left standing there, reaching. The switch is so fast everyone freezes, dazed, like we've just seen magic. No one, not me, not Pete, not his son, sees what's coming next. My old man pokes Pete square in the teeth with the end of the ax handle. Pete staggers backward and covers his mouth.

"How's that, ya fucking Joe Bag-a-donuts?" asks my old man.

I pull Elena out of her chair and push her toward the door. My father waves the ax handle. Vinnie comes around the counter holding a baseball bat as if he's about to step to the plate.

"Vinnie," I say. "Come on, don't—"

"You think you can come in here like I'm nothing, huh?" One swing and he'll knock my head through the window. I look for my father, but he's working the other guy over.

April's yelling, "Stan, hit him."

The bat trembles in Vinnie's hands, until Pete pulls it away from him and swings wildly at my father. Blood first. I step and throw my punch like I'm pitching a fastball. Pete's nose almost runs into my fist, then rides on my knuckles, sending him over backward. The punch throws me off balance and my left hand slides across the sausage pie, sending me crashing onto the table. I bang my chin hard and the sensation travels into my head and rings in my ears. The table tips and I land next to the wall, near April's long legs.

Pete scrambles like a crab and grabs my ankle. His nose is bent like its made of putty and blood flows from it across his lips. Under the window, I hold the baseboard radiatior and try to stand, but he gets to his feet with my ankle under his arm and I'm back on the floor.

The first strike of the bat glances off the side of my shoulder and connects just above my ear. Elena is screaming something and my father is near the counter, smacking the other guy with the ax handle. Pete's braced himself with his body on the wall and, rapid fire, over and over, the bat stabs me. I block with my hands, my arms, until it feels like my index finger breaks. From the corner of my eye, I see April going out the door with two slices of pizza folded on a paper plate. Pete's kid is right behind her.

"You filthy, raping spick, son-of-a-bitch bastard," Pete growls at me through his bloody mouth. I kick like I've gone crazy and scramble to my feet. I back against the cigarette machine. Elena hits Vinnie on the side of the head with the oven board. Then my father swings the ax handle into Pete until he crumbles on the floor.

Elena pulls me away. I try to thank her as she steers me through the door, but I have nothing left. We hurry across the parking lot. Sandy comes up behind us.

"Man, your father can kick ass," she says.

I climb behind the wheel and adjust the rearview mirror to look at my face. Even in the dark I can see my lips are bloody and swollen. Under my eye there's a knot, like a small golf ball. Elena opens the passenger door. In the distance police sirens wail. I start the engine, rev it, and place my palm on the skull shifter. I press the clutch and feel a bone, somewhere in my hip, click.

"Maybe you should go to the hospital," says Elena, sliding over the console.

Sandy leans in Elena's door. "Let me come with you guys," she says. "The cops are coming."

I tell Sandy to stay out of the car, but she squeezes next to Elena

anyway. With my foot on the clutch I yell, "Get out of my car."
She leans her head forward so her hair covers her face, but she
doesn't move. The police sirens are getting louder.

Like a man on the side of the road who just climbed out of a
wreck, my father stumbles toward my headlights.

"You ought to run him over," says Sandy.

I throw a string of curses at her, telling her to keep her mouth
shut. I swerve next to him and roll down my window.

"If the police pick you up," he says, "just remember, keep your
mouth shut. I'll take the heat on this one. You got that?" He wipes
the blood from a cut on his forehead, but it has already run down
his face and neck and ruined his cowboy shirt.

In a few seconds, I pass the instant photo booth near the exit
and my father is a small figure in my rearview mirror. After a left,
he's out of sight and the road rises over the Meadowbrook Parkway.
If I get arrested for this fight, there'll be no doubt in anyone's mind
that I'm my father's son. "You saw it," I say to Elena. "I had to hit
that guy."

She picks a slice of pepperoni off my shirt and flicks it out the
window and I realize half of what I thought was blood is tomato
sauce.

We pass the little drunken boat captain welcoming us to Freeport. On the left, just before Zuro's Deli, the blinking orange neon
cocktail glasses at the Villa Rosa flash by, then the raceway with
its tall dark lights over the track, followed by the recreation center.
I downshift and spin onto Main Street past the senior citizens'
housing, past my grandfather's old apartment, and bang the left
into the driveway of the Old Oyster Wharf. The Road Runner rolls
past the rows of hedges, past the antique shop, to the end of the
dock where the *Glory* rests in the canal. I cut the car's engine and
Elena gently turns my face. "I'm okay," I say.

"You sure?"

I take a deep breath and rub my tongue over my teeth. They are all there. She kisses me softly on my swollen cheek that's hard as a knot of cold fat. "You did the right thing," she says.

"That your boat?" asks Sandy.

I look out over the dashboard. The boat sits on the shining water like a giant sleeping swan.

"Man, it was Elena to the rescue," says Sandy. I open my jaw and pain shoots into my ears. "And, don't worry, Eddie, I'll get you out of trouble with the cops," she says. "Your father said he was going to get me into a movie."

I'd like to laugh but it would hurt. All his girls get the same line and are promised, "Ten grand at the back end, standard deal."

"Could he do that?" asks Elena.

I roll down my window. A wind kicks up and rattles a sailboat stay against its aluminum mast. "If she's got a quality," I say.

"Can I spend the night?" asks Sandy. "It's big enough, right?"

"You could wait for an invitation," says Elena. I take my hand off the steering wheel and she examines my finger, it's fat as a sausage. Sandy opens the car door, gets out, and heads toward the dock. At the hose she kneels and, holding her hair, takes a drink.

"I'm sorry," I say. "I never wanted you to have to do something like that for me."

"Eddie, it's okay."

I tell her it's not okay, and she pulls me toward her. "You know I'm not like my father," I say.

"I know."

"I'm really not a fighter," I say. "Maybe I shouldn't have even hung with the hitters." I take a deep breath.

"He's nothing compared to you," says Elena. She takes a tissue and blows her nose. "I don't know why I'm crying."

"My old man," I say, "he's the real thing."

Sandy stares at the *Glory*, floating a few feet from the ladder. Elena says, "I don't know where she's going to go."

"Who cares," I say. "Let her stay at the shelter." Sandy sits on the bulkhead. When she gets up, there will be a ring of tar on her pants. Maybe then she'll put them into retirement. Probably not. I tell Elena I've got to see somebody.

"Eddie, they'll be looking for your father," she says. Her eyes are worried. "You're hurt. You did enough."

I remind her where I hide the cabin key, then kiss her. Reluctantly, she leaves the car and slams the door.

I pull out.

Chapter Sixteen

The street light from Atlantic Avenue shines across Loopy's large bare back. He's lying on his stomach with his arms above his head, a rumpled sheet wound around his legs. I glance out the window that's propped open with a beer. The street is deserted. Not a car, nothing.

"Douche," I say, taking a step toward his bed. "Hey, Douche. Come on, wake up."

"What?" he pushes up on one arm. "What the . . . ? Eddie?"

"Yeah."

"What time is it?" He turns on the light, squints, and reaches for his Marlboros. "Shit, it's the middle of the night." He lights a butt with a throwaway lighter, and for a moment his face reminds me of someone much older, someone Loopy might be in twenty years. The smoke comes out his nose and he yawns, "You come in the basement?"

"Nailed my head on a pipe."

"Man, who did that number on your face?" he asks, putting his bare feet on the floor.

"I hit a guy that had a bat," I say. "Then he hit me."

Loopy touches my swollen cheek and whistles. "Looks like he hit a home run."

"I broke his nose." I fold my swollen knuckles and stiff fingers between my knees.

Loopy smokes, looking at the floor. "I could get Joey to fix him," Loopy says. "Break his legs or something."

"The guy's Italian, so forget it," I say. "I'm putting a plan together. Maybe I'll pull outta here."

"Yeah, sure." Loopy shakes his head. "Like your mother."

The words seem to hang in the air, then fall to the floor. Sometimes after a bottle she'd close her eyes, flip off her shoes, and wiggle her crooked toes on the worn stoop and tell Loopy about San Juan. "Blue water," she'd say. "Like a sky." She'd shut her eyes, "And good girls, not like the ones here."

Loopy stands and flicks his butt out the window. "You ought to put some steak on that shiner." He lifts my chin to the light. "We got some left over in the refrigerator."

"Asshole," I say. "It's got to be raw."

"It's medium rare." In his drawers he heads to the door. "Drain the radiator," he says.

The old house creaks under his footsteps. Years ago Mrs. Loop would throw musty sleeping bags on the floor next to the bed. Sitting at the window, Loop and I would stay up trying to call out the make and models of the cars that passed. Sometimes we'd sneak out to the 7-Eleven, beg and plead with dudes to buy us a bottle of Boone's Farm and cigarettes. Back then Grandma Cabbage wasn't a vegetable, and was just Grams. She could walk and talk. In the morning she'd mix pancakes and try to swat us with a wooden spoon if we got out of line. It seemed like Loop and I never got tired of each other.

Loopy's stereo speakers are the size of small phone booths. The system can vibrate dishes out of the kitchen cabinets. On them sits his dusty collection of chrome Mack truck dog emblems that we ripped from dump truck hoods and truck fenders. We did a lot of stupid crap.

"Remember them?" he asks, coming back into the room.

"Loopy, Sandy told me what happened," I say, replacing a dog on the speaker. "Why'd you lie to me?" He screws up his face like I'm crazy. "You raped her, didn't you?"

"I already explained all that to you."

"How about explaining it again."

"You don't believe me?" he says. "Man, I thought you and I were brothers." I run my tongue on the inside of a cut in my mouth and wait. From his nightstand he hands me a letter. "That's from Dirty Drawers."

Leaning toward the light I read the rounded script.

Dear Loopy,

    I'm writing everything down because there's no one to listen. Plus, when I talk to you I forget what I'm saying. I hope you are satisfied. You think that you can do anything to anybody anytime? Well you can't. I told you that from the beginning. But now everything's a mess. I feel like I am all by myself and something is missing. I'm sorry that I went to the police. I imagined it to be easy, but they made me feel like I was the one who did something to you. And now that's how I feel.

    I am always going to love you, I always did. I guess what I found hard about our relationship was you never called me and we never went out on real dates. You just expected me to be there waiting for you like I had nothing better to do. If you want to stop this, call me. I'd like to ask you something.

The police said I have to go before a grand jury and tell them the whole story, even about the way things were between us.

Love,

Sandra

P.S. I'm two weeks late.

I hand him back the letter.

"What? You never knocked a girl up?" he asks, stuffing the letter back in the pink envelope.

"This is different," I say. "She told me you raped her. You haven't told me jack-shit."

"Man, this ain't you talking. You working for the cops?"

"Be square with me," I say. "What happened?"

"What difference does that make?" he asks.

"It matters. To me, it matters."

"If you're asking me if she said, 'Give it to me, give it to me,' she didn't."

"I'm not asking you that," I say. "Either you raped her or you didn't."

"Hey, come on, you're going to wake my mother."

"Oh, now you're worried about your mother?"

Loopy puts his elbows on his knees and drops his face like he's about to puke. "Eddie, Sandy was always saying one thing, doing another." He groans. "Playing her games. I swear to God I didn't know she was pissed off until we were on the boardwalk." He gets up and opens and closes the blind like he's sending a message to someone in the street. "I didn't think I raped her." He looks at me. "It was business as usual. She was telling me, 'Stop, the sand's too wet. Stop, there's no blanket,'" he says, imitating her. "After we got into it she didn't say boo."

"She says stop, you're supposed to stop," I say.

"Eddie, she always said that. Look, I called her," he says. "She wants me to marry her." He closes the blinds. "This ain't rape, it's blackmail. You know what Joey says?"

"What does *Joey* say?"

"Joey says it's cheaper than getting a lawyer."

I stand and twist my neck to the side. It's sore, feels like I've been lifting crates of chickens all day. Probably, Sandy won't have the baby. It'll wind up like the others, in a steel bucket at a clinic, another bad day for her, another mistake to think about when she's alone, maybe half-drunk or stoned. Loopy slips a sweatshirt over his head and pulls on his jeans. "Hey, let's go fishing," he says.

Loopy follows me down the stairs. A Mother Mary nightlight shines at the foot of the hall. Propped on a pillow, Grandma Cabbage sleeps sitting up, facing the small television set. A homemade afghan is around her shoulders, and a green army sleeping bag is folded across her lap. Her teeth and pink plates soak in a glass of water with white powder at the bottom.

In the kitchen, Loopy grabs my shoulder and turns me around. "Come on, we haven't caught a fish in a long time. It would be like old times."

I open the refrigerator, take out a can of beer, and hold it to my eye. At the kitchen table, where I played my first round of blackjack, I pull out a chair and sit.

"You want me to kick anybody's ass, anybody's, your old man's ass?" he says. "It's done."

"Loopy," I say but can't continue. I'm exhausted.

Loopy sweeps a pile of wash to the floor and plops into a vinyl kitchen chair. "What are you so pissed off about? You ain't the only one with problems," he says. "Joey's got me running around Roosevelt," he says. "Collecting money from the brothers, then going back and forth to Staten Island, delivering it to the bosses.

That's what Joey calls 'em, 'the bosses.' " He reaches into a cereal box and puts a handful of corn puffs in his mouth. "I could use a day on the ocean."

"Forget it," I say, thinking about the girls.

"You'd think weed is an easy way to make a few bucks," he says. "But man, it's day in and day out."

"Get caught," I say. "Then talk to me about day in and day out."

"Joey says the more you sell the better known you get. That's why you got to change things up."

"They're using you," I say. "Soon as you get in a jam, they won't know you."

"But for now, Eddie,"—Loopy raises his eyes—"weed is king. You hear me, king." He waves his hands. "I haven't touched a shovel in three weeks." He goes to the closet and swings a fat gray sock onto my lap. "Check that out."

The wool sock feels like it has two big potatoes in the toe. I untie the knot at the top and pull money, wrapped tight as fists, out of the sock. Once my father called me into his bedroom and threw me a wad of bills, wrapped the same way. It bounced off my head. He and my mother laughed and laughed. Over breakfast my father imitated my surprise and the bills ricocheting off my head. The two of them laughed all day about it.

"It's yours?" I ask.

"Fucking-A." Loopy grabs a wad of bills. "Joey says I can't put it in the bank, calls it play money, only condition is it's got to be spent, and spent smart. That's what he says, 'Spend small, spend smart, nothing flashy.' "

A few days after the day the money hit me in the head, my father bought a speed boat, used, but real nice, a V-hull with a Mercury engine. The boat was behind a bar called Franky and Johnny's. We towed it out of the weeds, then out toward the road. My father and one of his cronies, this guy he called Cappy because he looked exactly like the comic strip guy Al Capp, were bullshitting and celebrating. "You just about stole the thing," Cappy said. I was in the backseat, looking out the rear window at the boat. It's obvious now that my father was going too fast. On a sharp turn the boat, strapped tight to the trailer, broke off the hitch and sailed right by us. I yelled but my father kept bullshitting and laughing. Our car turned, but the boat kept going straight and hit the dog and cat cages at the Humane Society. "Dad," I screamed, pounding his shoulder. Finally they both turned and we swung a wide U-turn. My father was spitting his curses. We got out and he grabbed my collar. The fence had ripped the hull open like it was made of Styrofoam. "You see that boat?" he said. "It never existed." He yanked his face to mine. "You understand that?" When we pulled away, I looked back over the seat, and the funny thing was none of the dogs had run away. They just stood in the back of the pens barking and fighting.

I tuck the money back in the sock. "What you gonna buy?"

"I don't know." He shrugs. "The other night, out at the Top Hat, I stuck about four hundred bucks in that bald go-go dancer's g-string."

"Nobody's gonna trace that," I say.

"You want to borrow some?"

"You were better off shoveling dirt," I say.

"Oh yeah, and for how long?" he asks, facing me. "How long was I supposed to break my back at the end of a cement chute? Huh?"

"That money's not worth squat in jail," I say. "You got rape charges hanging on both of us. Now you're the king of weed." I shake my head. "Ask my old man how it feels to be locked down right though Christmas, Easter, the Fourth of July."

"You worry too much," says Loopy. "Let's go fishing."

"Elena's on the boat," I say. "Maybe Sandy too."

"For real?" He looks at me like he just discovered Pontiac is made by Volkswagen. I shake my head and open the beer. "This is perfect," he says. "We've got to go. I'll get things back to normal between me and Sandy before you throw the anchor over."

"I don't know." I try to picture the four of us on the thirty-two-foot boat.

"I got gas money," he says, hitting his back pocket.

I agree to go and he insists on paying for everything. Loopy raids the refrigerator and cabinets, filling grocery bags with Pop Tarts, bread, butter, jelly, a carton of eggs, and bacon. "You want anything else?" he asks.

We pull out of the driveway, past the rusting Winnebago with four flats, that Mrs. Loop bought used, promising us we'd go to the Grand Canyon.

With dawn an hour off, the street lights seem to waver between on and off. It's strange to have Loopy riding shotgun with me behind the wheel. "Man, this thing's cherry-pie," he says when I give the Road Runner the gas. "It got any balls?" On Mill Road I power shift into third gear and roar past old man Seaman's deli. I ease off the gas, and Loopy holds out his palm. "Come on, don't leave me hanging."

When I don't slap him five, he throws his arm around me. "I'll get the Louperino charm working," he says. "Get her back in love." We roll down the driveway of the Old Oyster Wharf. The wide hedges scrape the side of the car. I'm tired and pull too far to the left, almost running over two metal garbage pails.

Chapter Seventeen

•

When my grandfather cruised up the canal, he always stopped at the bait and fuel store, even if he had full tanks and plenty of bait. With both tanks almost empty, I ease the throttle to neutral. Tim, an old friend of my grandfather's, comes limping down the floating dock. From the bridge, I zip down the ladder and catch Tim's line. The *Glory* slides in, barely touching the fenders along the bait store dock.

Tim never liked me much. Once he yanked my hair and told me I needed a haircut so, whenever I was with my grandfather, I stayed out of his reach. He gives Loopy a once-over, then unscrews the gas tank cap and starts pumping marine-leaded.

I follow Tim up the long dock, lined with small fiberglass runabouts with outboard engines. In front of the bait shop there's a barrel bearing the sign *Beware of the rare red bats.* A heavy wire mesh covers the barrel. Inside are two plastic baseball bats secured to a two-by-four with a coat hanger. When I was a kid, getting someone to peer in the can was a big joke. Today a gray-and-white seagull stands on top of the wire mesh looking into the light breeze.

The bait house is thick with the aroma of coffee. Tim hops on a stool behind the counter and opens the *Newsday* to the sports section. Walls are covered with contraptions, hooks, and lures. Through the years my grandfather probably purchased every kind and a few of the same, over and over. I spot a white, cone-shaped lure with a feather and a heavy hook. The lure has a happy face and is called the "Smiling Jack." My grandfather used the lure for trolling and once caught a striped bass that set the record for the summer.

"That the boy who got into trouble with you?" he asks.

I glance out the window. Fifty yards down the floating dock, the *Glory's* blue engine smoke rises from the canal. Loopy stands on the deck, filling the gas tank. "You heard about that?" I ask, wondering if every Freeporter over sixteen knows about that night in Long Beach.

"I read the paper." He taps the front page.

"It was a mix-up," I say.

"That so," says Tim, pouring coffee.

"The girl"—I hunt for the right word—"lied, at least about me."

"What about your friend?" Tim bends at a half refrigerator and removes milk in a glass bottle.

"He thinks he's innocent."

"What do you think?"

I shove my hands into my jeans pockets and raise my shoulders.

"So," he tips the milk and fills the cup to the rim. "You lose a fight?"

I touch my cheek. It's hot and swollen. When I breathe, my ribs ache down my left side. At the dock, Loopy lifts the gas hose from the stern and hooks it back into the pump.

"Let me give you a little advice." Tim points at me with his finger that's missing the last digit. "Get yourself some new friends. You think your grandfather would like any of this?"

I sip my coffee. My grandfather never liked Loopy much. When

we were about twelve, Loopy stole a pair of pliers from my grandfather's toolbox. Don't ask me why. He didn't need them. My
grandfather went out and bought Loopy a Sears tool kit, gave it to
him, and told him to stay off the boat unless he was invited. After
that he wasn't invited.

"It's the friends that can drag a good kid down," says Tim. "I've
seen it."

Loopy heads up the dock. At the ramp, he grabs the handrails
and takes long strides toward the bait house. The girls are in the
cabin. Elena tried to apologize about Sandy being aboard, but I
put my finger to my lips and told her to stay in the bunk, and that
we were going fishing. We kissed softly, then she closed her eyes.
Sandy slept with a strand of her black hair in her mouth. With all
the makeup washed off her face, she looked about fourteen years
old.

"Any blues out there?" I ask, still facing the window.

Tim grunts that the "oily bums" are running off Ambrose, a
lighthouse about five miles off the Jersey coast, twenty miles from
the Jones Beach inlet. "Give me five small ones," he says, "and
chum's on the house." Tim pushes up off his stool. "Come on,"
he says.

Outside, Loopy leans on the "Rare Red Bats" barrel. "I put in
twenty gallons," he says. A tern shrieks, caw-cawing over his head.
He flicks his cigarette into the air and the bird for a moment takes
off smoking. "You see that?" he yells.

"Big jerk," says Tim.

Around the side of the store, Tim removes a brass hook from his
belt that holds about two hundred keys, unlocks a battered icebox
door, and swings it open. The strong smell of fish wafts out and I
remember Skate and the fish case at the supermarket. Like someone who suddenly knows his wallet is missing, I realize that I'm

never going back. The same way I stayed away from the high school after I graduated, the same way I'm staying away from my house, I'll avoid Kurt and the butcher department.

Tim slides two white buckets of chum and a bucket of whole menhaden across the slick floor. "Use eighty-pound test," he says, puffing from bending over, "and wire leaders."

Today there are no party boats out of the Woodcleft canal to follow. The sun will burn off some of the fog, but for now I watch for buoys and picture my course along the channels. The Glory's wake disappears in the murk. Spray shoots over the bow, splashing the white gunwales, and green water runs crystal clear against the layers of paint. On the flying bridge, squinting into the murk, Loopy leans into the wind.

Past the inlet, maybe a mile off the West End jetty, the sky changes from lead to a brighter gray. The Glory plows into the swells, and the fog rides with us. Loopy rocks, his arms folded and his eyes half open. The steady rise and fall of the ocean has put him in a trance. "Take the wheel," I say, poking him.

I swing off the bridge and open the cabin door. In the indistinct early morning light at the front of the V-bunk, Elena and Sandy are curled on their sides under my grandfather's old blanket. Through the windows, the ocean swells like dull green mountains rising and falling. I tie the door open. The ocean air will have them awake in a few minutes.

I lift a hatch and pull anchor line out until it turns to chain, then I heave the anchor on deck. I toss the anchor over. Line races out around the cleat and disappears in the water.

Loopy jumps off the bridge. "What are you doing?"

"Having breakfast," I say.

"In the middle of the goddamned ocean?"

"It's not the middle." On the bridge I cut the engine. The wind whistles in my ears. If Sandy panics when she sees Loopy, I'm only half an hour from the dock.

Loopy swings up on the bridge and sits next to me. "So what am I supposed to say?" he asks, just above the ocean lapping on the side of the boat. "It was her fault."

"How could it be her fault?"

"I guess I ought to play it cool," he says, ignoring me. "She never had it too easy." He grabs the back of my neck. "Steady Eddie," he says, squeezing. "Always wanted to take them on a real date."

"And don't call Elena nothing but Elena."

"Elena who?"

"You know who."

One thing, we have enough eggs. I whip four in a pan, add milk, and turn the burner on low. The ocean swells lift the boat up and down, up and down, and the eggs slide from one side of the pan to the other, turning white from the heat. I slice a block of Velveeta cheese.

"This is kidnapping," says Sandy from the bunk. She pushes her sleep-tangled hair away from her face and sniffles.

"It's called"—I place the cover on the eggs—"fishing."

"You could have asked me. You could have told me *he* was coming," she says.

On deck, Loopy smokes a butt. He hasn't come into the cabin. Elena, hair in a high ponytail, squeezes out of the head and slides up behind me. "This is a stupid idea," she says in my ear.

"You want to go back to the dock right now?" I ask both of them. Elena looks at Sandy. " 'Cause if you want to. . . ."

"It's okay," says Sandy.

"Nobody feels sick?" I ask. They both shake their heads. "Loop's not going to throw you overboard. He's the same asshole he was two weeks ago."

"No, not quite," says Sandy, narrowing her eyes into tiny slits. "He's a bigger asshole."

"What is he doing out there?" asks Elena.

"Trying to figure out what to say," I flip the first omelet onto a paper plate. "Sandy, come on, eat something."

She slips in the booth across from Elena. I pour her a cup of instant coffee and she holds it with both hands. "This is only like my second time out on a boat," she says. "First time was those boats with the pedals in Eisenhower."

I break more eggs into the pan and pull a loaf of Wonder Bread from the overhead bin. When water boils in a small pot, I pour Elena a cup of coffee.

"He say anything about me?" asks Sandy.

Elena looks my way. Probably Sandy told her about the baby. I know *sorry* would be better than *congratulations*. I swirl Elena's omelet around the pan. In Freeport, on the other side of Atlantic Avenue, where the houses are nothing special, just two-bedroom slab jobs, there's a bar where white mothers in stretch pants and supermarket sneakers, either no makeup or too much, line up with strollers. If Sandy has the baby, she will be on that line, her little dark-haired kid trying to climb out. I glance at her; she cuts her omelet with the side of her fork and puts a large piece in her mouth. "Well, did he?" she asks.

In the doorway, wearing his black T-shirt and jeans, his tattoos showing below his shirt sleeves, Loopy hooks his hands on the top deck, hangs for a moment, then swings into the cabin. Inside, it's a few inches too low for him so he ducks his head. Elena watches him. Sandy keeps her eyes on her plate. He takes a slice of bread, folds it, and takes a bite.

I break the remainder of the eggs into the pan. "Sandy thinks she's been kidnapped," I say.

"No, I don't," says Sandy.

"I don't want to hear any nicknames," says Elena.

"What nicknames?" asks Loopy.

"The nicknames you've been calling us since day one."

The boat lurches as if it's been hit by a whale. Everyone, even Loopy, looks out the window. "It's the anchor line," I say. "Must have gotten caught when the boat was turning." We listen to the wind whistling, the ocean lapping against the boat, and wait for another pitch.

"You sure you know what you're doing?" asks Sandy.

"We both know," says Loopy.

"You don't know shit," says Sandy.

"I know you," he says. "I know your true colors."

"Come on," I say, stepping between them. "Sandy, I told Loop you were going to talk to the police. You know, and, fix the story."

"Fix it?" she says. "Fix it for you. Not him. He can rot in a heap of garbage."

"Yeah, right, put on a show," says Loopy. "Then tonight call me crying, begging me to talk to you."

"Yeah right," she says. "In your dreams."

Elena pushes the button for the weather band radio. A crackly voice announces that the day will be clearing. Small craft warnings have been lifted. Loopy sits at the edge of the V-bunk. He puts his omelet on a piece of bread and douses the eggs with ketchup. From above the sink, I pull out the peanut butter and jelly and push in next to Elena.

"I need air," says Sandy. Loopy moves his legs, and she slides across the bench and heads out of the cabin.

"Jeez, woke up on the wrong side of the boat," says Loopy.

"Don't you care at all?" asks Elena. "She was good enough for you all those nights, good enough to put out for you."

"You don't have to say it like that," I say.

"It's the truth."

I go to the cabin door just to make sure Sandy isn't leaping overboard. She sits on the deck with her body pulled into a ball, hugging herself.

"She turned on me," he says. "Benedict bitching Arnold."

"Who do you think you are?" asks Elena. "King of the hitters, king of the white-trash jackasses?"

"The little shampoo girl getting herself all in a lather," says Loopy. "Go soak your head." He goes out on the deck.

Elena's coffee slides across the table. She grabs it. "I'll never know how you consider that asshole a friend."

I put the top piece of bread on my peanut butter and jelly. I'd like to tell her that maybe it should have been someone else, but it wasn't. I didn't pick him out of a store. He wasn't much, but he was all I had. From the window the fog clears and the horizon appears, then disappears behind the steel-gray Atlantic.

The weather band tape starts again from the beginning. *This is the national weather broadcast short term marine forecast for Sandy Hook, New Jersey, inland Long Island and outer costal areas to Montauk Point* . . . I slide in next to Elena. *Windy conditions will diminish during the day, and the cloudy conditions will be clearing, seas will diminish to two feet. Small craft warnings have been lifted* . . . I shut the radio off and remember Elena telling me on the boardwalk in Long Beach that she never caught a fish.

"Let's give it a try," I say. "Maybe get you a few fish."

*   *   *

Dead reckoning puts me about twenty miles south off the Verra-
zano Bridge, five miles off Sandy Hook. I'm searching for a dump
area off the Jersey Coast called the "Acid Waters," where New York
City barges dump some kind of acid-crap full of iron. Mixed with
salt water, the ocean turns orange. My grandfather wouldn't fish
the Acid Waters or any of the Jersey dump sites. Whenever guys
talked about dump fishing, he'd put on a face and shake his head.
"I wouldn't eat that sewer-trout," he said one day, examining a
bucket of lings. He held up one of the small, slender fish with black
eyes, a soft white underbelly, and dainty barbels under its chin, and
opened its gill. Inside, yellow worms squirmed like boiling spaghetti.

There's no real way to predict where schools of blues gather. My
grandfather's only theory about bluefish was that they are as pre-
dictable as their hunger for their favorite food, menhaden. "Lots
of menhaden, lots of blues, and vice versa," he'd say. Supposedly,
in the spring the blues followed the schools of menhaden north.
But some years, when we fished for blues, we were lucky to get one
strike on our lines. Guys coming in from the Jersey dumps would
have garbage pails full of fish.

Some fishermen think it's the color of the Acid Waters that
attracts the fish; their big yellow eyes seem perfect for peering
through the murk. Some say it's the smell. Since my grandfather's
death, I've fished almost all the dumps, just because I like to catch
fish. Today, I'd head to the Mud Hole, a place where barges dump
New York Harbor muck, but it's too far.

After about twenty minutes on a southwest run, the ocean turns
orange-brown. With the throttle slowed, Loopy holds the wheel
steady. "Keep the compass right at forty-five degrees," I say.

I hook flashing metal spoons on two lines and, holding a rod under each arm, feed the lines into the rusty swelling waves. Just under the surface of the water, plastic bags and something yellow, some kind of meat, float by, which could mean that the Cholera Bank, a medical dump area, has drifted south. The Cholera Bank is supposed to be about ten miles southeast of the Ambrose Tower. I get the creeps just thinking about it, but continue letting out line. Today would be a bad day to get skunked.

The fog hasn't completely burned off. I can barely see where the line runs on an angle into the water. If I get a hit, I'll circle the boat and lob in a half bucket of chum. Blues run in schools and like to herd the bait into a tight mass, then slash and rip through them, vicious as piranhas feeding. I'd seen the water turn into a churning mess of half-bitten fish heads and ripped-apart bodies.

The cabin door opens and Elena, trying to get her sea legs, comes toward me, still wearing the clothes from last night. I stick the rods in the pole holders. She puts her arms around my neck and kisses me. "Who's driving?" she asks.

"Loopy."

"Loopy?"

"Hey, you wanted to catch some fish."

She lowers her eyebrows and mouth, a look that I've learned to mean she's worried, very worried. Just then the line on the port sizzles and whines. I grab the pole and loosen the star-drag. "Here," I say. "Hold this."

"I can't," she screams.

I thrust the rod in her arms and hook a fishing belt around her waist. I put the butt of the pole in the worn leather cup. The rod bends and vibrates like it's attached to a train. "What do I do?" she yells.

"Reel it in," I say. "Nice and easy."

On the flying bridge, I slow the engines and circle. Loopy leaps down the ladder and grabs the other rod.

"The chum," I yell.

We pull into hundreds of screaming terns, stabbing the water, snatching pieces of small fish. A large blue leaps out of the ocean. Loopy's reel starts screaming, the line sizzles into the water. Dead slow, watching the outside of the school, I circle. The school may only last a few minutes, so I hop off the bridge and grab the large aluminum net.

Reeling steadily, Elena's face is set and determined. The fish takes line. She takes it back. I move around her and tighten the drag. "Land it," I yell.

"What's 'land it'?" she shrieks.

About ten feet off the stern her hooked blue leaps in the air and the fish's silver bottom flashes like gun powder. Elena shrieks again. The fish is easily an eight-pounder. For a long minute she reels. "My arms are getting tired," she yells.

"Walk it," I say, leaning over the side with the net. Elena comes around and I scoop the big fish into the net and hurl it up over the side to the deck.

Sandy has come out of the cabin. The fish bounces two feet in front of her and she dances back into the cabin entrance.

Loopy flings his fish to the deck. Now, both fish bounce, snapping their tails and bodies, gnashing their teeth. With a wooden mallet, I pummel Elena's fish senseless. Blood sprays across my face. Then I pound Loopy's fish that's easily five pounds.

On one knee, Loopy rips his lure from the mouth of the gasping blue. I twist the lure out of Elena's fish.

"Sandy," I yell, holding out the pole. "Come on, take this."

She comes out of the cabin, watching the birds that are overhead and diving near the boat. With a small smile on her lips, Sandy takes the pole. She looks at Loopy, who's already hooked another fish. I dump the entire bucket of chum in the water.

In a split second Sandy's line takes a strike and she's almost knocked to the deck. I grab her shoulders and she yells, "Take it, take it."

The few times my grandfather chartered the *Glory*, he always made the women reel them in, all the way in. I hook another fishing belt around her waist and put my hand over hers. "Reel it," I say.

Elena waves the net and snags Loopy's fish. I fetch the hammer, but she's got it before me and winds up pounding the deck. I grab the hammer and crack the fish's skull in one blow. Loopy gives me his pole and gets behind Sandy, wrapping his arms around her, so there's four hands on the pole. The ocean is churning like a washing machine. Every five seconds a blue leaps out of the water. I race up the bridge and tighten the circle around the school. But, just as fast as they came, they're gone. The birds linger for a moment, then seem to disappear.

Eight bloody blues gasp their last breaths on the deck. The sun shines from a break in the low clouds. Loopy comes over and slaps five with me. "All right," he whoops.

"That was wild," says Elena.

"Where'd they go?" Sandy looks over the side into the orange water.

"Come on," says Loopy, climbing the ladder to the flying bridge.

On the bridge I scan the ocean for the birds and push the throttle. I won't tell Tim that we caught them in the Acid Waters. It'll ruin it.

By the time we reach the inlet, it's midafternoon. Loopy and Sandy are in the cabin. Elena leans her head on my shoulder. The outgoing tide has the buoys bent at forty-five-degree angles. I cruise straight through the crossed currents. The white stucco Short Beach lighthouse displays only the Coast Guard and American flags. The small craft warning advisory flags that were flapping in the fog this morning are long gone. I inhale a deep breath, smelling Elena's hair. I've been doing that lately, smelling her. I dig the way she smells, which is kind of funny, given what I used to call her.

Around the Coast Guard station there's a short row of dock and an octagon-shaped snack bar. Smoke pours out of the small chimney, which means someone's frying burgers. Today, a few runabouts are tied to the dock, and two houseboats one tethered side by side. In the summer every docking space is filled by 9. "Go get Loopy," I say. "He can help me dock."

Elena, like she's sleepwalking, rises and goes down the ladder.

Sunbathers dot the small island across from Short Beach. It's too cold for swimming, so children play at the shoreline with buckets and shovels. A few guys about my age stand around a cooler drinking beer. I wave and they wave back. Around the bend the beach is muddy, a good place to dig cherry and chowder clams. Farther down, at low tide, steamer clams shoot water from tiny holes in the sand.

"You're not going to believe this," says Elena, coming up the ladder. "I go in the cabin and they're right in the middle of doing it. Loopy's such a pig, he didn't even stop, and Sandy, she's waving me out of the cabin." We both start to laugh. It's really not that funny, but we crack up. "He was grunting and everything," says Elena, trying to get her breath.

At Short Beach I rear-end dock. An old salt catches my line, while two others, wearing Bermuda shorts and boat shoes, watch. The salt drops to one knee and loops the line around the base of the cleat, bringing it up and over diagonally, around and under one arm of the cleat then over, around and under the other, securing the bitter end by tucking it under the last crossover. It's called belaying, and my grandfather would have invited this guy aboard for a drink and a cigar.

With the stern secure, I hurry to the bow poles to tie her in; not too tight, because the tide here moves fast. I catch the cleat on the pole with a bowline loop and try belaying the line on the bow cleat. Through the window I get a glimpse of Loopy on his back smoking a butt. Sandy's got her head on his chest. I give Loopy the finger and he smiles at me.

Chapter Eighteen

The black canal, still asleep, shines. I rub the night out of my eyes, then, with an old towel, wipe the dew off the transom. In the thick morning the faint rumble of a commuter train, streaking to the city, rises in the humidity and leaves like a ghost. A boat engine sputters, catches. A seagull calls out. In the cabin, Elena's still in dreamland. Soon, she'll be knocking around, getting ready for work. A chill passes through my spine and I tell myself to remember this quiet moment, that promises nothing but a day of painting the Miller's boathouse and going out with Elena.

The brightening pink sunrise appears over the factory roofs. Next to the boat, a square of canal water is illuminated. Barnacles wave white tentacles and grass shrimp cling to the green bulkhead. In the opaque surface I study my face, my thick lips, my hair that's grown to my shoulders. I mimic one of my father's expressions by narrowing my eyes and cocking my chin. A grass eel. I reach into the water. The eel zips to the canal's bottom.

"You lose something?" asks Elena. I jump. She smiles and puts her arms around me. "Who's this?" I ask, putting on my father's expression.

"Charles Manson," she says.

In the cabin Elena plugs in the fan. In the small space in front of the bunk, she bends, beginning her morning yoga. A bead of perspiration runs down the center of her spine, winds through fine dark hairs at the small of her back, then vanishes into her bikini panties. She straightens, stretches her neck to one shoulder, then the other shoulder. We've been on the boat almost two weeks, I've seen her routine every morning, and I'm still amazed and watch her every move. It's hard to believe that this little six-pack from the parking lot knows how to do anything except suck a Schlitz, but she does, and it makes me wonder what the hell I know besides chopping chickens and sailing this boat.

Yoga over, she irons her white uniform shirt on the boat cushions. She turns toward the fan and raises her arms. She blows a wisp of her hair out of her face, reaches around my back and pulls our bodies together. Our kiss is hot and wet. She snuggles against me. "You want breakfast?" I ask.

"I don't have time," she says and leans her wet, warm forehead on my chest. "I just want it to be Saturday," she says.

I run my hands over her ass and lift her into the bunk.

"I'm going to be late." Her mouth tastes like toothpaste and her skin is salty from the warm night. I grind into her and unbuckle my belt. "You're so bad," she says, sliding away from me.

We do it fast and furious. I don't hold out very long. I never do when I'm on top, but it's just long enough for her. Sopping wet, I slide off her. Telling me that she didn't have time for "it," she slips her bra on her shoulders, then pulls on a fresh pair of red bikini panties.

At the recreation center, Elena piles out of the Road Runner, lugging her makeup case, her bag and uniform. "If I have time," she says, poking her face in my window, "I'm going to take a sauna." She kisses me.

"You're not hot enough?"

"I like it hot." She smiles at me over her shoulder. In her cutoff shorts, faded Keep on Trucking T-shirt, flip-flops snapping her heels, she steps into the varnished doors of Freeport Recreation. Weekdays, she pays a dollar to take a shower. I've been soaping up behind a plastic shower curtain on the deck. Afterward, in her white uniform, she catches the Merrick Road bus to work.

I pull out to Mill Road and head back to the *Glory*.

The boathouse at the Old Oyster Wharf leans to one side and looks like it's going to fall over. I lift a wooden ladder above a wild patch of yellow climbing roses and let it drop against the roof. With my shirt wrapped around my head like a sweatband, I climb the ladder holding a half gallon of oil-base barn red and a stiff bristle brush.

From twenty feet up, I follow the quiet canal toward the bay. The canal bends at the bait shop, then goes out of sight. Today there's no boat traffic. Most of the boats are owned by weekend warriors who rip though the channels on Saturdays and Sundays, headed to Fire Island and the Hamptons. Only the *Irma C*, a big black iron clam boat, and about a half dozen skiffs go out weekday mornings.

I tie the paint can to the top rung of the ladder, balance the brush on the can and pull a paint scraper from my back pocket. Without much effort, the hard flakes of peeling paint crack off the dry cedar shingles. I don't mind the work. Last week I replaced twenty feet of rotting dock boards. Week before last, I cut fifty yards of hedges down to waist level. Mrs. Miller pays me four dollars an hour off the books and lets me keep track of my time.

A gray-headed tern lands at the peak of the roof and watches me with one black eye. Mornings and evenings their cries ring across the canal. Sometimes they bombard the *Glory* with half-dead spider crabs or clams, then swoop down to feast on the deck. Elena feeds the gulls as if they were begging dogs. When we eat on deck, the gulls gather around, some old and beaten, some in their first summer. They watch and wait and strut up and down. If Elena tosses a hotdog, all hell breaks loose.

Across the canal the retarded kids file out of the brick building into the yard. Most of them go to the fence and clutch it like they're watching a baseball game, but there's nothing there except the canal and a few white ducks paddling past the boats. The teacher cups her hand over her forehead, looks over at me. If I was in charge of the school I'd give the kids fishing poles. From a baited line off the front of the *Glory* I've caught a few eels that were thick as my arm. Elena would not eat eel even after I barbecued the meat and smothered it with onions. I tell her it tastes like chicken. "So why bother?" she says. "I'll eat chicken."

By noon, I'm soaked with sweat and have been stung on the back of my hand by a yellow jacket. I run the hose over the welt, douse my face, then head out for lunch. On Sunrise Highway I drive past my house and pull into the truck stop. A trucker sprays down an oil rig. Water and black heating fuel puddles over the sewer. After draining through some tremendously long pipe, the oil is probably emptying into one of Freeport's canals. There's always ribbons of gasoline floating on the surface of Freeport Creek.

The still half-painted house is falling apart. The small wooden stoop is so crooked the house appears to be pitching backward. Could living in a cockeyed house make someone crooked? Of course I know it's not possible, but it seems like everything in my life has been bent or crooked. My bedroom window doesn't have a shade or a drape. For a moment I imagine a younger me framed in the window, looking out at the truck stop and traffic. People going by may have noticed me in the window and remarked, "There's that kid in the crooked house." Maybe someone's wife or mother or grandmother bent her head toward the rear window and said, "That must be his mother on the stoop." They must have thought it was a shame that a kid's mother drank out on the sidewalk in front of a crooked house. Some of them must have hated me for being part of something so ugly, an eyesore that all the cops gave a good once over before they turned into Wetson's Hamburgers or 7-Eleven. At least my father's hotel room was off the main road. Only the guys in the bar watched him and his girls come and go.

At this hour my mother's working, so I pull off and hang a screeching U-turn across the double yellow lines. The Road Runner's power snaps me out of my mood. I goose the gas and the car surges forward with the force of a giant wave.

The cement-block building is marked LAUNDRY. The windows are painted white from the inside with shoe polish and the door is held open by an old leather boot. Laundry is a wash-and-dry operation. Customers drop off and pick up their clothes across town at Pristine Cleaners, a flashy joint with air conditioning, magazine racks, and plants they spray from plastic atomizers. My mother once told me that, if she didn't have a Puerto Rican accent, she'd be a counter girl at the other store.

Inside, it's got to be over ninety degrees. Past the pressing machines and the hanging clothes, my mother sticks her head and shoulders inside a washer that's about eight feet across and five feet high. She comes out with an armful of wet clothes. A red bandanna is slipping down her thick wiry hair. I wind around a

Chinese woman working a sewing machine. She smiles and points at my mother.

We settle at a green picnic table next to a broad swamp maple with a rough trunk. From a radio, Led Zeppelin drifts into the park. The wind comes up and sunlight filters through the tree branches. A long time ago my mother would bring me here to play on the swings. She'd sit at this exact table drinking beer or wine, smoking, staring across the monkey bars and swings to the Wood-cleft Canal's bars and party boats.

My mother slides in on her side of the bench. Being away from her for a few weeks makes me notice that her face is drawn and her hair is shot through with gray. With her jeans and shirt prac-tically falling off, the biggest thing about her is her hair. She's combing it out into an afro. I can almost hear my father, "What the hell? You trying to look like a hippie? Huh?"

My mother places a bag with beer on the table. I unwrap two steaming Ranger burgers. "So what about the police?" asks my mother. "You still in trouble?" She narrows her eyes and small vertical creases appear above her lip.

The fight in Violetta's flashes in my head. The word is out that Pete's nose was broken in two places and he's threatening to go to the cops. When I learned the news, Elena saw my face and told me not to worry. "We're leaving," she said, "remember?" All week I had been stocking the boat with canned goods, fuel, matches, rain gear, flashlights, extra parts, hoses, sparkplugs. I checked the cooling system, cleaned the fuel pump filter, made sure all the fastenings were tight. I even went underwater wearing a diving mask and examined the propeller. If the cops came looking for me, I'd be out of Freeport and on my way. All it would take was untying the lines and starting the engine.

"No," I tell my mother. "That blew over." I go through Sandy
dropping the charges. My mother watches me with a puzzled look.
I try to explain why Loopy got me involved, but even to me it
sounds screwy.

"So then, good," she says. "You stay away from him and that
girl." She takes a large bite out of her burger. On the end of the
table, I knock the caps off two bottles of Miller. I don't want to
drink beer this early, but I don't want her drinking alone. She
takes a gulp of beer. I think about Sandy swearing Loopy raped
her, him swearing he didn't. "Loopy's planning to marry that
girl," I say.

"The girl he raped?" My mother shakes her head, then laughs.
For a while we talk about Sandy's plan of renting the hall above
the firehouse. She's already volunteered me for setting up and dec-
orating the hall for the reception. Loopy's asked me to be the best
man. I told him thanks, but no thanks. He told me that I was
forgetting where I came from, then he put his fist through a wall.
Jesus, he's a gorilla. Elena's the maid of honor. She's already talking
about shoes, dresses, and crap.

"So, your girl?" asks my mother. "You got her on that boat.
Living without hot water?"

"She showers at the rec center."

"And what about you?"

I smile at her. "First you say, don't get into hot water," I say.
"Now you complain I don't have hot water."

"Wise guy," she says. "Always with the jokes, right?"

"No, not right," I say.

"Yeah, you and your father," she shakes her head. "Think I'm
dumb because I'm Puerto Rican."

"Don't be stupid, Mom. I'm Puerto Rican too."

"You're not Puerto Rican," she says wiping the ketchup off her

lips with the back of her hand. "Your father, he's more Puerto
Rican than you, and he's German."

I recall my reflection in the canal. Sometimes, I'll catch myself
leaning with my legs crossed just the way my father does, or even
laughing his strangled laugh and, I guess, that's what she sees. "I
broke a guy's nose for him," I say. "He tell you about that?"

"All he ever says is he's broke?" She picks up her hamburger.
"You ever meet a guy so broke that dresses so snazzy?"

I shake my head. "You want another beer?"

"So what about this girl, she don't mind no hot showers?"

"Look," I say. "All you got to know is she's nice."

"You don't need nice," she says. "She take care of you, she rub
your back, she cook?" I make up a story telling her that Elena waits
on me hand and foot. That's what my mother wants to hear. Truth
is, I do almost everything around the boat. Maybe I'm neater than
Elena, maybe I notice things first, but that's the routine we've
settled into. Sometimes, though, Elena's a royal pain in the balls.
She expects me to have all the answers. "What are we going to do
when we get to Florida?" That's one of her favorites. "How are you
going to make money? What am I going to do? Start at the bottom,
start sweeping hair off the floor again?"

I've told her that I have a strategy. All I've got to do is get a job
painting houses, cutting lawns, anything until I get the fishing char-
ters going. "Right," she said. "There's probably no other guys in
Florida already cutting lawns. They need hitters from Freeport to
cut their lawns. The Cubans, they must all be too busy, so they
need Freeport spicks." In a rage I reminded her I was half Puerto
Rican. "Half," I screamed, charging off the *Glory*. I don't know how,
but Elena found me dozing in the Road Runner in front of the
Freeport Historical Society where they display old lobster pots,
whaling harpoons, and pictures of the town before families like

mine moved in and ruined everything. Elena cried on my chest, begged me to forgive her.

"Elena takes good enough care of me," I say to my mother. "She give you a good breakfast today? You can't work on an empty stomach." I think of me standing at the small stove serving her breakfast. "And don't let her know too much." My mother takes another bite. "That's the secret. With your father I finally laid down the law. He's not barging into the house anymore. I told him he's out."

"But you'd take him back?" I ask.

She wags her head considering it and I know my parents will never change. In her best "nice" voice, she tells me about the guy with the blue pickup. "Artie would like to meet you sometime," she says. I tell her that I already met him. "You're crazy, you never met Artie," she says. I listen to her go on about Artie, who can build anything out of wood, who built the stage at the Nassau Coliseum. "Custom," says my mother. "All custom for that rock band with the makeup." I ask her if it's KISS but she isn't listening. "Artie's a union man," she leans across the picnic table. "Union," she says wide-eyed, chewing a mouthful of burger. "What you were gonna be." She watches me. I pull a slice of onion from my burger. Like someone building a fire, she throws more and more fuel on Artie of the blue truck and the union carpenter's job, trying to make him seem bright and warm. "Artie got work at the next car show," she says. "Only the inside guys get that work."

"Sounds like he's got it made," I say. In her eyes I see her hope that this guy will be different. But, none of the Arties she brought home were worth a damn. He's after something. They all were. Most left in the morning, before breakfast. One guy stole the television. Maybe this "Artie" needs a place to crash. Maybe his wife threw him out. My bet is in two months she'll be back at the

Tropicana meeting a new Artie or sitting on the stoop watching the traffic for his blue truck.

Beyond the trees and the spiked wrought-iron fence, the cars on Grove Street turn right, then head up the Nautical Mile. Two young mothers come around the bend, pushing strollers with sleeping children.

"You taking drugs," says my mother, grabbing my hand. She presses her fingers into the yellow jacket sting.

"It's a damn bee sting," I say, yanking my hand.

"Looked like something I once saw on your father from a needle."

"He shot drugs?"

"Not while he was out." She scratches her head. "And don't ask me what drug. He did what they all did."

"Was he hooked on it?"

"I don't know," she says.

"Well, what did you think?" I lean forward.

"I don't think," she says. "You think, then you might start thinking you know something." She raises her eyebrows and nods and I picture him in his orange prison uniform, sticking a needle in his arm. "It was a long time ago," she says.

A group of kids throw their stingray bikes on the grass and run toward the swings. They jump on and begin pumping, their Keds and Converse sneakers pointed to the blue sky. My mother watches them and I wonder if she remembers all the times I played there and she sat here. Those were the good times, the quiet times.

"Ma," I say, touching her hand. "I'm thinking about leaving, taking off in the *Glory*."

"Leaving," she says. "Where you going?"

"I don't know, maybe Puerto Rico," I lie, hoping this may make it easier for her.

"Don't go there," she says, grabbing my hand. "Too many spicks." She forces herself to laugh.

"You taught me not to say that word," I remind her.

"I thought you never listened to me." She coughs and leans toward me. "Just take off with your new little girlfriend, not a worry in the world." She releases my hand and turns away.

"I'll call you," I say. "When I get to where I'm going, maybe you can come down and visit."

She looks around the park. "Nah, you two go. Me, I like hot water." She waves her hands toward the swings, the bars lining the canal. "I know," she says. "You want to go to where you feel free of all this." For a short time she sits at the end of the bench, looking into the stiff dry grass. She slips her hands between her legs and pulls her shoulders forward.

"You cold?" I ask.

"It's going to rain." She finishes her beer. "I can feel it in my bones." I ball up the wax paper from the burgers and stuff the garbage into the burger bag. Muttering something, she throws the empty beer bottles into a wire trash can. When she returns she stands in front of me, smaller and frailer than ever. I'd like to warn her about Artie but she'd never listen. I remember a day a long time ago when I saw her coming down Main Street, pushing our laundry in a Woolworth cart. I was with the guys and Loopy asked, "Hey, isn't that your old lady?" I shook my head at him and we all kept walking. I was never much of a son to her. She smiles and I hug her. She feels weak as a bird, like her ribs are coming through her back. There's tears in my eyes and I sniffle.

"You got allergies?" she asks.

"I miss you," I tell her.

"Hey, Popi, you going soft on me?" She squirms out of my arms.

"You going to be all right?" I ask her, knowing she won't be, that some day in the heat and humidity of that laundry, or in the smoky haze of the Tropicana, or right in the front room of the house, she's going to disappear. Something will happen.

"You know me." She shrugs.

In front of the laundry, my mother lingers in the Road Runner with her door open and one foot on the curb. "I hope you're coming by soon," she says.

"I'll come by," I say.

"Artie says he wants to go out on the boat," she says. "He wants to catch fish in, what do you call it?"

"The Acid Waters?" I ask. "I'm not fishing there anymore."

"Then you'll take us where you go?" I tell her sure and she smiles. "Goodbye, Eddie." She leans over and kisses me on the cheek. She gets out, holding the bag with the leftover beers. The door to Laundry is still wide open, and she heads in.

Chapter Nineteen

All afternoon on the ladder, I paint the boathouse and go over our conversation in the park. Somehow, I feel relieved and upset at the same time. She probably only told me about Artie so I wouldn't worry about her. I spread the barn-red paint on the scraped shingles and imagine my mother tumbling from our kitchen chair to the floor, lying very still, with her eyes half open. I have to shake my head to get rid of the picture.

I climb down the ladder. The side of the boathouse shines with new paint. In order to finish, I cut back the climbing roses. The thorns scratch my forearms and small dots of blood appear. After five minutes, I look like I've been in a fight with a cat. I flash on my mother in the bathroom, her head and shoulders jammed in the small space between the sink and the toilet. One time I found her like that. Her pants and panties were down and she was very still. Her skin was cold. I pulled her out, sat her against the hamper. I was just a kid, maybe the fifth grade. I saw her wide patch of dark curly pubic hair. I knew it was wrong to look, but I looked.

I hop aboard. Out of the bright sun, in the dim cabin I can barely see. I press my head against the sweating varnished wood in the cabin. The boat bounces and Elena calls my name. I come out of the cabin and she's smiling, holding up a plastic bag with a bottle of something inside. "Friday, Friday," she chants. "Party, party."

I have to smile and she kisses me. "You finished?" she asks, looking over at the boathouse.

"Almost."

She pulls a green bottle of champagne from the bag and begins untwisting the wire guard over the cap. "I don't know, I just feel like celebrating," she says.

After a quick dinner, we pack the champagne in ice and cruise to the beach at West End Two. Elena sings along with a Bee Gees' song from *Saturday Night Fever*. The movie sounds pretty dumb, some guy working in a paint store, getting his rocks off by dancing disco in a white suit with no tie. Elena's been bugging me to take her.

The highway is empty. I punch the pedal, and the narrow channels and marsh grass whiz by in a blur. Elena puts her hand over mine and we shift the gears together and blow through the empty toll booth doing seventy. When the speedometer needle bounces toward eighty, the entire dashboard vibrates. Elena digs speed.

At the parking field, we swing in next to a few cars that have fishing licenses on the dashboards. I remember being here with her just a few weeks ago and skinny-dipping in the freezing rough waves. Barefoot, arm in arm, we cross the long stretch of flat sand toward the dunes. In the approaching dusk a few nesting terns fly above us, but they're nothing to worry about.

Where the jetty separates the inlet from the ocean there's a smooth buildup of windswept sand. We spread a worn quilt and bury the corners. The ocean breathes with steady rolling waves that crest at the end of the jetty, then rumble in with white water.

Down the beach surf casters whip their long rods toward the waves. A few miles out a trawler works. No one else in sight. For a while we listen to the surf rushing across the black rocks of the jetty. Elena pours two plastic cups of champagne. I think about cutting out, pulling the boat's lines at the Old Oyster Wharf and not coming back. I dig my heels into the cold sand.

"What are they fishing for?" Elena asks, looking down the beach.

"Blues, mackerel, whatever's running."

She digs through her pocketbook, juggles it around, and comes out with a round brush. She gives her hair a few hard strokes. "At lunch I got one of the girls to drive me home, I wanted to get these shorts." She pulls a thread on her cutoff jeans. "This was on my makeup table." She removes a letter from her pocketbook. The envelope is postmarked from Los Angeles and sliced open at one end. Elena smiles, taps the letter out, and unfolds it. "It's really nothing that great," she says and places her head on my lap. It's from her brother and she begins to read, " 'Dear Little Sis, Your letter came just in time, it really made my day.' " The letter describes how he accidentally knocked over his new Harley, " 'Damage. Not major, but damage,' " Elena continues and we both smile. The letter backtracks: he bought a Harley because he blew the engine in his Volkswagen van. He describes his dogs and how they get into the garbage at his apartment, he describes Elena as " 'sounding more positive, or should I say less negative.' " It's a long, rambling letter. Elena reads it slowly, enjoying it: " 'Mom called and told me you moved out.' " Elena turns the letter over. "Then he asks a bunch of questions about you," she says.

"Let me see."

She hands me the letter. I read it through, then go back and reread the last part. " 'Sis, I played your demo tape to the guys in the band. Everyone thinks you sound mighty fine. You got better and you better get yourself out here. Warren thinks you'd be perfect.' " I fold the letter and hand it back. She slips it into the envelope.

"Who's Warren?" I ask.

"He plays the organ," she says. "Eddie, what are you thinking?"

"I'm thinking," I say, but can't continue because my throat's so damn constricted. After a moment I tell her it's great news. She says that she didn't tell me she was sending her brother tapes because she thought I'd think it was a waste of time.

I take a few measured breaths, then ask her if she's going. "I don't know," she says.

"But you want to?"

"I don't know what I'm going to do." She tightens her jaw. "Maybe you could come with me."

"To do what?"

"I don't know," she says. "It's probably a lot like Florida."

"You think they need a spick to shake the maracas?"

"Don't," she says.

"Or maybe they don't have enough spicks out there in L.A. to mow the lawns." She shuts her eyes, but I continue, "What am I to you? A chico, a taco-head?"

"What are you so mad about?"

"I'm not mad." I think of that night on the boardwalk when Elena unbuckled my belt in front of a couple strolling by. I don't know whether I want to punish her or try to make her Armpits again. At least then I didn't give a rat's ass about her.

She gets up and walks toward the water. I'd like to hold her, tell her that I don't want her to go, but I think about the bottle of champagne, and her chant, "Party, party." Some party. She gets invited to go to California and it's the happiest I've seen her in weeks. Where the hell do I fit? Is she going to invite me to stay at her brother's apartment? Is there room? Could I sleep with a guy's sister right under his nose? Is this *it?* Is this the end of us? Is she just going to split, start fresh?

I pull my knees to my chest. The coming night has turned the ocean a dark blue and has strengthened the black frothing waves. The trawler is on the edge of the horizon, just about gone. Elena returns and sits next to me. She nudges her head back onto my lap. "Don't do anything you don't want to do," I say. "You want to go, just go, okay?"

Chapter Twenty

Elena pulls the Road Runner's rearview mirror over to check her hair, it's piled on her head and braided tight as rope. "I don't feel like a maid of honor," she says. She looks like one of the women on the cover of a fashion magazine.

"I don't feel like a best man," I say. "And don't do that to the mirror. The damn bolt fell out three times."

"What crawled up your ass and died?" she asks.

"You try looking in a loose mirror. Everything looks like an earthquake." It's the most we've said to each other all day. Man, I thought the boat was small when we were getting along, now it's like a freaking closet. She doesn't like to admit it, and she gets pissed off at me if I say anything, but we're history. She answered her brother's letter and told him she'd be flying out the end of July. With phony enthusiasm, I told her she was doing the right thing.

I straighten the mirror and roll by the fire truck bays, searching the half dozen volunteer firemen for a familiar face. One of them is washing the black wheels of the hook and ladder. The others stand in a half-circle watching. Soap runs down the slanted concrete driveway to the metal grate in the sidewalk. I squeeze the Road Runner between two cars.

We cross the wet cement toward the firehouse. My brand-spanking-new black shirt is right out of the cardboard and itches my neck. I'm supposed to wear a rented fagged-out tuxedo, but tough. My old Dingo boots and jeans will have to do. Boat living. No shower, no hot water, no closets, no tuxedo. I didn't want a part in this wedding, but Loopy and Elena wore me out.

The volunteers, their sponges motionless against the four-foot rubber tires, stare at Elena's miniskirt, sweater, and burnt-orange platforms that lace up her ankles.

"Forget them," she says. "We're getting out of this town."

We're getting out. *We're.* She says it like *we're* going together.

We cross in front of the fire truck, and I feel their eyes and the heat of the engine. They must have just shut it down. The volunteers continue staring hard. In high school guys wouldn't ogle my girl's ass (at least not with me around). I turn, and Elena tugs my hand.

Afternoon sun streaks across the polished tile floor of the empty fire department hall. At one end is the glass-enclosed trophy case, jammed with chrome- and gold-colored trophies, ribbons, and old burnt fire hats. At the other end, Sandy bends over a folding table pulling the legs upright. As usual, she's wearing her bell-bottom jeans with the holes in the ass. There's a new ring of bulkhead tar around her bottom. Twisted white crepe paper, taped to the fluorescent lights, winds randomly around the ceiling, the way kids toilet paper the trees on Halloween. Chairs are stacked against the far wall. We cross to Sandy, and I pull the last leg of the table straight.

"Thanks." She lifts the bottom of her T-shirt, revealing her still flat stomach, and wipes her forehead. "I'm a freaking nervous wreck. Where the fuck is Loopy?"

Elena looks at me.

"He's probably on his way," I say.

"I brought help," says Sandy. "But they're no help." In the corner of the room, under a cloud of cigarette smoke, three older women sit at the only table that's not leaning against the wall. Their stiff, blond, beauty parlor hair looks like straw baskets.

"When are you getting dressed?" asks Elena.

"It's all out in the car," she says. "The blow dryer, makeup, my dress. But I can't even think. Look at this." She holds out her thin hand and it's trembling like a drunk's. "I was throwing up. I don't know if it's nerves or the baby. Everything is going to be terrible. It's the story of my life."

"Everything's going to be fine," says Elena.

"Not this," she lifts a piece of her straight black hair. "I was supposed to get it set at Speedy Cut and Blow, so I go over there and it's closed." They hug for a moment and over Elena's shoulder Sandy says, "He better get his ass here."

I flash on Loopy, standing on a bridge with nowhere to go, except into the river. I pull up three chairs. Sandy sits and cradles her head. "I was at the apartment," she says. "Loopy never painted."

"You guys never finished?" asks Elena, looking at me.

"When was I supposed to finish?" I ask. "I don't even have the key."

"If Joey's got so goddamn much money," says Sandy, without looking up, "why doesn't he have the place painted and carpeted?"

Joey's footing the bill for the wedding and a honeymoon at some club with a heart-shaped bathtub in the Jewish Alps. He also hooked Loopy and Sandy up with an apartment on Brooklyn Avenue near the train station. A few days ago, Loopy bug bombed all the rooms and swept up half a grocery bag of roaches. Sandy made a big production, walking from room to room choosing paint colors. But at Richmond Hardware Loopy bought all the same color, this pissy nut-house yellow. I wasn't going to tell her.

Elena and Sandy head out to the parking lot for Sandy's dress and veil. I set up tables, then place metal folding chairs around them. They return, lugging bags bulging with hair spray, and disappear into the ladies' room in the corner of the hall. I climb a ladder with a roll of tape in my mouth and basketball-size crepe paper wedding bells in my hands. Under each bell it says HAPPINESS.

Sandy's aunts and mom rip open packages of plastic cups, paper plates, paper napkins (all with wedding bell designs). The paper tablecloths have flowers around the borders with large glowing candles in the middle. Sandy's mom, leaning on her aluminum walking cane, rises. Her dress has enough material for a car cover. She reaches around and pulls it out of her butt. It's bad news for Loopy if the bride turns out to look like her mother.

The aunts join Loopy's mother and the three of them, almost perfect circles—round as they are high—work their way across the hall and stand at the bottom of the ladder.

"Gorgeous," says Sandy's mother.

"Absolutely gorgeous," agrees one of the aunts.

I climb down the ladder.

"What about the centerpieces?" asks the mother.

"We'll go with the fake," says one of the aunts. "They got the most beautiful displays at Woolworth."

"The fake last," says Sandy's mother.

The aunts yank their pocketbook straps to their shoulders, fix their cigarettes in their lips, and head to the door.

"Get blue," yells Sandy's mother. "They have the most beautiful blue."

At the corner table, I unfold a tablecloth. Sandy's mother helps me pull it across the table. "Where's Loopy?" she asks.

"I'll have to give him a call."

"You mean he's at home?"

"Soon as we get set up, I'll go find him."

"What do you mean, 'find him'? Is he hiding?" She takes her cigarette out of her mouth. "He better not pull any crap," she says. " 'Cause I've had it." She coughs and the heavy flesh around her face turns from gray to pink. Coughing, she lumbers back to her command post next to her brown paper bag, and pulls out a beer.

I stop the Road Runner at the Louperinos'. Mrs. Loop's on the porch in a lounge chair, holding a sun reflector under her chin. She drops the reflector, then waves. I climb the rotted steps and stop a few feet from her.

"Grabbing some color so that I don't look like death," she says. Below her tight shorts, her long white legs are crisscrossed with blue and maroon veins.

"The wedding's in a couple of hours," I say.

"Don't I know it." She reaches, snaps open her pocketbook. "Loopy had to go in today. They're finishing up a big job in Oceanside, putting an extension on the mall at Times Square Store." She pulls out a slip of paper. "You want to know something, I've never even met my future daughter-in-law. How do you like that? Never even laid eyes on her." I have no idea what to say. I take a step down the stairs. "I know it's a shotgun wedding. That's what we called them when I was a girl, a shotgun wedding. Make everything nice as pie." She squints into the sun and the cat pokes its head out from under the lounge chair.

"Still got the cat," I say.

"This character," she says, "was spraying my curtains again." She swats him on the side of the head and he scoots off the porch. "Eddie, you don't know what I put up with," she says, pulling a cigarette out of her pack of L&M's. "Everyone in my office knows." She waves her chrome lighter under the cigarette that's wagging in her lips. "Talking behind my back."

On Atlantic Avenue the light changes and a line of traffic streams by. I'd like to get going but Mrs. Loop is looking at me like I owe her an explanation. "How's your mother?" I ask. "Still watching her programs?"

"Her TV is all fuzzy, a goddamn snowstorm."

"I could look at it for you."

Mrs. Loop snaps her purse shut. "You don't have to, the thing never worked right."

"Well," I say, looking down at the worn wooden steps. "I better . . . get." I point to the car. "I'll see you at the wedding."

"At least he's out of trouble." She waits for me to say something. "The kid won't be a bastard," she adds. I can't imagine Loopy doing anything with a kid except swatting him in the head. "I had Loopy when I was seventeen and his daddy took off like a . . ." She mutters something. "You think this world needs another kid running the streets not knowing his daddy?"

"I know mine," I tell her. "It's not all that it's cracked up to be."

"You know what hurts?" she says. I don't want to know, but I nod. Being Loopy's mom isn't any bargain. I think of my own mother taking breaks in the cinderblock alleyway next to the warm exhaust from the dryers. "I never got a written invitation to my own son's wedding."

"No one did," I say.

"But I'm the mother, the mother."

"You need a ride to the firehouse?" I ask.

"Don't you have enough to do?" She holds out the paper from her purse. "That's for Loopy's tux. It has to be picked up before three." I take the rental receipt. "Light blue with the navy piping," she says.

It's exactly like the one I was supposed to wear.

Oceanside is on the way to Long Beach. I pass the blocks where we raced the Firebird on Saturday night just a few weeks ago. What if we hadn't picked the girls up that night? I would be in the store cutting chickens, fetching coffee and tea. I'm not relieved, but at the same time I'm not exactly sorry either. So far, being with Elena has been nice. Last night, while sanding the deck, I caught her watching me. That's a great feeling.

The boat's getting into shape. Shipshape, my grandfather would say. Lately, I get the feeling that he's guiding me, letting the work come easy. The entire flying bridge is sanded and varnished. The decks are varnished. Near the engine compartment, I've cut the dry rot out and replaced it with new wood. The engine starts on the first crank. The leaks around the head gaskets sealed themselves. The only thing that's stopping me from pulling out and not looking back is Elena. With charts that Tim dug up from the back of the bait shop, I plotted a course along the intercostal waterway that ends at Key Largo. I showed Elena where the *Glory* would be on day one, all the way to day twenty.

"Florida?" she asked. "Where they got all those lawns?"

The entire area around Loopy's job site is fenced off. A backhoe and bulldozer are parked at the foot of a mountain of sand and rubble. No one's around. It could be the lunch hour, but I doubt it. Someone would stay behind. At a makeshift gate, the fence is padlocked. I turn around and head back.

Where Freeport meets Baldwin, there's waterfront bar built adjacent to the bridge, a hole called Duckey's. Loopy's Goat is parked next to the bar with its ass sticking into the street.

Inside it's dark, smoky, and dead. A guy that runs a skiff in the bay hangs over his beer with his loose rubber green waders around his waist. He raises his head like an old tired watchdog then goes back to his beer. The jukebox lights flash, but nothing's playing. Loopy's at the end of the bar talking to Icky Vicky. Two years ago on New Year's Eve, with everyone counting down to midnight, Vicky found me in the crowd of screaming drunks and drilled her tongue down my throat and breathed, "I want you to be my first in 'seventy-five." I hung around until she locked up. We shoved the half-spoiled, ransacked trays of pickles, pigs-in-blankets, potato salad, noodle salad, to the back of the pool table and climbed on the chalk-stained felt. Being with her reminded me of the Himalaya ride at Coney Island. Balls to the wall for two minutes and, when it's over, you wonder why the hell you did it in the first place. I wound up getting mustard all over my back.

Vicky leans over the bar in a low-cut shirt that's hardly street legal. Patches of acne start at her forehead and appear to be drifting like dinky red buoys down her neck into her chest, then into the large space between her little tits. Loopy's got his face about six inches from them and about four inches off the bar.

"Douche," I say.

"Asshole," says Loopy, giving me one of his thumb-lock handshakes that turns into a bear hug. "My main man," he says, "my main stain." He stinks of sweat, beer, and cigarettes. I pull out of his grasp. They are polishing off a pitcher of melon balls.

"What's happening?" I ask Vicky.

"Same ol,' same ol,'" she says. "Except he's marrying Sandra Gass." Smiling, she pops the top off a bottle of Miller. "What I don't get," she says, "is last month she was accusing youse guys of rape." Loopy doesn't move, just stares at her perfect little acne-covered chest. In the dim light, her skin looks like someone beat her with a wire brush. "You don't think that's sick?" she asks me.

"Don't ask me," I say. "I'm the best man."

"Fucking A." Loopy grabs me. "The best of the best."

"He really buy her a one-carat ring?" asks Vicky. After Loopy presented Sandra with the one-carat zirconium, that she still thinks is real, she dropped the charges.

"There's more carats in carrots," I say.

"What?" Vicky gives me a puzzled look.

"Quality," says Loopy, laughing. "Only quality."

"You still didn't explain anything," says Vicky.

I tell her that I wasn't even under the boardwalk, that the whole thing was a mix-up. She eyes me suspiciously, as I suppose almost everyone always will. Maybe, though, the true story will leak out. One day last week when I took a break from painting the Miller's boathouse, I met Detective Sack in Seaman's Deli. He was dressed in the same baggy suit that he wore when he arrested me. "I should have listened to my gut," he said, tearing the plastic lid on his coffee. "I had a bad feeling about Louperino's statement. Ninety-nine and nine-tenths of the time I'm right if I follow my gut."

"I wouldn't mind if you tell that to the papers," I said. He laughed and threw two quarters on the counter for my Coke. "I'm not joking," I said.

Larson was outside the deli waiting for Sack in the same un-marked car that I was cuffed and tossed into. "Trottman," he called. Just hearing his voice spooked me. He followed me with his finger. I tried not to notice. "Yeah, Trottman, you, I got your num-ber."

"Hey," says Vicky, poking me. "Earth to Eddie." I grab her hand.

She leans across the bar and kisses me near the mouth. "I didn't think you did it," she says.

"Oh, my gosh," says Loopy in a sappy voice. "I'm gonna cry."

I tell them about the hall, the decorations, about Sandy's aunts. Loopy whines and looks around. "What time is it?" he asks.

"Half past a cow's ass," says Vicky, stirring the bottom of the pitcher of lime-green melon balls. Whips of her blond hair held in place by two fake-looking plastic lobster-claw clips fall across her face. "This is supposed to be the happiest day of your life," she says, picking up her shot glass.

"You know how many times I've heard that?" says Loopy.

"I hear Eddie's next," says Vicky.

Just to throw her off balance, I'd like to ask if she's gotten her foot caught in the pool table pockets lately, but I just let out a breath. After New Year's she called my house a few times, asked me to visit her, begged me to go see *A Star Is Born*. It wasn't just Barbra Streisand, I couldn't face Vicky. It felt like the time when I was a kid and pulled a dog biscuit out of the fourth-grade Christmas grab bag.

"Elena's still Sandy's best bud?" asks Vicky. "Isn't she?"

"Eee-lane-ah," sings Loopy to the tune of "Tammy." "Eee-lane-ah, my love." Loopy cracks himself up.

"She's setting up for *his* wedding," I say.

"Let's toast," says Vicky, refilling the shot glasses. Some guy that owns a dragger comes in and sits at the other end of the bar. "Be back," says Vicky. We both watch her wiggle down the bar in her skin-tight Wranglers.

"Icky Vicky," I say. We both laugh and down our melon balls. I can just imagine what Vicky thinks of us. Loopy getting loaded on his wedding day, tripping up the altar. Me, the best man, charged with accessory to rape—against the bride. Shit. Not that it matters one way or the other. The marriage probably won't last much longer than two kegs of Pabst at a fireman's funeral.

"Joey gave me a package to deliver," says Loopy, studying Vicky's ass down the bar. "I opened it. Money, a lot, stacks of hundreds."

"So what," I say. "Isn't that what you do? Anything but touch a shovel."

"Eddie, listen," he grabs my arm. "Remember that plan we had about taking off in the *Glory*? Me being your first mate, remember that?" He opens his wallet and removes the Twinkie package cardboard that lists supplies and expenses. The ink is almost worn off. "That money, it's enough to cover it fifty times over."

"Enough to get whacked for," I say. "That's what guys like Joey do. Whack people."

"They'd never find us." He smiles. "We could be on our way, nobody would find us. Think about me being married, waking up with Sandy, going to bed with Sandy." He frowns. "Would you do that to your best bud?" I just look at the bar and he goes on saying that he'd come back someday and do better than his old man. "I haven't seen him in fifteen years." His chest heaves up and down. I don't think Loopy is going to do better than his father. "Come on, you and me." His eyes shine. "Forget Elena."

I can't even look at him. I'd like to tell him that Elena's already decided to go to Los Angeles, but he'd think it was great news. Holding her back is out of the question. For the rest of her life she'd be wondering if she could have had a singing career.

"You're telling me you'd rather live with old Armpits then get outta here with me?" He holds out his five-year-old cardboard full of figures. I wonder if he knows the nights of hanging out, cruising, are over. He looks at me like I'm suddenly someone he doesn't recognize. "Or maybe Armpits got you pussy whipped?"

I open my wallet, remove the tuxedo receipt, and stuff it in his

T-shirt pocket behind his pack of cigarettes. "We got an hour to get your head on straight, pick up your tux, and get to the fire-house."

"I'll call her Elena," he says. "No more Armpits, that make you happy?"

"It's not about her," I say. "Come on, let's get out of here."

"I'm backed up," he says pointing to an overturned shot glass.

"I'm going." Hoping he'll follow, I head down the bar. In two seconds I'm out under a sky that has turned overcast. I take a deep breath and pull my keys out of my pocket. He could get married, divorced, screw Icky Vicky, then Sandy, all on his wedding night. I don't want to give a damn.

I start the car and wait a long minute. Just when I'm ready to go back in to drag Loopy out, he barrels out of the bar.

"Hey," he yells. "Wait." He comes to the car window. "Man," he says, opening the door. "I left two free drinks on the bar." I let the clutch out. The Road Runner lurches and Loopy just about falls into the seat.

"Look," I say. "You don't want to get married, fine with me."

"Man, it ain't that simple," he says.

We cross over into Freeport and I pull into the beer distributor where we've parked on countless nights waiting for something to do, something to happen.

"It's that simple," I say. "Screw Joey, screw Sandy, screw Joey's money, we're talking about you, Loopy. Your life."

"Wait here," he says and gets out. I figure he'll walk down to the canal to think, but he turns into the distributor. A storm rolling in off the ocean has turned the sky gray. Across the canal, tree branches sway. Wash whips back and forth on a clothesline, and shiny fiberglass boats sway and rock.

Loopy comes out holding a six-pack of Miller and gets into the car. "It's gonna pour," he says, popping a beer for me. The beer is cold and tastes good. So many nights hanging around, drinking, waiting. I don't want to think of them as wasted, but I can barely remember a single thing about them. It's quarter after three. He's got forty-five minutes. If we don't get going, he'll miss his wedding.

"That night under the boardwalk," he says. "I . . ."

"Yeah?"

"Don't get pissed off." He gulps his beer.

"What? Loopy, it's three-fifteen."

"I did it," he says thickly and crushes the empty can in his hand. "The funny part is, I just kept thinking, I better stop, but I didn't stop." He presses his thumb into his temple and closes his eyes. "It was like if I stopped she'd win. Believe me, Eddie, I stopped plenty of other times. It's half her fault, she always strutted her ass around Violetta's like she was putting out seven days a week and twice on Sunday."

"Man, that's not a reason—"

"Half the time? Shit, over half the time, she gave me some excuse and I wound up at the Top Hat with a major case of blue balls."

Sandy's scream from under the boardwalk goes through my mind. "You thought about it?" I ask. "When you were raping her, you thought about it?"

He takes his hand away from his head and tries to laugh. "I know," he says. "That sounds bad, right?" I take a swallow of beer, not surprised that he's been lying to me, but shocked that he did it deliberately. "I never really gave a shit about it until that day out on the water," he says. "That was the only thing that wouldn't come off me." I look at him and he's got his mouth tight with regret. "Maybe I owe this to her."

"You can't change what you did by getting married."

"I know." He looks at me. "I ain't fucking stupid. If it don't work, then it don't work. But she wants to get married more than anything else in the world." We sit for a minute, neither of us saying anything. I start the engine. "You know what Sandy told me once," he says. "She said she never won nothing. Never."

"So, what."

"I don't know, I just thought . . ."

"You think you're some kind of prize?" I ask. "You're the booby prize."

"Not to her I ain't," he says.

I'd like to tell him that he should be in jail and that marrying Sandy won't erase anything. I hope the night under the boardwalk stays on his shoulders like extra gravity. "Promise me one thing," I say. "Promise me you won't hit her, or ever"—I try to find another word for rape, but can't—"rape her."

"That's a done deal," he says. "A done deal."

I pull out and head to the tuxedo place on Merrick Road. Rain dots my windshield and the smell of the concrete rises from the road. Loopy opens another beer. "I'm gonna be late," he says. "Late for my own wedding. Ain't that a song or something?"

"It's supposed to be just an expression," I say. He laughs, and I grip the steering wheel. I won't forgive him. It wasn't just stupid sex under the boardwalk. He knew what he was doing.

"I'm getting married," he screams out the window at some old lady crossing the street. "Married."

Chapter Twenty-one

In the corner of the firehouse men's room, between the slop sink and a frayed green sofa, Loopy tries to snap the back of his tuxedo bow tie. I tell him to stand still and hook the small metal clasp. He squeezes into the jacket of the light blue tux. "Man, this is like torture," he says. The pants are above his ankles. "You think this looks okay?" he asks me.

He resembles a *Saturday Night Live* skit. "Looks okay to me," I say.

Loopy plops onto the couch. I've heard that late on Friday nights the firemen hustle whores into this men's room. Loopy leans forward, picks his jeans off the floor, and reaches into the pants pocket. "That cost me a half-a-yard." He holds out a gold wedding band. "Take it," he says. "You're the best man."

"It's inscribed," I say and read, " 'L. C. loves R. Q'?"

He grabs it from me and holds it to the light, then puts it between his teeth and pretends to bend it. "That little Jew at the pawn shop."

"It's gold," I say. "Better than her engagement ring." He extends his hand, but I don't take it.

"What's your problem?" he asks.

"You," I say, just wanting to get it over with and be through with him, his wedding, and his pawn-shop wedding ring.

"Oh, man," he mutters. "I'm getting married." He places both his palms on the sink and stares into the mirror. I hop up on the flat-topped trash can and sit. From his back pocket he pulls out a brush and tries to flatten his hair. Finally, he sticks his head under the faucet and slicks his hair back. "That'll do? Right?"

An old guy comes in wearing a suit that looks like it's got ten pounds of sand in the jacket pockets. "You're getting a crowd out there," he remarks, stepping toward the urinal. "I'm Sandra's uncle," he says, and faces the tiled wall. "Her Uncle George."

"I'm Larry," says Loopy. "Everybody calls me Loopy. That over there, that's Eddie."

"Rained on my wedding day, too," he says. "Didn't rain for the whole month of July, then the sky opened up."

"Rain don't matter," says Loopy. "It's good for the flowers." He smiles at me. "So you related to Sandra or something?"

The old guy gives Loopy a look. "I told you," he says. "An uncle."

For a moment we listen to Uncle George pissing. "That don't mean you automatically got to be related," says Loopy, looking at me for help. "Does it?" I'm trying not to crack up, smiling so hard my face hurts.

"Nice meeting you," says Uncle George, zipping up and heading for the door.

"You didn't wash your hands," calls Loopy. Uncle George pushes out the door.

" 'Automatically got to be related,' " I say.

"Hey," says Loopy, laughing. "I'm just trying to make a first impression."

I poke my head out the door into the hall. Elena and Sandy are nowhere in sight. I suppose they're in the ladies' room getting

ready. Near the iced kegs, guys I hung with in high school toss back
plastic cups of Pabst. "Looks like old home week," I say. "All the
fellas from the cave are out there."

"You were king of the cave," says Loopy, like it's supposed to be
some special honor. The cave was just an underpass at the high
school where all the hitters played handball and smoked. I wasted
whole school days cutting classes in the cave, slapping pink Spald-
ings until they split open. "You ever think I'd get married before
you?" he asks. "Bet you never thought that."

The truth is, I never thought about it at all until these past few
days. Marriage was for the "older" crowd. It was years off, like re-
tirement or death. Most guys I knew got married for bad reasons.
Loopy's cornered the market on just about all of them. Marrying
Elena to keep her from Los Angeles would be a gigantic mistake.
But, Jesus, all the shit we've gone through in the past few weeks.
I slip the ring on my pinky. It fits.

"Why the hell do people get dressed up for their wedding anyway?" Loopy squares his shoulders. "Seems like I ought to be able
to wear whatever I want." He stares in the mirror wearing the worn
face of someone coming off a long stretch of night shifts.
"Should've shaved," he says.

"I saw your mother," I say. "She was catching a tan."

"A tan in a rainstorm," he says. "That figures."

"She's pissed 'cause she never met Sandy," I say.

"Armpits ever meet your mother?"

"Maybe someday." If nothing else they could talk about hair,
manicures, and makeup.

"Don't get your thousand-mile stare going," he says. "I'm the
one getting married."

I think about Elena in Los Angeles, and my stomach gets queasy.
If she's late from work, I'm wondering what the hell's keeping her.

How will I feel when she's actually gone? When my old man's under the hood of a car he always says, "Life is timing."

"Let's get this over with," I say.

Loopy's little brother, Meatball, places the needle on his turntable and the heavy bass notes of Chicago's "Color My World" vibrate around the room. Loopy and I wait next to Captain Guy, who's wearing a white captain's jacket. Just about everyone south of Atlantic Avenue knows Captain Guy from the Helm Bar and Grill, where he stands day after day, week after week at the bar, just left of the door, drinking and reading. Captain Guy, at least at one time, was a real boat captain, but he has rheumatoid arthritis that's turning his joints into hard knots of bone. He walks stiff legged like he's frozen. When anyone asks him what's wrong with him, he removes his pipe from the corner of his mouth and yells, "I'm an incurable romanticist in love with the written word."

When Sandy's aunts finish lighting candles at the tables, a hush falls over the hall and Elena emerges from the ladies' room carrying a bouquet. She starts across the floor and everyone sort of holds their breath. Even the jokers around the keg quiet down and place their plastic cups of beer on the bar. Elena takes slow, deliberate steps, like a real church wedding. She looks so good, so sexy. Just thinking that, I know every inch of her turns me on. She comes up beside me and her hair spray and perfume almost knock me over. She snakes her arm through mine and smiles at me.

Sandy steps out of the ladies' room and crosses the dance floor in her white mini wedding dress. If someone had told me she'd be a beautiful bride, I would have thought they were joking. But, there she is, with a veil over her face, her hair in ringlets like Shirley Temple, wearing white platform heels, a bouquet of cloth flowers, and she's beautiful. Someone, I think Whitehead, whistles over the music. Sandy breaks into a wide smile and everyone starts clapping, actually applauding, like she's just won first place in the Miss Nautical Mile pageant. I've never seen her smile like that.

Captain Guy runs his finger across his throat and Meatball kills the song. Elena and I hold hands and, for some reason, it feels like the first time I ever held a girl's hand. Captain Guy opens his black book, looks into it, then closes it.

"We are gathered here," he says in a heavy tone, "to join Sandra and Larry into the sacred bond of matrimony." He looks at both of them with a serious face and goes on describing marriage as "a voyage that takes a lifetime." He throws in some corny clichés that might fit another couple's wedding, but not this one. "Without love on board you won't make it," he says. I look at Elena and she's looking at me. Then Captain Guy opens the book and starts reading the standard lines: "Do you, Larry, take this . . ." Even with the emotion of the moment swimming in everyone's eyes, and the few drinks I've had, I think about Loopy raping her, not stopping, hurting her, bruising her, him knowing full well what he was doing.

Sandy's staring into Loopy eyes like she's in a trance. Loopy's eyes are still glazed over from the melon balls. Across the dance floor I spot Mrs. Loop's sunburned face. She fooled the weather. Her white lipstick and eye shadow make her look like she's under a black light. She smiles at me and I smile back.

I give the ring to Captain Guy. Loopy slips it on Sandy's finger. "I now pronounce you man and wife. You may kiss the bride."

Loopy makes a big deal out of the kiss, bending Sandy over dramatically. Snickering, he slips his tongue down her throat and hikes up her miniskirt. Everyone's clapping, whistling, going crazy. Sandy wiggles out of his arms and almost falls to the floor. Then, it's over. They're married.

To "You Ain't Seen Nothing Yet," Sandra and Loopy shuffle around the dance floor. He hugs her, engulfs her. The stuttering lyrics blast around the hall. Loopy stamps around doing the bear-hug waltz, bending Sandy's back so that she's practically looking at the ceiling.

Next is "Stairway to Heaven." Everyone hits the floor, the kids, the old hitters from high school. Only the fat aunts and Sandy's mother are left at their tables.

The slow notes ring out and the familiar flute plays. Elena wraps her arms around my neck, pulling me onto the floor. "You look so handsome," she whispers in my ear and presses her face next to mine.

"You want to get a picture of me," I say. "You can put it on your dresser in L.A."

She pulls away from me and picks up a new partner, one of Sandy's cousins from Brooklyn, who really knows how to dance. The DJ changes the song. From the crowd, I watch her strut to the disco that all the girls keep requesting. Loopy's out on the floor, doing a humping dance against Sandy's hip. At the bar with my old crowd, I watch the zipper head twirl her around.

The keg is running into pitchers, then being poured into glasses. Squirrel has taken on the duties of bartender. Whitehead, Loopy, Ferth, Grady, we're all back together again like old times, but it doesn't feel like the old times. "You hear about the psychic Puerto Rican who knew the exact time he'd die?" shouts Whitehead. "The warden told him." Everyone breaks out laughing. Loopy appears out of nowhere and grabs Whitehead. The guys hold Loopy back while Whitehead repeats that it was only a joke. "Jesus, Eddie can take a joke." Squirrel pours Loopy a beer, and he drinks it in one gulp. "Eddie can take a joke," says Whitehead. "Right?"

"You're a joke," I tell him.

Sandy's aunts file in, each carrying a covered aluminum tray. They put the trays down on a table that's set with chafers and Sternos. Sandy's mother comes alongside me. "All home cooking," she says in my ear. "Sausage and peppers, potato salad, ziti, and Italian bread—nice spread, right?"

I don't say anything, so she continues on about how she wanted something nice for "her Sandra" because "she deserves it." I look around, trying to slip away. She unsnaps her shiny white pocketbook. "You ever see a cuter baby?" She unfolds a plastic folder containing photos of an innocent dark-haired child. "That's Sandra," she says.

"You got a lot to be proud of," I say.

The fire whistle blows. The whine of the alarm drowns out the music and everyone on the dance floor stops bouncing up and down. Fire engines rev and the building seems to shake. Kids cover their ears and run in circles screaming. When the whistle dies, "The Hustle" blasts across the hall. All the girls, the fat aunts, the kids, rush the dance floor, forming loose lines.

Sandy's the only woman not dancing. I wind around the floor to her. "What's the matter," I say. "You're a natural hustler."

"Like you're not," she says. On the dance floor the lines of clumsy dancers are stepping forward and pointing in the air. A kid gets knocked on his butt. I'd like to tell Sandy to be careful around Loopy. That if he got out of control she could call me, but all I ask is if she feels any different.

"I don't know." She sips her beer. "Gonna have this baby, that's different."

"You going to wake Loopy for that?" I ask.

"You don't stop, do you?" She punches my arm and pulls a pack of Kools from the sleeve of her dress. "Elena told me she's going to California. Let me tell you something." She puts the cigarette between her lips. "Come out and say it, just say it, 'Don't go.' I bet she won't go."

"I know," I say.

"Then say it. You two got a thing going."

"Like you and Loopy?"

She lights a cigarette and blows smoke out the corner of her mouth. "I know Loopy better than you think," she says. "This is what he really wanted. He's all an act."

I think about Sandra pinned under Loopy, fighting in the damp sand.

"And believe me," she says, "his act ain't hard to follow." I'd like to tell her that I know he raped her, but I won't, can't. Not at her wedding. "Loopy told me about the Puerto Rican joke," she says. We both turn and look at Loopy, he's sound asleep. His long wet hair on the table. "He really loves you," says Sandy, "probably more than me." She hits her hip into mine, just the way Elena does. "You better get some food," she says, "before it's all gone." She shimmies away, waving to some girl holding up two shot glasses.

The open area between the tables is crowded with dancers, mostly girls in their stocking feet. Elena's headed toward me but is intercepted by a girl in an orange jumpsuit, who pulls her back into the dancers. Everyone is getting drunk. In no time the kegs will be floating in their ice water. "Got to talk to you," says Whitehead, pointing toward the men's room. I shout above Barry White's "Let the Music Play" that I want to get some food. Whitehead tugs my arm and I drop my cup. Beer splashes across the floor.

"What's your problem?" I ask.

"They're gonna arrest you," he says, cupping his hands around my ear. A bead of sweat runs down his forehead. "Larson's outside waiting for you."

I follow him into the men's room. "Waiting for me?"

"One of the firemen dudes told me. Larson's got a warrant." I lean against the wall. "You and your old man tool some guy up in a pizza parlor?" asks Whitehead.

"A warrant?" I repeat, not wanting to believe it.

"Arrest warrants," says Whitehead. "They'd come up and get you but the firemen don't want a fight and the place wrecked." I'd like him to crack up laughing but he just stands there waiting for me to say something. "Man, I'm talking square shit," he says.

I wash my face with cold water. Whitehead hands me a paper towel and rambles on about how I've got to get "the fuck outta here."

At the window I turn a small crank and the bottom pane opens. The Road Runner gleams in the crowded parking lot. Beyond the lot is the back of the Tropicana. Trash cans are lined up next to a metal door. The rain has ended and the sky is clear. In the corner of the public parking lot, kids are shooting hoops on a rim attached to a light pole. I pass the toilet stalls and sit on the arm of the green couch. Whitehead is looking into the mirror examining something on his forehead. That night in the pizza parlor, Pete had the ax handle. There's four witnesses. That day in Seaman's Deli, Sack just about apologized to me. But, Larson couldn't let it go.

"I wouldn't get too comfortable," says Whitehead. "Guys get done on that couch."

In the hallway I call my old man and, for the first time in a long time, I'm relieved to hear his voice. I tell him about the arrest warrants. After a silence he says, "Get outta town.

"I'll take the heat. Straighten this shit out."

"Where am I going to go?"

"You got a boat," he says. "Go to Hawaii."

"The Millers owe me a hundred bucks," I say. "I don't get paid until Wednesday. I got ten dollars in my pocket."

"Meet me at the *Glory*," he says and hangs up.

Elena's still being twirled around the dance floor by Sandy's cousin. One moment he's behind her and the next she's whipped out, then pulled in. Grady throws his arm around my shoulders. "Are we gonna kick Larson's ass?" he asks, smiling. I get out from under his arm. "We could do it," he says. "There's twenty of us."

"You could do it yourself, Grady." He's so full of shit. "Why don't you go do that."

"Huh?" he says. "Myself?"

Elena spins around and I seize her hand in mine. Our eyes meet. Panting, she comes off the floor and follows me into the hall. The door shuts behind us, muffling the music. "What's wrong," she asks, catching her breath.

"Elena," I say. "I'm leaving tonight."

"This early?" she asks. "The guys went to get more beer."

"Not just the wedding," I say. "Larson's outside with a warrant."

"Wait," she says. "You mean you're *leaving?*"

"The *Glory*'s tanks are full. By morning I could be in Jersey, then I just head south. I showed you the course."

A girl pushes out the swinging doors, sees us, and heads back in. "So where does that leave me?"

I shake my head. I'd like to ask her to come with me, but remind myself that she's going to California.

"You don't have to leave, not tonight." Her eyes are wide and wet. I put my arms around her and she presses her cheek into mine. "Can't you just hide out for a while?" Her body is hot from the night of dancing and drinking. I run my hands over the slippery material of the dress. In the morning she'll still want to join her brother's band. I could be in jail.

Loopy has come to and he's swaying over a near empty keg like a guy standing in a round-bottom boat. Grady has everyone fired up. The hitters are around him talking about kicking ass. I pull Whitehead out of the pack. "We're gonna turn the mother out," he says like a chant.

"Forget it," I say, handing him my car keys. "I've got to get out of here. Get the Road Runner and drive it around. Anywhere, go down the Nautical Mile then come back. If the cops pull you over, tell 'em that I lent you the car and I'm still at the wedding. When you're sure you're not being followed, meet me over at the 7-Eleven on Grove Street. Got it?"

He salutes me.

Elena and I hurry down the stairs and push into the side emergency door. The alley leads to the front of the firehouse and is fenced off at the other end. She follows me along the cyclone fence to a metal dumpster. I grab the metal top and hop up on the side. "I can't do that," she says. "Not in these heels."

"Come on," I say, extending my hand.

"Oh, for Christ's sake." She slips off her shoes and I hoist her up. We stand on the closed lid that's a foot below the fence. I scramble over the fence into the high weeds. Elena drops her orange shoes and pocketbook to me. "Eddie," she says, gripping the top of the rail. "If I fall, you better catch me." She hikes up her dress, swings her legs over the fence, and tumbles into my arms.

Hidden by a line of trees, we trample through tall weeds littered with empty wine and beer bottles. We cross the lot as if we're under enemy fire. I look back and spot Larson's car parked in front of the firehouse. In a small crowd of firemen, he's drinking from a Styrofoam cup. There's two patrol cars near the curb with two uniformed cops next to them.

The winds are calm, the night sky cloudless with a melon slice of moon. The ocean will be dirty from the storm but flat, the stars brilliant. A few miles out, away from the shoals and sandbars, I'll set a course and navigate using lights from the shore.

The 7-Eleven's lot is jammed with cars. Inside, people wait on line to buy beer, ice, chips, and pretzels. Elena and I stand near the pay phones. The field has stained and soiled her shoes and stockings. Grass sticks to the straps. Tied to a post under the awning a German Shepherd watches us and wags its tan-tipped tail.

"You don't have to go to the boat," I say. "I can put your stuff in the trunk of the Road Runner. The key will be in the hiding spot."

"What are you going to do with the car?" she asks.

"My father can sell it for me."

She pets the dog's head, then lets her hand fall to her side. "You want me to go with you?" she asks.

I take her hand. She already knows I want her to go, we talked about it for two weeks. "I'll visit you in Los Angeles," I say, wanting to tell her that I understand. I tell her that she's got a good voice and that her brother's band could make it someday, the next "Captain and Terrible." She smiles and tears streak her cheeks.

"You don't have to leave tonight," she says. From down the block, I hear the sound of the Road Runner's engine. Whitehead is revving the engine like an asshole.

"If I don't, Larson will—"

"Don't give me that bullshit," she says, wiping her cheeks with her palm. "You could hide out anywhere."

She cries and then begins to sob. I rest my face on the side of her tight hairdo and bite down on my bottom lip. I never wanted to feel this way about her, never thought I could know her so closely. "Come with me," I say.

The dog puts his tail between his legs and sits quietly. People pass, eying us. Elena catches her breath. Whitehead pulls into the lot and revs the engine. He hangs out the window, smiling. "He's such a little turd," she says and lets go of my hand.

I should kiss her. It could be good-bye.

"I love you," she says in a choked way.

"Me too." We hug, then I hurry between two parked cars.

"Man, you called it," says Whitehead. "The cops pulled me over coming out of the lot." He smiles. "Told them I was making an ice run."

I thank him, but practically have to yank him out of the driver's seat. When I pull away, Elena's standing in front of the phones next to the dog. At the red light on Sunrise Highway, I think about turning around, but when the light turns green I hit the gas. Even with the air rushing in the window, Elena's scent lingers.

Chapter Twenty-two

At the Old Oyster Wharf, I roll down the driveway and cut around the boathouse. My father's leaning on the back of his Caddy. He's dressed for a Saturday night; black slacks and a red shirt. He drains the end of a Schaeffer and tosses the can near the rose bushes. "The fugitive," he says, coming up to my window.

"Who do you think will be picking that can up?"

"Not you," he says. "Not anymore." He smiles and points at me like he's got me again.

"I'm not in the mood," I say, getting out of the car.

"Come're," he says. "Got something for you." My father opens the trunk of the Caddy and removes a large box tied with yellow rope. "Going-away present," he says, heaving the box up. He drops it on the ground. From a leather pouch on his belt he removes a pocket knife and pulls the blade out. "Go ahead," he says, cutting the cord. "Look." I lift the flap. Inside is something yellow. "Inflatable life raft," he says.

"Where'd you get it?"

"Never mind where I got it. It's yours." He pulls out an instruction manual. "Guy that I got it from said all you got to do is pull something and it inflates."

"You steal it?"

"No, I didn't steal it." He kicks at the shell driveway. "You want to see what I paid for it." He opens his wallet and unfolds a yellow paper. "That's the goddamn bill'a sale."

Anyone else I would believe, but with my old man I have to make sure. The bill is from Paul's Army Navy, stamped paid. "I just don't need any trouble," I say.

"You satisfied?" he asks. "Don't want to read about you being shark bait."

"Don't worry," I say. "I'm safer in the middle of the Atlantic than in this town." We lug the raft over to the dock. He hands the box down to me and I place it in the corner of the deck.

"You mind if I come aboard?" He climbs down the ladder and steps on the transom with his pointy boots. He shouldn't be on the boat with those soles but I don't say anything. With his shoulders raised and his fingers stuck in the pockets of his jeans, he takes a quick peek in the cabin. "Goddamn, it's looking sharp," he says. "Never did get to go out on it." We stand across from one another. We're about the same size. "Do me a favor," he says, taking out his Camels. "You check in with me every once and a while." He lights up. Smoke comes out his nose and curls around his face. "And don't forget I'm your old man."

"You do me a favor," I say. "Stay away from Mom."

He smiles. "Can't promise that," he says. "She's worse than these cigarettes."

In the cabin, everywhere I look I find something of Elena's. I fold her clothes and slide them into a duffel bag. In a drawer where my grandfather kept his knives, I remove her panties and bras, run my fingers inside the cup of a purple bra, thinking of all the lovemaking the past few weeks, all the laughs, all the hot nights holding each other. The cabin's silence is screaming loud.

My father looks in. "You two get in a fight?"

"Nah," I say. "Just taking a break."

"That's what she told you?" He laughs. " 'Cause that's what I usually tell them."

On the hood of the Road Runner my father holds his lighter over the car's title and registration. I sign the back of the registration where it's marked "Seller." He folds them and sticks them in his shirt pocket. "Nice and quiet down here," he says, counting out eight one-hundred-dollar bills. He puts them in my hand.

"It's worth more than that," I say.

"Beggars can't be choosy." He tugs at the back of my hair and I pull away.

The car's trunk is open and the small dying bulb inside illuminates Elena's duffel bag of clothes. On top is her "Keep on Truckin' " T-shirt. I always hated that saying.

"How come you ain't taking your little woman," he says.

"I'm just not." I feel the wad of money in my pocket. "Look, for once, can I trust you?"

"That's a shitty attitude," he says, "after I bought you the lousy life raft."

"Elena's at the firehouse at Loopy's reception." I peel off four one-hundred-dollar bills. "Give this to her."

He takes the money and promises me that "it's in the bank." I don't know if he'll ever deliver the money, but I have to believe him.

"Tell her it's for her airfare," I say.

The *Glory*'s engine putters and spits canal water. Moths dart around the stern light. My father unties the lines and tosses them to the deck. I ease the throttle forward and the she slips out of the docking spot. Smoke hovers on the dark canal. I cut the wheel hard right. The Martin Luther King School passes on one side and the Yankee Clipper Restaurant on the other. I look back. My father's standing on the dock. He flicks his cigarette, and the ash drops to the water.

The bait store light is on so I pull in to the floating dock. Over the freeboard, I secure a line on a cleat. Tim comes limping down the planked walk.

"Late for you," he says. "Going blackfishing?"

"Just going," I say. He ties another line on the bow and pulls the *Glory* until she bumps the car tires bolted to the dock.

In the bait store, Tim taps coffee into a paper filter. "You look lower than whale shit," he says. He gives me a look and pours water into the coffee maker. "There's blackfish running out by the bridge." Tim selects a package of hooks from the wall. "They're biting on these with a clam on it."

I take the package. The coffee is strong and tastes good. My head's fuzzy from the beer and the night. I have a hard time imagining what Elena's doing at the wedding. I don't see her doing the Hustle, or getting drunk. Tim goes on about blackfishing. "At the inlet bridge some guy pulled in a twenty-five pounder," he says. "That's got to be a record for this time of year."

The bait shop door opens and my old man pokes his head in.

"Hey," he says. "You forgot something." He swings the door open and Elena is behind him. She holds her ruined shoes, not saying anything. Our eyes meet and I get off the stool. She comes in the door and buries her head on my shoulder, then starts to cry.

"She was walking down Merrick Road," says my old man. "And I said to myself, that's Eddie's girl, and sure enough." My father goes on and on explaining how he pulled over and shouted, "Hey, you ain't Elena, are you?" How she got in and they drove the entire length of Freeport Creek looking for the boat. "Then she says to me, try the bait shop."

Elena takes a long breath. "I thought I'd lost you," she says.

Twenty feet off the docks at Short Beach I toss anchor. I'm tired, beat, the inlet is crossed with breakers, it can wait until morning. In the distance the Inlet Bridge is stuck in the open position. The arms of road reach up like a picture of Jesus my mother has tacked in her bedroom. Glowing car headlights stretch for miles on both sides of the bridge. Maybe Larson's waiting in the traffic. Most likely, he's at the cop bar on Smith Street drinking whiskey, thinking he'll nab me tomorrow. There's never any trouble finding local trash. Hitters never go anywhere. They're stuck in the ground like gas pumps and fire plugs.

Under the bridge, red and green stern and bow lights glitter on the channel. I remember my grandfather always called blackfish by their real name, tautog. He'd throw a line around one of the bridge's wide cement columns and tie the *Glory* off so the current ran into the bow. Around one a.m., he'd tell me to hit the hay. In the morning I'd rise and he'd always have a few tautog in the fish well.

I pull Tim's gift of blackfish hooks from my tackle box and carefully pull one from the plastic package. He gave me chowder clams for bait. I should try fishing near the docks, but I'm too tired. In the sky I find the pan-shaped Big Dipper, then the Little Dipper. I've read that the galaxy has over a hundred billion stars. There's got to be somewhere I can go. I can't say I'm not scared. I've never really left anything before, but it feels right.

The current strains the anchor line and the lapstrake sides of the *Glory* groan. Elena steps from the cabin holding the lantern.

She's naked, but there's no one around and it's practically pitch black. She twirls, giggles, and wags her ass at me. "Come over here," I say, but she races back into the cabin and slams the door. She's still high from the wedding.

I let out more anchor line and sit for a moment. The arms of the bridge are still reaching to the heavens. Across the channel, a light snaps off in a bay house. I put the hooks back in the tackle box and lay my fishing poles on the deck. I dip the bucket of clams over the side. In seawater they'll live for a week or so.

"What's taking you?" Elena's standing with her hip pushed to the side, her elbow cocked against the cabin door. "I'm counting to ten," she says. "Ten, nine, eight, seven . . ." At three I put my arms around her and she stops counting. Even naked, she's warm. "Time for bed," she whispers in my ear.

In the cabin we climb into the V-bunk. "You think we're gonna be all right?" she asks.

"Sure," I say and remember the four hundred I gave my father. I ask if he gave it to her.

"What money?" she says.